Innocent Eyes

by

Gabbi Black

In Their Eyes, Book 3

This is a work of fiction. Names, characters, places, and incidents are either the product of the author's imagination or are used fictitiously, and any resemblance to actual persons living or dead, business establishments, events, or locales, is entirely coincidental.

Innocent Eyes

Cover Art by *Diana Carlile*

The Wild Rose Press, Inc.
PO Box 708
Adams Basin, NY 14410-0708
Visit us at www.thewildrosepress.com

Publishing History
First Edition, 2022
Trade Paperback ISBN 978-1-5092-4561-1
Digital ISBN 978-1-5092-4562-8

In Their Eyes, Book 3
Published in the United States of America

She's a diligent student.
He's a masterful teacher.

He's here.

Tarah's breath hitched in her throat. Saturday at midnight and, like clockwork, Sebastian Merrick was home.

He wasn't alone, of course. He was never alone. Tonight's companion was a blonde with a short skirt, tight blouse, and heels at least five inches tall. Her tits were falling out of the blouse.

Her IQ is probably lower than her bra size.

Okay, uncharitable thought. *Take a proverbial step back to get the entire picture.* Big Tits looked up at Sebastian with dreamy eyes and leaned on him because she teetered on those ice-pick stilettos.

"Good evening, Mr. Merrick."

As usual, Sebastian inclined his head, didn't meet her gaze, and made his way to the elevator. The blonde gave her a quick wink, and Tarah gaped.

That was a new one.

Settling back into her chair, Tarah sniffed diffidently at the nauseating scent the woman left in her wake. Probably had doused herself in a bottle of the stuff. No clue whether that was an expensive scent or drugstore perfume. The blonde had probably skimped. Spent all her money on the boob job. Or, more likely, someone had bought them for her. *Whoops, need to pull in the claws.*

Maybe those were real. The woman could be a CFO for some fancy corporation…or a lawyer or maybe a pediatric surgeon at the children's hospital. Maybe she had bought them herself. Big Tits could be the most intelligent woman in Vancouver or just the luckiest.

Dedication

To The Wild Rose Press team who took a chance on me and who have supported me all the way—Rhonda, Josette, Diana, Lisa, and the entire crew.

Chapter One

He's here.

Tarah's breath hitched in her throat. Saturday at midnight and, like clockwork, Sebastian Merrick was home.

He wasn't alone, of course. He was never alone. Tonight's companion was a blonde with a short skirt, tight blouse, and heels at least five inches tall. Her tits were falling out of the blouse.

Her IQ is probably lower than her bra size.

Okay, uncharitable thought. *Take a proverbial step back to get the entire picture.* Big Tits looked up at Sebastian with dreamy eyes and leaned on him because she teetered on those ice-pick stilettos.

"Good evening, Mr. Merrick."

As usual, Sebastian inclined his head, didn't meet her gaze, and made his way to the elevator. The blonde gave her a quick wink, and Tarah gaped.

That was a new one.

Settling back into her chair, Tarah sniffed diffidently at the nauseating scent the woman left in her wake. Probably had doused herself in a bottle of the stuff. No clue whether that was an expensive scent or drugstore perfume. The blonde had probably skimped. Spent all her money on the boob job. Or, more likely, someone had bought them for her. *Whoops, need to pull in the claws.*

1

Maybe those were real. The woman could be a CFO for some fancy corporation…or a lawyer or maybe a pediatric surgeon at the children's hospital. Maybe she had bought them herself. Big Tits could be the most intelligent woman in Vancouver or just the luckiest. She was upstairs with Sebastian Merrick right now while Tarah manned the security desk.

Life just wasn't fair.

All quiet. The security monitors confirmed that assertion. Boasting thirty-eight stories of soaring glass and concrete, the building housed some of the richest and most powerful of Vancouver's elite.

Five floors were full of rental suites that hosted actors, directors, and musicians intermingled with businessmen and women, from a week to several months.

Tarah snapped to attention, rising to greet the older couple approaching. "Good evening, Mr. Lansing, Mrs. Lansing. Did you have a pleasant evening?"

Camille Lansing offered a genuine smile. "Mr. Lansing surprised me with tickets to the symphony with dinner and dancing after that." She gazed at her husband with adoration. "The best thirty-fifth anniversary present I could ask for." Her eyes shone, bespeaking her love for him. "Oh, and he gave me this."

Camille twisted her wrist so Tarah could admire the bracelet. Identifying the metal and the stones was beyond her. "It's lovely."

"Eighteen karat white gold with diamonds and alexandrites." Mrs. Lansing kindly saved Tarah from the humiliation of being unable to comment intelligently. The Lansings weren't expecting her to be knowledgeable, but she strove to be more erudite. Maybe

2

then Mr. Merrick would see her as more than a concierge or security guard.

Her admiration of the elderly couple couldn't have been clearer to Tarah.

"Mr. Lansing is a considerate husband." The older woman gushed her praise, her eyes bright.

Said husband blushed under his wife's lavish praise but also beamed with pride. Mixed with love.

Thirty-five was a significant event these days, and Tarah's heart gave a little stutter of wistfulness. *Will I ever find that kind of happiness?* "I wish you both a wonderful evening."

The carnal look passing between the couple had her fighting not to blush. Clearly, not too late in the evening to engage in some horizontal dancing. The couple headed to the elevator, still on cloud nine, and Tarah glanced over at the monitors before resettling in her ergonomic chair. Surreptitiously, she pulled her class notes from under the clipboard. Developmental psychology. Not her favorite class, but the most important on the road to being an elementary school teacher.

At the rate she was going, her dream would require another five years to attain, and she'd be thirty before she ever saw the inside of her own classroom. She allowed a moment to feel sorry for herself, then she redoubled her efforts to learn about autism spectrum disorders.

No use. Her mind wandered where it should not. Upstairs… *Sebastian Merrick.*

Even the name implied a sense of authority. He was over six feet tall with thick black hair and brown eyes so dark they appeared black. Those eyes, on the few occasions his gaze met hers, had been intense, and she couldn't hold eye contact. Sebastian's gaze seemed capable of boring directly into her soul.

And what does he see when he looks at me?

Surely, not the sexual attraction that overwhelmed her. The man was pure animal magnetism and had to know it. Women swooned at his feet. If this evening's nubile companion, and all who had come before, were any indication. All his companions were stunning. Tarah couldn't help comparing herself to them…and coming up lacking every time.

Unlike those tall willowy beauties, she was all of five-feet-six, and since she never wore high heels, that wouldn't change. Although she was on the slim side, her breasts—on a good day—were a B cup. Hair, mousy brown. Face, unremarkable. But her eyes. Pale blue, they seemed incongruous with the rest of her features. The world considered her plain and boring, and she couldn't disagree. She was nothing like the women Sebastian preferred. She hung her head for a moment before straightening and looking around.

He's too old for me anyway. And he's too successful to notice a lowly security guard.

So she'd continue to have a crush on him, and he would remain ignorant of her racing heart each time he walked by.

Like clockwork, Big Tits reappeared at four a.m. Tarah held the door open for the woman, watching to make sure she made it to her cab. Although that service wasn't in her job description, she believed prudence was important. It wouldn't do to have one of Mr. Merrick's companions get injured and sue the strata corporation.

After watching the taxi depart, she took in a deep lungful of frigid air before turning back to her desk.

Sebastian Merrick leaned against her console.

She stopped dead in her tracks.

"Good evening, Miss Peters."

She froze, rooted to the spot. Never in her wildest dreams had she imagined he might know her name.

"Good evening, Mr. Merrick." Morning had almost dawned, but she followed his lead. "How may I help you?"

His gaze was intense and unwavering.

Maintain eye contact. Don't let him see how he affects you.

She tried to hold his gaze, but in the end, she couldn't. His eyes were too incisive, too piercing.

"You get off work at six, yes?"

She swallowed convulsively. Damn dry throat. "That's correct."

"I'm taking you out to breakfast at six fifteen."

That would give her enough time to change from her uniform into street clothes. "That w-would be f-fine." *Stammer much?*

He inclined his head and strode to the elevators. Of course, one waited for him. Even an elevator wouldn't dare defy him.

When he disappeared into the car and the doors slid shut, she let out the breath she hadn't even been aware she was holding. Sitting because her legs couldn't hold her any longer, she snickered. It'd never occurred to her to say no.

Another thought popped into her head.

Sebastian lived in apartment 313.

That apartment.

A former owner, Rielle Reid—now Rielle Clayton—had needed Tarah to retrieve some clothes when she was in the hospital. Tarah hadn't thought twice about it. She'd entered the condo, heading straight for the master suite. The image of that room would forever be indelibly imprinted on her brain.

A dungeon.

The master bedroom had been converted into something resembling a medieval dungeon. The walls were painted black with raised stucco to approximate stones. A set of manacles hung on one wall. Another was covered with…tools? Okay, a whip, handcuffs, and a dildo, but what were the rest of those implements? She could guess, of course. She even contemplated searching on the internet, but that seemed…weird.

In one corner was a large cage—like a dog kennel. Finally, she spotted an odd wood-and-metal contraption with four manacles. That one was beyond bizarre.

When she spotted four shackles, one at each of the four posts of the bed, disturbing arousal swelled within her. Steeling herself, she opened the walk-in closet and…gawked. Fetish wear for every occasion hung there. Leather, spandex, and latex were the primary fabrics. Amazingly, she'd never seen Rielle wear any of these clothes or anything resembling their style. Maybe she wore them under a trench coat, unknown to Tarah.

Since she found no clothes suitable to wear home from the hospital, Tarah made her way to the spare bedroom. There, to her infinite relief, were Rielle's street clothes. Selecting jeans, a blouse, a wool coat, socks, and shoes was easy. These represented the Rielle she knew. When she delivered the clothes to the hospital, Tarah wondered if Rielle would mention the dungeon. Tarah never asked, and Rielle never told.

Soon after, Rielle had moved to the suburbs with a

man she loved. Now they were married, had a nine-month-old baby girl, and Rielle was four months pregnant.

Smith MacLean had bought the condo, and to the best of Tarah's knowledge, he hadn't renovated. Within six months he'd moved to the suburbs with a woman he had fallen in love with, Alessandra Soriano—now Alessandra MacLean. The condo had never even gone on the open market when Sebastian Merrick bought it.

Again, without renovations.

The dungeon is still there.

Truthfully, she could guess some of the things he was doing with those women every Saturday night. What surprised her was how much she wanted to be his focus—the woman at his mercy. So much it made her insides clench and ache.

Or maybe it was the other way around. Maybe he was at the mercy of the women. As quickly as the thought flickered through her mind, she scoffed at it. Sebastian Merrick was an alpha male. No way did he bow at the feet of some woman. A Domme, according to research she'd never admit to having done.

Nope, he was in charge.

So why was she having breakfast with him? Actually, more like he'd commanded her to have breakfast with him. His eyes—pools of dark brown—had drawn her in, and she'd been powerless to deny him. Not that she wanted to.

Sebastian Merrick had asked her to breakfast… *Her*. Little, unremarkable Tarah Peters.

Developmental psychology. With a final exam she had to ace on Wednesday morning. She *could* do it. After taking one more look at the security monitors, she returned to reviewing her notes. Two hours. She only needed to focus on her studies for two hours and put Sebastian Merrick out of her mind during that time.

****

Tarah was ready five minutes early. Marvelle, her replacement, eyed her as she waited for Mr. Merrick. In hindsight, she should've agreed to meet him someplace else. Now she'd likely be the subject of gossip. She hoped Marvelle was as professional as she and that the woman wouldn't mention it later.

She didn't want to do anything to jeopardize her good-paying job. She'd landed this position when she was eighteen and had just graduated from high school. Her mother's boss, Mr. Joseph, lived in the building, and when he heard Tarah was looking for an overnight shift, he put her name forward for consideration.

Her work history had proven she was responsible. She'd been working since she was fourteen as an after-school caregiver for three kids. Every day, from three until ten, she'd babysat, successfully balancing the kids and her schoolwork. Although she'd scrimped and saved every penny she could, it only paid for one full-time semester at university before the money ran out. When she'd realized school was too expensive to continue, she set out to find a job she could do while continuing part-time studies. This security job had been a godsend. For most of her coworkers, like Marvelle, this was a permanent and lifelong job. Tarah couldn't conceive of doing this for the rest of her life but respected those who did.

Two minutes.

Why the hell did you agree to this?

Yes, he'd asked, and truthfully, curiosity was

8

driving her, but she felt more. He knew her name. He knew when her shift was over. He knew she'd say yes. Should she have hesitated? Made him think she wasn't a pushover?

Too late.

Mr. Merrick stepped from the elevator, looking handsome and refreshed despite having only slept two hours. Probably less, by her calculations. He wore a white shirt, khaki pants, and carried a leather jacket. He pulled off sexy with minimal effort.

"Are you ready?" The question, at first, seemed offhanded. The intensity of his gaze, however, was anything but casual. That animalistic veneer never left him and was on full display right now.

Tarah desperately hoped Marvelle couldn't sense the obvious tension, although the woman would have to be dense not to. She bobbed her head, not trusting herself to speak. They stepped out of the lobby and into the dawn, walking side by side in silence. Early December had descended, and the air had a distinct chill to it. Pulling up the lapels of her jean jacket, she matched his stride. He set a brisk but not unreasonable pace—his long legs eating up the ground they covered.

"I thought we would eat at The Georgian."

She wasn't dressed for that kind of establishment but remained silent. He could see she wore jeans and a blouse. He knew the place they were going.

Before his invitation, she'd planned to hop the bus back to East Vancouver and the two-bedroom walk-up she shared with her roommate, Ainsley. Their schedules were so different they rarely saw each other—and that was okay. Intensely private, Tarah was the opposite of the gregarious and outgoing Ainsley. Strange, when volunteering in a room of preschoolers, she controlled the kids with ease. Adults, on the other hand, were hard for her to figure out. Toddlers said what they thought, showed their emotions, and loved unconditionally, whereas adults weren't so transparent.

The restaurant, in a famous landmark hotel, appeared too soon, and Mr. Merrick held the door for her. The hot air hit her with a blast, and she hesitated for a fraction of a second, letting the warmth roll over her. It felt as if she'd opened her mother's stove to pull out dinner. She stepped forward. She tilted her chin up and straightened her shoulders, trying to act urbane. Trying to act as if being here with Mr. Merrick was no big deal.

The lobby was deserted at this early hour. The desk clerk gave a discreet gaze of appreciation when she glimpsed Mr. Merrick. As if noticing Tarah's glare and realizing she'd been caught, the young woman offered a genial smile accompanied by thinly veiled surprise.

She was probably wondering what a gorgeous man like him was doing with a dowdy girl like Tarah.

Stop it.

How often had she pored over books about self-esteem and how to instill it in her students? How often had she looked in the mirror and repeated those mantras? How often had she looked away, not believing a word?

No good answer for that.

The hostess of the restaurant smiled as they stepped forward, Sebastian's hand firmly at Tarah's back. Not that guidance was needed. Although Tarah wasn't the shiniest penny in the jar, she definitely wasn't the dullest. No, this gesture was to stake his claim—to make his ownership clear.

But why?

"Mr. Merrick, so nice to see you again. Are you meeting someone, or is it just the two of you?"

The woman was stunning, even at this early hour. Perfect makeup—subtle yet clearly used for enhancing. Not that she needed the help. Long dark lashes, matched by bronze skin that glowed in the low light, fringed her stunning dark eyes. The sensible pumps provided her with height while her straight spine and regal posture afforded a picture of the perfect woman. Far more elegant than Big Tits. Far more sophisticated than Tarah.

Oh, for fuck's sake, knock it off.

But it's true.

"Just the two of us, Celia, thank you."

"Your favorite table is available." She led them to a secluded table and waited patiently while Tarah sat on one side of the booth, Mr. Merrick on the other. Then she placed the menus on the table, either oblivious to the tension or, more likely, trained to ignore it unless someone was under obvious duress.

And since Tarah had agreed to this foolish idea, duress was not a word she could assign to this…event. Stress? Definitely. Insanity? Absolutely. But duress? No, she'd been willing enough, overcome by the same lust that plagued her every Saturday night.

"Coffee, juice?"

Celia's question brought her back to reality.

"We'll both have orange juice, and I'll have the Columbian blend, and Miss Peters will have decaf."

Celia's perfect teeth shone, even in the dim light. "I'll have Kristoff bring those right away. Enjoy your meal." With that, she departed.

Dumbfounded, Tarah gaped. She was perfectly capable of ordering her own drinks—had been doing so most of her life. On those rare occasions she ate out, that was. In this moment, though, she stayed silent. Mostly because he ordered exactly what she would've chosen. As much as she craved caffeine, her body would revolt, keeping her tossing and turning when what she needed was a good sleep.

Shrugging mentally, she offered, "Thank you."

"You're most welcome."

He looked at her with such intensity she was forced to again look away lest he see her discomfort. Lest he see past her defenses. Lest he see into that part of her soul she shared with no one.

"Please look at me."

A command, despite the quiet tone. *Damn it.*

Powerless to disobey, she met his gaze. What did he see when he examined her with such purpose?

"I am glad you decided to join me this morning."

As if I really had a choice. "And I appreciate the invitation, although I'm not sure why you asked me."

He smiled, a slow lazy curling of his lips.

"But you're curious, aren't you? You're a very curious young woman. You see things, but you ignore them. You know things, but you feign innocence. You have access to the deepest and darkest secrets of hundreds of people, yet you use discretion as your weapon."

Tarah snickered softly. *As if.* She waved her hand airily. "I hardly have access to people's...deepest and darkest secrets. And I don't use weapons." She turned the idea over in her mind. "Sure, I'm discreet, but that's part of the job."

"But the innate curiosity is in direct competition with the need to keep silent. Do you talk to anyone?

Share the secrets with anyone?"

The denial was swift and immediate. "Of course not. I really need this job. I like this job. I'd never do *anything* to jeopardize this job." Her gut twisted. What was he thinking? What did he know? A false accusation could cost her everything. He seemed honorable, but that didn't mean she was correct or he wouldn't coerce her.

"You keep my secrets." His face was a proverbial stone—inscrutable and unreadable.

"What secrets? You don't have any secrets." *Liar.*

He tisked his disapproval. "Don't lie to me, Tarah. Don't *ever* lie to me. I can tell. Your face is transparent and your thoughts written across it."

Her cheeks heated with embarrassment. "Even if I knew your secrets, they belong to you."

A brow arched. Whatever he was about to counter her assertion with was set aside when their waiter arrived, two mugs of coffee and two glasses of orange juice at the ready.

"Have you decided what you're going to have this morning?"

"Miss Peters will have the pancakes with fresh blueberries on the side, and I'll have eggs Benedict. I would like the eggs hard."

"Of course, sir." Kristoff bobbed his head.

A younger man, probably no older than herself. Attractive—blue-eyed, shaggy blond hair—but not nearly as entrancing as Mr. Merrick.

"I'll have them for you shortly."

As soon as the waiter was outside of hearing range, she rounded on her host. "Mr. Merrick, I appreciate the consideration. I really do. However, I *am* capable of selecting my food."

"Sebastian."

Derailed by the non sequitur, she gaped. "I'm sorry?"

"My name is Sebastian. If we are going to have breakfast, you should call me by my given name."

Since she'd always thought of him as Mr. Merrick, this was a sharp and unexpected turn. She never considered addressing him—or any tenant—so informally. "I'm not sure I'm comfortable with this."

"Well, get comfortable." His tone was deceptively mild. "How is your psychology course going?"

That stunned sensation, which hadn't really abated, came back with a vengeance. "How do you know about that?"

"Your mother's boss casually asked how your studies were progressing, and she was a fount of information. She's very proud of you."

Tread carefully.

"I'm surprised Mr. Joseph was so interested in my schoolwork."

Sebastian made an offhand gesture. "He probably wasn't, but when I inquired after you, he made some discreet inquiries of his own. I doubt your mother realized she revealed your secrets."

"It isn't a secret I go to the university." She attempted diffidence. Regrettably, it didn't work. If anything, his gaze intensified. Her jaw tightened so hard her teeth clacked. "May I ask what else my mother said?"

He appeared to contemplate whether he was going to answer her, but then he did. "You're twenty-five years old, studying English and psychology because you aspire to be a grade-school teacher. You can't afford to go to school full time, so you work while going to class whenever you can." He took a breath, or a pregnant pause, then continued. "Your father had cancer, which left him permanently disabled, so your mother is the breadwinner in the family. That's why there is no extra money to fund your education."

"I'm an adult and perfectly capable of supporting myself." Every fact he enumerated was accurate. *Damn him.* Finances forced her to work full time while going to school part time to finish her undergraduate work. Teacher's college was a one-year, full-time program, and she needed to save enough to get through that year. Her anger that he appeared to know all that bordered on irrational, but she didn't care. This was getting out of hand.

"You're not dating anyone at the moment."

She narrowed her eyes at him as her gut tightened. "There is no way my mother knows that, nor would she say anything about that to Mr. Joseph."

Sebastian's smile was indolent. "You're right, of course. You have now confirmed my supposition. Secrets." He leaned forward, holding her gaze. "You can't keep them from me."

His voice was barely above a whisper, but his message came through loud and clear. Unease swept through her, and a shiver crawled up her spine. "Why did you ask me here?"

The food arrived, preventing him from answering her question. Her annoyance intensified. Sebastian attacked the food like a man after weeks in the wilderness, surviving on berries. Her stomach growled. The pancakes looked delicious, and fresh blueberries were her favorite, so instead of making a scene, she dug in to the savory concoction.

She repeated her question again once the meal was consumed. "What am I doing here?"

"Having breakfast."

A statement as simple as the man was complex.

"Keeping me company."

"If you hadn't sent your companion home so early, she could've kept you company." *Shit.* She clapped a hand over her mouth. "I'm sorry, that was rude of me."

He inclined his head. "But very true. Barbie, however, was not looking for breakfast. I gave her what she was looking for, and she left."

Tarah wanted to ask what Barbie—*seriously, Barbie?*—had sought, but knew better. He still hadn't answered her question, infuriating man. *Why am I here?* "Look, Mr. Merrick—"

The look of disappointment crossing his face stopped her mid-sentence.

"I told you to call me Sebastian. I expect you to do what I tell you."

Not menacing, but not upbeat and happy either.

Her eyes widened, but a frisson shot up her spine. *What?* The intensity of his stare overwhelmed her senses and fried her nerve endings.

Breathe.

"Okay." Once air returned to her lungs, the oxygenated blood shot to her head, and her heart rate was back under control, she spoke. "Sebastian. Maybe you could tell me why I'm here."

"I have a proposal for you."

She frowned at him and lifted an eyebrow. "What kind of proposal?" Her voice was steadier than she.

"You spend six months with me, and I pay for the rest of your education. I don't just mean tuition. I mean rent, textbooks, and incidentals. Everything you need so you can become a teacher."

What the fuck?

Her throat went dry. She gulped her orange juice, then cleared her throat. She tried twice before she said, "I don't understand."

Sebastian's brow arched. And was that a smirk on his face?

"I'm sure this sounds bizarre to you, but I'm hoping you'll see how we might both benefit. I'm lonely and looking for a companion. No sex, mind you, just company. You feel the same way, and this is a way for you to alleviate some of that loneliness. You'll continue to go to school part time, but the rest of the time, you'll be with me."

The band around her chest tightened. She had a million questions, but one came to the fore. "Why me? You could have any of hundreds of women, thousands, probably. Why pick me?"

His penetrative stare returned. "Because we understand each other. We'll be able to satisfy each other's needs."

"What do you get out of this?"

"I told you—"

She shook her head violently. "No, I want to know the actual reason. Not some bullshit story about you being lonely."

"Language, Tarah."

His reprimand was mild, but disturbing steel laced his tone. Heat flamed in her cheeks at the chastisement.

"I won't tolerate that kind of disrespect."

Laughter bubbled in her chest, and she resisted the urge to give in to the hysteria overwhelming her. "I'm not a prostitute. I won't be propositioned."

An ominous shadow passed across the man's face. "I never called you a prostitute nor did anything to indicate I thought of you in that way. Don't put words in my mouth."

A lick of fear enveloped her, but something more encased her. Something elemental about the way he looked at her. Snakes coiled in her belly. But this thing between them—this electricity. Did he feel it too?

"You want this, Tarah. I'm offering you everything you've ever wanted, and all you have to do is give in for six months."

She took another sip. "Give in?"

"You surrender yourself to me, and in return, I give you freedom. Freedom to pursue your passion."

"What do you mean, *surrender*?" At first, she'd believed his expression unreadable, but the current between them informed her, even with her inherent naiveté, more was going on. Just below the surface, for both of them, the stakes were high. Higher than anything she'd faced in her entire, unremarkable life.

Now he took a sip of his coffee, relaxed as ever except for the grip on the handle. His knuckles were white. "You agree to be my submissive for six months."

She sucked in a breath. "That sure sounds like a whore to me."

He tisked again. "Not a whore. I said no sex. Mental submission differs greatly from sexual submission."

"I sure don't see a difference." Sarcasm laced her return volley.

His eyes darkened, the brown disappearing and surrendering to black pupils. "Once you move in with me, I'll teach you the difference."

Unable to help herself, she laughed. "You want me to move in with you and believe it's not about sex? I didn't just fall off the turnip truck."

"No one said you did."

His eyebrow arched in that sexy way, and she was momentarily distracted. What if it was about sex? Would it be so bad to surrender in bed to a man so sexy? So predatory? So knowledgeable and, at the same time, oddly charming?

Would that really be so bad?

His words yanked her back from that image.

"As you well know, there are two bedrooms in my condo. You'll have one, and I'll have the other. There's a lock on your door if that makes you feel any better."

"What's stopping you from molesting me in the kitchen?"

"My word that I won't."

He was serious. He believed she'd take his word for it. She pushed back from the table. "Thank you for breakfast, Mr. Merrick."

As she passed him, he snagged her arm. Not wanting to make a scene, she stopped.

"I won't take *no* for an answer." He pulled a business card from his pocket. "I expect to hear from you before your shift tonight." He released her and resumed sipping his coffee as if the last fifteen minutes hadn't taken place.

She stared at her arm where he'd gripped her. Startled when he'd grabbed her, she was equally stunned to be released. Her arm tingled, even though the grip hadn't hurt and had been too brief to transfer the warmth of his hand to her chilled skin. She wanted to make some witty and brilliant comment but didn't dare. She needed to keep her job. "I thank you for the offer. Mr. Merrick, it would be impossible for me to accept."

"Fourteen hours." Deceptively casual yet phenomenally strong and overwhelming words. "Not a minute longer."

She rolled her eyes as she left the restaurant. Fourteen hours, fourteen days, fourteen years…it didn't matter. She was never going to become Sebastian Merrick's submissive.

Never.

Chapter Two

Rolling over and punching her pillow again, Tarah tried to find the sweet position so she could sleep comfortably, but the battle proved useless. Noon. She'd lain awake for three hours, debating, disagreeing, relenting, and then restarting the arguments. The pros and the cons. Then she flipped over and started the whole debate again. On its face, the proposition was patently ridiculous. How could she possibly become someone's submissive? What did that even mean? Sebastian said the submission was mental rather than sexual.

Yeah, right.

Now he was Sebastian. Only natural after he propositioned her.

What did she know about Sebastian Merrick? What did she know about any of the owners in the building? He'd been correct when he asserted she understood discretion.

Since sleep proved impossible, she flipped on her bedside lamp, rolled out of bed, and stumbled over to her computer. The machine had been acquired in a surplus sale at her mother's job. Lynette bought it for her daughter as a birthday present. That was seven years ago, and Tarah did her best to baby the machine since she had no money to replace it.

The only reason she even had internet was Ainsley needed it to research. Her roommate attended the

University of British Columbia full time as a medical student so was always in the lab or studying for a test or going to Gross Anatomy class. When she was home, though, she needed the internet and never considered asking Tarah to contribute to the cost.

While her machine booted up, she grabbed a caffeinated soda from the fridge. The computer still churned when she returned to her room. The sound reminded her of a coffee machine, chortling away, and she drummed her fingers on the desk. That Sebastian debate raged as the computer came online. The minute she connected to the internet, she searched him.

She gleaned little info. Owner of Merrick Enterprises, which, in turn, owned a chain of family-oriented restaurants. Already in Western Canada and the Pacific Northwest, the company was in expansion mode. Over forty locations and still growing, although no financials available on the privately held company.

Aside from a few photos of Sebastian at fundraisers and galas, she located nothing about him. Unsurprisingly, he didn't have a large digital footprint. Like herself, he didn't have Facebook, Twitter, or Instagram accounts—or not in his name. She located nothing she could use to ferret out personal information about him. He was rich, and he donated to worthy charities. Nothing new there.

His business card in hand, she pressed her finger to the black embossed lettering, as if some divination would come from the words.

Six months.

In terms of her life, this represented such a small time period. If she agreed to this, she could finish her undergraduate degree in one year. Another year at teacher's college…in two-and-a-half years she could stand in front of her own class. Responsible for encouraging little minds. Third grade, because something about ten-year-old children appealed to her. Perhaps because her own third grade teacher had been so amazing—had such a profound impact on her life.

Six months.

On an impulse, she googled submissive.

Three hours later she was even more conflicted. Rather than enlightening, the search had confused her. Most blogs by submissives spoke of great enjoyment of their chosen lifestyle. On the other hand, she located blogs that equated submission with mind control.

She found articles about how submission and surrender of mental and emotional struggles could lead to deeper introspection and understanding. Other articles were written by Dominants about why they chose the lifestyle and what they expected of their submissives.

How could it be so simple? Someone submitted and someone controlled? Someone gave up who she was, and someone rebuilt her in the image of what he wanted. And it went both ways—men who submitted and women who dominated. Even the words held strong connotations. Her parents had been egalitarian. In health they'd been equal partners, and now that her father was ill, her mother took on more of the burden, but they still shared the emotional load evenly. Her mother might nag a bit, but she did it out of love. She'd rarely tell her husband what to do, and he'd never acquiesce without a definitive reason.

Tarah had no point of reference. She'd never faced giving up part of herself as necessary to make a dynamic work, and rarely needed to decide between her needs and someone else's.

Had she missed out?

She'd always told herself she was happy being alone. Convinced herself she didn't have time to cater to a man's needs. Believed she was a complete person without a significant other. And she was right. Being so busy, she had no time for a man or for someone to pull her focus away from her goals. She wanted a classroom of her own. Simple. And if she was lonely along the way? Well, surely worse things in the world than keeping one's own company existed.

Focus.

Back to her research. Despite the odd dynamics, the people involved made it all seem so reasonable. Virtually every website encouraged a contract between the participants.

Would she have a contract with Sebastian?

Was she really considering this?

Six months.

The words had become a mantra. No one had to know. Ainsley was never around. Her coworkers would speculate, but they'd be her former colleagues. He'd promised to set her up with her own space and to pay all her expenses. Who cared what anyone else thought? She wasn't going to advertise her situation, so it likely wouldn't be an issue.

Scrutinizing her too-cramped room, she attempted to visualize what living with Sebastian would be like. His condo was huge, each room bigger than the next. The white room, the room he promised her, was double the size of her current space. With that room being located across the condo from the master bedroom, a vast distance existed between the two spaces. They'd be sharing a bathroom, but she'd shared plenty in the past, and what difference could that possibly make? She'd stay out of his way, right?

All she had to do was follow his orders and commands.

Six months.

Twenty-four weeks.

One hundred and eighty days.

No simple answer was forthcoming. And because of that she couldn't leap forward. Being cautious was less likely to cause problems. She'd have to turn him down.

Giving up on the offer and the dreams they'd inspired, she crawled back into bed, begging the deities for at least a few hours' sleep.

****

At eight o'clock Tarah stood at the door of 313, hand poised to knock. She owed Mr. Merrick the decency of turning down his proposal in person, so here she was. The respectful thing to do. The security guard on duty, Carlos, had given her an odd look but waved her through. Grateful for the trust, she'd ridden the elevator with nerves drawn taut. Three floors were not enough time to make any monumental decisions, and taking the stairs would've been more logical. Logic, however, had fled tonight. Not that complicated. *Thank you for your generous offer, but it's just not for me.* How hard could that be?

Before she lost her nerve, she knocked on the door. She was not known for her patience with anyone except children, so every second was an interminable wait. Each of those seconds featured a debate on whether to stay or run as fast as her feet could carry her.

She jumped when the door opened.

Sebastian, dressed in a black silk shirt and black linen trousers, looked like the million bucks he was worth. According to her research, he was worth more than that.

How much more? Not that money was important. A bank account did not determine a person's worth. That being said, the more wealth, the more likely people gossiped behind their backs. With gossip came speculation, and undoubtedly, she'd be caught up in that vortex.

"Nice to see you, Miss Peters." He stepped to the side. "Won't you come in?"

She wanted to refuse, but the inevitability of it overrode common sense. Having the discussion in the hall where nosy Mrs. Wannamaker might hear wasn't an option. The old woman made an irritant of herself, and all the security personnel were well acquainted with her machinations. She was a pesky busybody.

As Tarah stepped into Sebastian's suite, all thoughts of meddlesome neighbors fled. Prominent over the couch, in a space that had once been empty, was a large oil painting of a woman.

A totally nude woman.

A modernist piece as opposed to something in the classical vein, but then she was no expert in art. A beautiful piece, though, to be sure.

"A Carlyle."

The name meant nothing to her. "It's stunning." Although she wouldn't have picked it for herself, it suited the taste and the aesthetic of the man by her side.

Deep breath. Stay calm.

"I just wanted to come by and thank you."

"I need to show you something."

Apprehension ran up and down her spine. "Really, I just—"

"Follow me."

Despite her misgivings, she obeyed his command. He crossed to the door of the white room, opened it, then beckoned her inside.

The room was still white, with very little having changed from when Rielle lived here. On the desk sat a laptop, an e-reader, an MP3 player, a tablet, and a cell phone. A flat-screen television was set up in one corner with a DVD player. Everything brand new. *When was the last time I owned something new?*

"Mr. Merrick—" His eyebrow rose, and she stopped. "Sebastian. I'm not sure why you're showing me this. I can't be bought."

His disapproval radiated. "I'm not trying to buy you. I'm showing you what would be at your disposal. If something's missing, just tell me, and I'll acquire it. You need to concentrate on your studies, and this space is designed to help you do that. It will also be your sanctuary."

He wasn't using the future conditional. He spoke as if this was a done deal.

"Monday and Tuesday will be your days off. You'll have weekdays to yourself, but I may require you for evening engagements. Plan on spending most of the weekend with me. I will, of course, be supplying you with clothes to suit the various occasions. As this is the holiday season, there are several events for us to attend."

"Sebastian—"

He took her hands in his.

Her first instinct was to yank her hands back and run as fast as she could. His hands were warm, the pads of his thumbs smooth as they made circles against her knuckles.

"Six months. Everything you've ever wanted, and all I ask from you is six months."

His nearness disconcerted. A light scent—not aftershave nor cologne—but something more natural, more elemental.

Focus, damn it. Desperate to come up with even one objection, she surveyed the room. One reason she shouldn't do this. She was a smart woman, so surely, one argument why this was a terrible idea would pop into her brain.

Slowly, his rhythmic stroking of her knuckles broke her defenses. The self-protective wall she'd used as a barricade for so long started to crumble. Glancing at their entwined hands, she blinked several times, then gazed back up to meet his all-too-seeing eyes.

"All right. I'll do it." Her tortured whisper pushed past a clogged throat.

Where she expected smugness, she found only…tenderness.

"You won't regret this."

I already do.

"When's your final?"

"Wednesday morning."

"Then I'll meet you at your apartment Wednesday afternoon, and we'll get you packed to move here. We should be done by nightfall."

Why bother asking how he knew her entire life could be boxed up and moved in one afternoon? Nor how he knew where she lived. She didn't ask anything at all.

"You have an hour before you go on shift. Perhaps we can—"

"A contract." She blurted out the critical word, voice trembling. "We need a contract."

Apparently unfazed, he indicated she leave the white room. His hand at the small of her back was strong and offered unwavering guidance. "I'll bring it from the office. Why don't you sit down? Or help yourself to something to drink in the kitchen, if you would prefer. I'll be back momentarily."

She wasn't surprised he had a contract ready. He seemed prepared for everything.

Too nervous to sit, she made her way to the kitchen. Snakes, wriggling their way around her gut, ate at her nerves. As much as she wanted an alcoholic beverage, decorum and her work schedule dictated she grab a bottle of sparkling water. With that bit of fortification, hopefully, she'd be able to sit still long enough to read the contract.

She headed back to the living room and collided with a wall of solid muscle. He steadied her by the elbows. She tensed at the unexpected contact—an instinctual reaction she couldn't control. "I was just getting something to drink. Did you want something?" She cringed at the inanity in her tone.

"I already have a scotch."

Of course he did.

"Why don't we sit at the table? It will be easier for you to review the document and suggest any changes you might see fit."

Would she have the guts to make changes? She sensed an inevitability to this. Her destiny had been set the moment she agreed to go to breakfast with him. Yet did she regret her decision to do that?

Taking the seat he offered, she allowed him to push

in her chair. Gallant, but not surprising. She removed the cap from her mineral water and took a sip as he placed the contract in front of her. She scanned the first page and looked at him in the seat next to her. She then skimmed through the next page, just in case the first was a mistake. No, she'd understood it correctly. A final glance over the last few pages had her apprehension climbing. Corrections, punishments, rewards…all words she understood in the colloquial sense but not in the Dominant/submissive sense. She'd never been corporally punished as a child and wasn't really looking forward to it now.

Putting down the papers, she met Sebastian's gaze. "I'm in over my head."

He inclined his head. "You need to read the contract carefully from beginning to end."

She pointed to it, desperation clawing at her. "Behaviors, punishments, corrections, rewards… This is…"

"A lot to digest, I know."

His gaze was inscrutable—no indication of what was going on in that masterful mind of his. He wanted this, obviously, but how much? Did he have reservations? He didn't seem like the type, but everyone had some qualms, right?

"You've done your research, Tarah, and you knew to expect this. Is there anything unreasonable here? Anything you can't handle?"

This time, she started at the beginning again and read every single word.

Was there anything unreasonable? Unreasonable was such a relative word. His standards would be high, punishment meted out if those expectations weren't met, but doing what he asked was all within Tarah's ability. And if she did, there'd be no punishments…

Six months.

She took the pen and, before she lost her nerve, signed her name.

I'm signing my life away.

"You needn't look panicked. You are perfectly capable of doing everything here. You may have to put your mind to it more than at other times, but I'm confident you can." He reached for another pile of papers, then exchanged them for the ones in her hands. "Here's your copy for future reference."

Silently, she promised herself she'd study and even memorize them as soon as her final exam was over. She slipped the papers into her sack. The punishments didn't sound too bad, but they progressed. She planned never to need punishment beyond level one.

She gazed at him, desperately wishing for some indication of his thinking. But nothing clarified or explained what was contained in those fathomlessly dark eyes.

"Do we shake on it?" What was the protocol for a situation like this?

He grinned. A wolfish grin. "Sure, we can shake on it." He held out his hand.

She placed her much smaller one in his, and the power when he closed his hand around hers jolted her. The handshake was firm but not painfully so. Yet this was much more than a sealing of a contract. She'd agreed to go swimming in a tank with a shark.

And he looked hungry.

Chapter Three

Tarah had only taken two hours to pack everything she owned. She did it during study breaks and still aced her final exam. The entire bus ride home had been a mixture of happiness and nervousness. With everything going on, she hadn't had time to contemplate the future. She'd given her resignation at work, apologizing she hadn't been able to give two weeks' notice. Not a problem, she'd been told. Apparently, they'd found a gentleman who used to work as a security officer on film sets, and he was ready to start Friday night.

When she finally tracked Ainsley down to tell her she was leaving, her roommate said some agreeable man had come around and paid the lease. What did he look like? Over six feet tall, black hair, brown eyes, and gorgeous as hell. Now, as she walked up her street, a moving truck and three men waited for her.

"Ms. Peters?"

She eyed the crew. "Yes, I'm Tarah Peters."

"We're here to move you."

Despite herself, she laughed. "He sent three of you?"

The man with the clipboard nodded. "Mr. Merrick said to move any furniture to the storage space he arranged, and to move your personal effects to his condo. He apologized for not being here in person, but a business matter came up."

She hadn't expected him to be there, so that wasn't a big deal. "You don't understand." Meeting the man's gaze, she tried to explain. "I rented the room furnished. I have two boxes of books and two suitcases of clothes. That's everything I have."

The man with the clipboard inclined his head. "Well, it won't take long. As soon as we're packed, we'll call you a cab and meet you at the building."

"I can take a bus—"

He shook his head. "Mr. Merrick's instructions were explicit. You take a cab and meet us there so you can oversee us. Make sure we don't break anything."

She was about to reiterate she only owned clothes and books, but the man was serious. *Fine.* Arguing was pointless. She led them into her building and up the two flights of stairs.

It took exactly one trip. She gave the keys to a neighbor as prearranged and slid into the cab the man had called for her. Without a backward glance, she left East Vancouver and headed into the unknown.

****

As with the move-out, the move-in took all of one trip. Marvelle was working and acted as if the entire thing was no big deal. And maybe it was. Maybe the problem was in Tarah's head. She shouldn't care what others thought. Wouldn't care. So what if they thought she was a mistress or some other sordid thing? She knew what she was, and that was enough.

Unpacking took mere moments. Now what? With nervous energy to spare, she paced the condo like a caged lioness. All the doors were open except the dungeon, and as much she wanted to see if the room was as Rielle had left it, she knew better. If she was meant to see the room, then she would.

Fatalistic much?

Her outfit was a little shabby. Maybe she should try to look good tonight—make a good impression. She stalked back to her room and pawed through her measly stash of clothes. Okay, she'd pair her one clean white blouse with her work pants. A shower was in order, so she crossed the condo again. Sneaking another peek at the painting, she gave up all pretense of not staring. The woman was both statuesque and stacked, with blonde hair on her head and…down below. Intimidating.

So why had he *really* selected Tarah when he could've had any woman he wanted? She had no simple answers as she entered the bathroom.

Nirvana.

She'd died and gone to heaven.

She found a separate shower with multiple heads and an enormous soaker bathtub. Tossing a mental coin, she decided she'd shower tonight and take a bath tomorrow. After turning on the water as hot as she could tolerate, she stepped into the spray. Soaping up, she did a leisurely exploration of her body. Amazingly, she could take all the time she wanted without worrying about a temperamental boiler and a small hot-water tank. Her hair went halfway down her back, so she had to use two handfuls of shampoo to get all of it washed.

Squeaky clean, she reluctantly left the warmth of the shower and stepped back onto the tile floor. Even though she'd flipped on the fan, she'd steamed the mirror. She dried herself using the obscenely expensive bath sheet. Such a decadent difference from the towel she owned, left tucked in her suitcase along with a few other things that'd never see the light of this place. She wasn't ashamed of her favorite wool blanket, but it had a couple of holes in it. Her sheets were for a single bed, whereas the bed in the white room was a king.

Plus, she'd found several blankets and extra sheet sets on the upper shelf of her closet. No, she'd hold on to her things but keep them hidden. She grabbed her bottle of dollar-store lotion, then she applied it to her body. Ever mindful of how dry her skin was, she tried to keep it hydrated.

Detangling her hair took some time, and then she set to work with the dryer. Time was passing, so she left it a little damp in favor of hurrying to dress and be ready for Sebastian's return. He hadn't given her a precise time, but she wanted to be ready. Should she put on makeup? *Five o'clock.* After crossing back to her room, she quickly put away her clothes and gazed longingly at the laptop.

Tomorrow. She had all the time in the world to explore tomorrow.

As she stepped out of her room, she heard the key in the lock. Nerves threatened to bring her to her knees, and she took a steadying breath before going to greet him.

His surprise was obvious, but his grin was also wide. He grasped her upper arms lightly and pressed a kiss to her cheek. "I enjoy being greeted at the door."

"I'll remember." *Why is my voice breathy?*

He stepped back to examine what she wore. "Put on some shoes and your coat. We're going out to dinner."

She swallowed. "Am I dressed appropriately?"

He gave her a once-over, and she tried not to squirm under the scrutiny.

"We're going to the restaurant around the corner, and it's fairly informal."

And very expensive. She returned to her room and slipped into her one pair of heels and her jean jacket.

Her reappearance caused him to frown. "It's cold out—don't you have a winter jacket?"

"This will be fine." *Back off—you're not my mother.* Not that her mother would care. "I wear it all the time." Her winter coat still sat in her suitcase because of the frayed sleeves. Her jean jacket wasn't as warm but was respectable.

Seemingly appeased, he offered his arm.

Hesitantly, she slipped her hand at the crook of his elbow. Twice now they'd touched, and it disconcerted her. Was it her imagination heat was coming off him and hitting her in waves? Probably. He smelled good. Not cologne or aftershave, but a woodsy, outdoorsy smell. Since they were in the middle of a concrete jungle, the scent was incongruous and illogical.

As if by providence, the elevator was there to greet them. When they crossed the lobby, Carlos wished them a good evening.

Suck it up.

And hold your head high.

As they stepped outside, the chill permeated her body—the jacket offered little protection in the wind. Were frayed sleeves really the end of the world? A gust of wind pushed her closer to Sebastian, and he placed his arm around her to hold her steady.

"They say it may snow tomorrow." He tossed off the line in a casual-conversation way.

"Well, it's cold enough." Amazingly, the thought didn't bring with it the normal concern. The heater in her old room had been, at best, temperamental and often hadn't worked. Facing a blast of winter in her old place would've been dicey. In Sebastian's condo, heat would never be in short supply.

Upon arriving at the restaurant, they were ushered directly to their table. He ordered a rum and cola for himself and a white-wine spritzer for her. He was being high-handed again, but she yielded to him. She rarely drank, and it'd go right to her head, so she planned to sip it slowly. He ordered the spaghetti for himself and the shrimp linguine for her. Lucky thing she wasn't allergic to shellfish.

"How was your day?"

He shrugged. "Like most of my days. I work hard because I choose to."

His offhandness rankled, so she persisted. "What does that mean?"

"That I have competent people working for me. Whether or not I'm there, they'll do their best."

She considered his response. "Are you a taskmaster?"

Now he became contemplative, his eyes a little less focused. "I hire the best and pay them well. I have high expectations, and more often than not, my people meet or exceed them." He met her gaze with dark intensity. "You have every potential of exceeding my expectations, Tarah."

"I'll do my best." She swallowed her trepidation. "I wanted to thank you for sending those nice men and paying for the cab."

A look of bemusement crossed his face. "A very short move, according to Cliff. They were undoubtedly pleased as they had a four-hour minimum charge."

"Oh." She wasn't sure how to respond.

Dark eyes sparkled in the candlelight. "I can afford

it—don't worry about it."

"Of course." Heat bloomed in her cheeks. "I didn't mean…well, thank you."

"Anything you need or want—you need only ask."

The ease of his generosity overwhelmed her. Seeking courage, she ventured, "It's too much."

Unexpectedly, he snagged her hand. His hands were always warm, a contrast to hers, which were often cold.

"In an odd way, you'll earn those rewards."

Her eyes widened in panic. "I thought you said I wasn't a prostitute." She hissed the words, mindful of the other diners.

Something flashed in his eyes. "Don't equate generosity with paying for favors. The contract specified rewards as well as consequences. Don't question my integrity, Tarah."

Shit.

Her cheeks warmed again. She dropped her gaze to their hands, which were still entwined. "I apologize. I'm not used to this. I come from a middle-class background with middle-class values."

"And I came from something one small step up from the gutters, but it doesn't define who I am." A self-deprecating edge to his voice.

Her gaze snapped up. "I didn't…I didn't know."

His thumb stroked the sensitive juncture where her thumb met her index finger. She suppressed, barely, the shiver running through her.

"If I were American, then mine would be the American dream story. Rags to riches. The truth is hard work and a determination to succeed bred success. I wasn't going to be defined by my circumstances."

"Admirable." She was genuinely impressed. Her

own aspirations paled compared to what his must have been. "Are you happy with your success?"

He pulled back, a brow arching. "I would never sit on my laurels if that's what you're asking."

She shook her head. *Frustrating man.* "I wasn't suggesting that. I was asking if you've found some measure of satisfaction with your life. If you died tomorrow, would you leave this world feeling fulfilled?"

"What an odd question." His brow furrowed. "I wouldn't have any regrets. Is that the same thing?"

Now she considered. The snakes-in-the-belly sensation was back. "I guess so. I want to say I made a difference. I'd say I'm not as happy as I envision I'll be when I become a teacher."

"What if you're wrong? What if you don't make a difference? What if you're a bad teacher?"

That was exactly what she ruminated on when she dug through linguistics and semiotics. When she tried to differentiate between Freud and Jung. When she trudged through all those damn electives, including French. Hadn't she wondered if this was all worth the hassle?

"I have to believe I'll become a teacher and will make a difference. Otherwise, the years of struggle have been for naught."

"I wasn't questioning you, Tarah. I have the greatest faith you'll succeed. I just want to make sure your expectations aren't so high you never meet them." His gaze softened, the little lines around his mouth relaxing.

She shook her head, adamant about this. "I need to aim high. I need to prove myself if only to me."

He relinquished his hold on her hand as the food arrived.

The loss engulfed her. *Idiot.* Holding hands meant

nothing.

"Thank you." She offered the words to the waiter despite the thickness in her throat. "It smells delicious."

"Can I get you anything else?"

"No, we're fine." Sebastian didn't break eye contact with her but inclined his head at the waiter. "Thank you."

The waiter stepped away, and she savored the aroma. It smelled like heaven. Dollar-store noodles and macaroni and cheese didn't have the same flavor.

"So expressive," he murmured with an odd expression on his face.

Instead of being embarrassed, she simply smiled. "I'm always grateful for good food."

"You see, Tarah, we have something in common."

In that moment she almost—almost—believed him.

****

Pleasant contentment enveloped her until they stepped from the restaurant, and she was hit in the face by not only the wind, but the first flakes of snow. "I guess the weather forecasters got it right for once." Her voice was dry.

Sebastian shrugged out of his jacket and placed it around her shoulders.

"You'll be cold." A token protest as the warmth from his coat was already enveloping her.

"I grew up in the cold." His tone was self-deprecating. "This is nothing."

Gallant. Seeing as she was cold, she didn't put up another argument, and they walked the few blocks in companionable silence.

Carlos stood when they entered the building. "Mr. Merrick, Miss Peters, I hope you had a pleasant evening."

"We did, Carlos, thank you." Sebastian gestured toward the enormous glass windows. "Drive carefully—it's started snowing. You have a long way to go."

Tarah didn't ask how Sebastian knew the older man had an hour-long drive to get home. He had to be omniscient. Or at least omnipresent. How else could he know so much?

When they stepped into the condo, she removed his jacket. "Thank you." She gave him a genuine smile as she handed it back.

"You are most welcome, Tarah." Lightly, he clasped her upper arms, tugging her toward him. They were almost—almost—touching. He pressed a kiss to her forehead. "Now, go to bed. You've got a big day tomorrow."

She frowned but decided not to question him. She was exhausted, despite the early hour, and bed sounded heavenly. About to step away, she took a moment, searching for the right words. "Thank you, Sebastian."

"You're most welcome. Tomorrow we start your training."

It sounded ominous, but she put all thoughts of submission from her mind, and when her head hit the pillow, she was asleep within moments.

The white room held no natural light, but Sebastian had installed a slow wake-up lamp that started out low and, by the time the alarm went off, was full bright. Tarah had set the alarm for seven so she could be up to see Sebastian off to the office.

After making her way to the kitchen, all she discovered was a note from him. He'd be home at ten, and she should be dressed by then. What kind of sloth did he think she was? Normally, she went straight from work to a preschool where she volunteered, then she went either to bed or to class. She rarely slept over six hours. The full ten last night had made her a little sluggish. A walk. After breakfast she'd take a walk in the fresh air.

Sebastian's fridge and pantry were well stocked, and she made herself toast with a cup of yogurt and a cup of black tea. Once she was finished eating, she took her tea to the windows and pulled back the blinds. Her heart sank. At least a foot of snow was piled on the balcony. Since her winter boots had a gap between the sole and the boot, she was going nowhere. The building had a pool, but she didn't own a bathing suit.

The stairs. She'd walk up and down the stairs. Fifteen floors up from where she was and fifteen down. Maybe that'd burn off some of this nervous energy. She changed from her pajamas to her sweats, grabbed the key Sebastian had left her, and headed for the stairwell.

By the tenth floor, she was questioning her enthusiasm. She had believed herself in shape but rethought that assertion. Determined, she kept walking up the stairs, at times dragging herself with her arms. At the top, her sense of elation was short lived as she looked down. Whether dizzy from the exertion or from vertigo, she opted to take the elevator back to her floor.

Relaxation came in the form of a soak in the massive bathtub. It'd fit two people, and her belly fluttered at the image of being in there with Sebastian. Fit and trim, he had the physique of a runner. He was handsome, even she could recognize that, but she sensed something more to him. Animal magnetism sounded hackneyed, yet sexy seemed trite. Those reduced him to the physical, and he was much more than that. The man was intelligent and incisive, and his ability to read her was terrifying. She never hid her emotions because no one cared enough to notice. Now she was living with a man who noted every single detail, making her a butterfly pinned to a corkboard, there to be examined, scrutinized, and found lacking. Because he'd find her lacking. Everyone did. Except the kids. They noticed her, loved her, showed her unrestrained affection. But adults? No, not them.

And Sebastian was nothing if not an adult.

At nine thirty, she pulled herself with great reluctance from the tub of cooling water. After hurrying through the drying of her hair, she dressed quickly in jeans and a sweater. Sebastian had been a little light on details, but he must have been aware she possessed few options.

At five minutes to ten, he entered the suite. Again, she was at the door to greet him. This time he merely smiled and indicated she follow him into the living room.

"I've asked a friend to come visit with you. I expect you to be on your best behavior and accept my wishes without question."

What the hell? "Why wouldn't I? I can manage respectful."

He merely inclined his head. "Remember, you promised."

A knock at the door brought a frisson of nervousness that shot through her. She now represented Sebastian Merrick, and her behavior would reflect on him.

Murmured greetings carried from the hall, and three women entered, pushing trolleys full of boxes and garment bags. Following them was a beautiful woman. Uncommonly tall, she commanded attention. The woman was reed thin and wearing heels. Her black hair with silver threads was swept up in a chignon, and her incisive blue eyes were already assessing Tarah.

"Mme Veronique, this is Tarah Peters. Tarah, this is Mme Veronique. She is a friend with impeccable taste."

Instead of preening under Sebastian's praise, Mme Veronique held out her hand to Tarah. "Miss Peters."

"Tarah, please."

The intimidating woman smiled warmly. "Tarah," she repeated with a slight accent.

Tarah had no ability to place it but would've pegged the woman as Eastern European.

Mme Veronique stepped back. "These are my assistants. Jeanne is a stylist, Kelci is a makeup artist, and Simone is a professional dresser. They all work in the film industry, but I was lucky enough to procure their services this morning."

Tarah offered her most genial smile. "I thank you ladies for being here to help." She glanced over to Sebastian. What was she thanking these women for?

Mme Veronique answered the unspoken question. "Simone is going to take you into your bedroom and get started on measurements while Jeanne and I select outfits that will match your coloring." She gave Tarah another appraising look. "You have the most stunning eyes. And your hair. Would you be averse to letting Kelci add some dark-auburn highlights? It would give you a more exotic and alluring look."

Tarah never even considered refusing. She gave the intimidating woman the bravest smile she could. "I'd be thrilled."

"Very well," Mme Veronique said, apparently giving her approval to the entire situation. "Simone, will you help Tarah?"

The younger woman nodded enthusiastically and led Tarah to the bedroom. *Led her.* The woman had obviously been here before. *Ugh.* How many women had benefited from Sebastian's largesse? Because she was under no illusions about what was going on. She was about to be thrust into the role of the young ingenue accepting gifts from the rich older man. *Don't fight it, or there will be consequences.* Since she didn't want to know what those were, she stripped for Simone and let the woman take her measurements.

****

They took a break for lunch, and then Kelci went to work on Tarah's hair. The bubbly young woman spoke about several of the actors she'd worked with. Her specialty was movies and fashion shoots, but she admitted she loved her private gigs. She'd been working with Mme Veronique for five years and had the greatest respect for the woman. She also confided Mme Veronique rarely did these private affairs, and Sebastian must be a very important man.

Well, she hadn't been that direct, but Tarah ferreted out the information.

So he had access to exclusive services. Why was she not surprised? Although she shouldn't have been, she was stunned speechless by the new hairdo Kelci had given her while Tarah sat on the closed toilet lid. The woman worked miracles. And without question, Mme Veronique had been correct—Tarah looked more exotic. Kelci also gave her hair a trim and made the most amazing bangs. Tarah'd never had bangs, but they framed her face beautifully and emphasized her high cheekbones.

The young assistant had also worked magic with

makeup, showing Tarah how to replicate the results and giving her a new set of cosmetics.

Another thing that made her chest tighten and her head spin. She'd had no use for makeup, figuring she was okay as she was. Looking at Kelci's handiwork, she was willing to rethink that assertion.

Kelci examined her with a critical eye and gave a wide smile. "I may have outdone myself, but I had an amazing palette to work with. Your skin is translucent. You wear sunscreen, right?"

"Um, sure." Actually more like she never had the time to go out and enjoy the sun. Usually, she was asleep when the sun was highest in the sky.

"Let's go show Mme Veronique and that man of yours."

Again, she made some sound which might be taken as assent. The two people in question were deep in conversation but broke off when she entered the room with Kelci trailing behind her. When she hesitated, the makeup artist gave her an indelicate nudge.

Mme Veronique scrutinized the results.

Tarah tried not to squirm, not willing to be found wanting. When she turned to Sebastian, though, she flushed. His gaze was predatory appreciation—raking up and down her body—settling on her face. His mouth curled up in a slow and appreciative smile.

"You look stunning," Mme Veronique pronounced. "Kelci, you have outdone yourself."

Sebastian swept out his hands to encompass all the women. "A bonus for each of you. Everyone tonight will be looking at my companion."

"And, of course, she must wear the pale-blue dress."

That dress was a strapless number that was short and

fit Tarah like a second skin. She could barely breathe in it, let alone wear underwear. Panty lines, Jeanne had explained, as if that made everything acceptable. Tarah had never once gone commando in her life. Tonight would be a first.

Before she knew it, Mme Veronique, the three assistants, and the now virtually empty trolleys were gone, leaving her alone with Sebastian.

She whirled on him. "I told you I couldn't be bought."

He looked bemused. "Do you have anything vaguely suitable for tonight and all the other events we'll be attending for the next six months?"

Good point. "But all the other clothes? Jeans, blouses, pants, turtlenecks, boots, shoes, coats…" She trailed off. Also the extensive lingerie collection and the slinky midnight-blue nightgown, but she wouldn't mention them.

"Again, it's simple. You represent me. What you wear reflects on me, and I put up a professional image."

She shot out the question uppermost in her mind. "How many times has Mme Veronique been here? How many other women have you bought?"

His eyes blazed fury. "Smith MacLean—a man you know well—introduced me to Veronique, and this was the first time I engaged her services. I warned you about fighting me."

She knew Smith MacLean. He'd owned this condo before Sebastian.

The penny dropped. "He did the same thing for Alessandra?"

Tarah had met Alessandra a few times and liked the warm woman with the kind heart. She flashed back to the first time she'd met the petite brunette. Alessandra had been passed out in Smith's arms, wearing a spandex catsuit and four-inch heels. Smith had been obliged to ask Tarah to unlock the door to the condo so he wouldn't drop the *lady*. She distinctly remembered rolling her eyes and muttering under her breath that Alessandra didn't seem much like a lady. As she got to know the other woman, a pang of guilt over the nasty comment had caused a knot in her stomach. She didn't know the entire story, but she now knew the older woman had been in an awful place when Smith brought her here.

"Yes, he did the same thing for Alessandra. She arrived with even fewer clothes than you did. Now, I want you to go lie down. Get up at five and get ready for this evening. It's a sit-down dinner, and we need to be there at six thirty."

What the hell? "You're ordering me to my room to take a nap? What am I, three years old?"

Sebastian simply inclined his head. "I told you to not fight me on this, and although you were well behaved when the women were here, you've been insolent ever since. Be glad this is the only punishment I'm meting out. Now, go before you annoy me any further."

Beating a hasty retreat, she went to her room. She wasn't going to take a nap—that was for sure. She eyed the pile of electronics and sat at the desk.

The laptop booted up in mere moments and was preloaded with everything she could ever want. Once she hooked the laptop up to Wi-Fi, she surfed right away. She pulled up more information about submissives. So far, she wasn't doing a very good job. Making a silent promise to do better, she read the instructions on how to download books to her e-reader.

Chapter Four

"You look stunning."

Despite herself, she basked in Sebastian's approval. This afternoon's spat had been forgotten, and they were headed to tonight's dinner in a cab. She fidgeted nervously with her purse. "What do I need to know about tonight?"

"We'll be sitting with Lucille and Gordon Forbes. Lucille is an investigative journalist from the *Vancouver Sun*. Joining us will be Marilyn and Lars Halston. Marilyn is president of Luxurious Cosmetics."

"That's the brand I'm wearing."

"All by design." He straightened the lapel on his coat. "A way for you to start a conversation if necessary."

She drew her finger along the intricate design of the beaded clutch purse. "And who am I?"

Sebastian angled himself toward her. "You're a third-year university student studying to become an elementary school teacher."

"Am I your friend? Companion? Mistress? Because that's probably what they'll think."

His laugh sounded more like a bark. "I don't give a fuck what they think. You're my dinner date. If you choose to tell them you're living in my spare room, that's up to you."

"They wouldn't believe me." She wasn't pleased

with this line of discussion. "I don't want to be seen as a money-grabbing little—"

"Don't say it." His voice was sharp. "There's nothing wrong with our relationship."

"Except you're twenty years my senior." *Whoops.* This might be not only a fight she'd lose, but a tone she should be avoiding.

"Thirteen, and don't get cute with me. You're giving yourself far too much importance."

Her face flamed. "I don't want to tarnish your image."

"My image will hardly be tarnished. I have been attending this event by myself for the past five years, so you'll garner some vague attention but nothing more." He made a sharp chopping motion with his hand. "Stop fidgeting."

Her hands immediately stilled. Just in time for the cab to pull up to an exclusive yacht club she'd never heard of. Calming the butterflies in her stomach, she waited for him to come around and help her from the taxi. He offered her his arm, which she took gratefully. She'd never worn heels over one inch before and was a little unsteady on these two-and-a-half-inch shoes. Several other pairs of shoes that'd been selected were even higher. Better practice in them when she had some time.

They checked their coats, and he led them into a large room that was festively lit. "Tonight is a benefit for the Children's Hospital." He pointed to an open floor area. "After dinner there will be several speeches and some dancing."

Dancing? She'd never danced in her life. *Suck it up—you can do this.*

They were the first to their table, soon joined by Marilyn and Lars. After introductions, Tarah complimented Marilyn on the quality of cosmetics, and Lars spoke up, pointing out the cosmetics weren't tested on animals. Pride for his wife shone in his eyes. He didn't seem concerned she was the higher-profile member of the couple. Well, everyone had an important role to play, and sometimes it was to be an asset to one's partner. She could do that. She could be an asset to Sebastian.

Lucille and Gordon arrived shortly before dinner was served, so the midway point of the meal had passed before Lucille directed a question toward Sebastian. "I heard Club Kink reopened. Have you been yet?"

Tarah nearly choked on her wine.

With a bland stare, he offered a casual smile. "Since Smith is now the owner of the club, it stands to reason I might visit, but no, I haven't gone yet. I hear it's busy these days."

"Notoriety will do that."

What the hell are they talking about?

Lucille looked at her. "Club Kink was at the center of a scandal involving Carl Jergen."

To Tarah's continued bewilderment, Lucille clarified.

"He was a powerful conservative judge who thought he could be the next prime minister. His proclivities, and the fact he killed a woman, ended his grandiose delusions. Word is he's planning to plead insanity."

"Will never hold." Sebastian placed his napkin next to his empty plate. "Aside from the fact the murder is on tape, women like Rielle Clayton and Alessandra MacLean have stepped forward to report his abusive and aberrant behavior."

"Rielle?" All the blood drained from her face, and nausea gripped her. Telling herself the heat was making her feel faint only got her so far.

Stay calm.

No one knows.

But they will if you keep this up.

"If you'll excuse me." She steadied herself when she rose, offering the bravest smile she was capable of in that moment. The other men at the table rose, but she was barely aware of them. Having scouted out the bathroom upon arrival, she threaded her way through the tables, beating a hasty retreat toward the promised privacy and security.

Rielle.

That meant Tarah knew Carl Jergen. He'd been the man who'd abused and tormented her friend for four years. For four years she'd sat back and observed, never saying a word. Discretion, Sebastian had called it. Cowardice would be the better term. She could have said something. *Should* have said something. The night Jergen kicked Rielle so hard he broke her rib and punctured her lung, Tarah should have spoken up.

Instead, following Rielle's lead, she corroborated the story of slipping on the bathroom floor and landing on the side of the bathtub. Why the doctor accepted that story with Jergen's footprints on Rielle's skin was beyond Tarah, but she deferred to the older woman's wishes. Rielle had sent her a bouquet as thanks for her help that night, and they'd never spoken of it again. That Rielle was now happily married with a nine-month-old baby didn't lessen Tarah's guilt.

"Are you all right, dear? You look awfully pale."

Lucille Forbes had materialized in front of her while she'd been woolgathering. The older woman's concern was evident.

She waved her hand. "A little nauseous, that's all."

"These things can be very warm. Good timing, though." Lucille joined Tarah on the richly upholstered bench. "The speeches are about to begin. The men won't even notice if we take a few minutes to fix our makeup."

Tarah nodded, appreciative of the excuse.

"I take it you're acquainted with Rielle Clayton."

Well, there went her hope of discretion. "I worked in security at Mrs. Clayton's building, although she went by Reid back then."

"Is that where you met Sebastian?"

She didn't speak, not trusting her voice to be steady.

"Quite a coup, landing one of the most eligible bachelors of Vancouver."

"I…I didn't land him. He asked me to join him here this evening as his companion."

Lucille inspected her closely as if checking for the veracity of her statement. Since she uttered only the truth, she didn't worry about her facial expression giving her away. Her crimson cheeks weren't helping her story.

"Sebastian is a very attractive man."

Tell me about it. "I won't argue."

"I wish you the best with him."

Tarah pulled her lower lip through her teeth. "I'm not…I mean we're not…" She let the thought trail off.

Lucille placed a hand on her knee. "I meant nothing by it. Sebastian has been a friend for ages. My interest in Kink is more because I did the exposé on Jergen and was thrilled to see him finally brought down. I respect both Rielle and Alessandra for what they did. Standing up to someone powerful takes guts."

Guts she didn't possess.

Inclining her head, Lucille smiled. "I can hear the applause, and that's our cue to rejoin the men. Chin up, my dear, you've made a good impression."

How had Lucille known she needed cheerleading? Well, it didn't matter. The compliment carried her all the way back to the table.

Sebastian stood and helped her into her chair. He leaned over. "Everything okay?"

She met his gaze, trying to dispel the cloud of doubt Lucille's questions had given her. "I needed to get out of listening to the speeches."

As hoped, Sebastian laughed. He glanced up at the dance floor filling with couples. "Ready to dance?"

Her panic must have been evident.

"A slow dance, I promise you. Just follow my lead."

Just follow my lead. How hard could that be?

****

When they arrived home, Tarah was barely through the door before she slipped out of her shoes. She let out a long sigh as her feet pressed to the cold hardwood floor.

"You did well."

"Thank you." She pressed a hand to his lapel. "You didn't do badly yourself." She slipped out of her coat and let him hang it up.

"What did you and Lucille talk about?"

The question was asked with deceptive casualness, but she caught the edge in his voice. "This and that. Girl talk, you know?"

"You and Lucille are both women. Somehow I don't think you exchanged beauty tips."

The geniality was back, but she wasn't fooled for an

instant.

"And before you answer, Tarah, remember I can see everything on your face."

She barely refrained from rolling her eyes. God, he could be exasperating. "We talked about Carl Jergen, Rielle, Alessandra, and how I landed a date with the most eligible bachelor in Vancouver."

Hoping he'd skip her first comment and laugh at the second didn't work.

"You were surprised at hearing about the arrest? Jergen's face was all over the news and in the papers."

She bit her lower lip. "I get wrapped up in my studies and my work. I honestly wasn't aware he'd been arrested."

"But you knew him."

Please don't make me answer the question…

Unmovable steel was more forgiving.

"Yes." She made the admission grudgingly. She was useless as a liar. "I knew him. I knew what he was doing to Rielle, and I did nothing."

Sebastian's gaze narrowed. "Were you really in a position to do anything? You were, what, twenty-two?"

"Something like that." No point in hiding the bitterness. "But old enough to see what was going on."

He pressed a hand to her cheek. "He could've hurt you and not just physically. You were right to use your discretion." He opened his mouth to say something else, then cut it off with a shake of the head. "It's late, so go to bed. Tomorrow I want you to go online and sign up for your winter classes. Three is a good number. Order your textbooks as well so you can get started on your studies."

She always did, wanting to make sure she was never

behind, but still his kindness overwhelmed.

He pulled a credit card out of his wallet. "Use this until I get you one of your own."

Stunned, she took the card. She'd planned to dig into her savings to pay for the courses. Slowly, step-by-step, she was becoming more entrenched in this relationship. With a resigned sigh she took the card and went to bed.

Only when she was slipping off to sleep, did she wonder what he'd almost said to her in the hall.

****

Friday morning Tarah took advantage of the pool. Now she had both a bathing suit and a bikini, so it seemed a waste not to take advantage of the building's amenities. Swimming had been a part of her childhood, and she'd taken the progression of swimming classes, each year improving her skills and abilities. As she stroked through the water, she was pleased to see she was still as proficient as ever. She'd missed this and planned to take full advantage whenever she could.

After returning to the condo, she showered and sat down at the computer to register for her courses. Abnormal psychology, French grammar, and twentieth-century Canadian literature. Slowly, course by course, she was whittling her way down to an English degree with a psychology minor. Little minds. All those little minds she'd be able to guide. To help. Ordering textbooks was easy. They'd be delivered on Monday.

Eleven o'clock.

What the hell was she supposed to do with her time? Weird to have time on her hands. She would've kept her volunteer position at the daycare except the owner's daughter was now a senior in high school with her mornings free. She too wanted to be a teacher, and she needed practical volunteer experience. Tarah had been thanked for her service and shown the door. That'd been three months ago. At first she'd reveled in the extra sleep she'd been afforded, but now the thought of endless days intimidated. She'd worked every day since she was fourteen, if not paid, then as a volunteer or as a student. Instead of enjoying the decadence of free time, she was edgy.

When she heard the key in the lock, she was flooded with relief and hurried to the door so she could be there when Sebastian stepped in. She came face-to-face with a beautiful woman. *Uh-oh.* Was this one of Sebastian's submissives? Did she know Tarah was living here? Was she supposed to go hide in the white room? And for that matter, where was Sebastian?

Swallowing her unease, and feeling silly, she held out her hand. "Hello, I'm Tarah."

"I know." The other woman gave her a smile. "Mr. Merrick told me you'd be here." She shook Tarah's outstretched hand. "I'm Gratzia, the cleaner."

"Oh."

"You stay out of my way, and we'll get along just fine."

"Oh." *You sound like an idiot.* "Fair enough. I guess that means you don't need help."

Gratzia gave her an evil glare. "I worked for Ms. Reid, then Mr. MacLean, and now Mr. Merrick." She eyed Tarah speculatively. "I know what goes on around here, but I keep quiet. I like my job."

"What goes on…" The shoe dropped. Gratzia was referring to the dungeon. "It's not like that…"

Gratzia waved her off. "I'm starting now. I start with the white room and finish with the black room."

Tarah couldn't help but laugh at the apt descriptions of the rooms. "I'll wait out here for you to clean the white room, and I'll make myself scarce."

Giving her a quick smile, Gratzia moved into the apartment toward the broom closet. "You see? We understand each other fine."

Thus dismissed, Tarah took up residence on the couch in the living room and waited until she could get out of the cleaner's way. Given the woman's lovely ebony hair, dark-brown almond-shaped eyes, and beautiful figure, she'd catch any man's eye.

Jealousy?

No…curiosity. The woman said she'd been cleaning here for years, so no reason existed to think she and Sebastian had anything but a professional relationship. Even if they did, Tarah's place wasn't to speculate otherwise. He could have intimate relationships with whomever he pleased. She was his submissive in mind only. She certainly didn't have a claim on his body, even if she wished it were otherwise.

When Gratzia gave her the nod her room was clean, Tarah made a quick escape. Taking her e-reader, she opened one book from next semester's lit class.

****

When five o'clock arrived, she was about a third of the way through an extremely dense book. Hugh MacLennan's *Two Solitudes* was an attempt to explain the differences between the French Québec and the rest of English Canada.

Needing a break, she headed to the kitchen. Sebastian hadn't said if they were eating out tonight, and she contemplated whether she should cook dinner. *What am I supposed to do?* Panic was setting in when she heard the key in the lock. For the second time that day, she went to the door.

Sebastian entered.

Thankfully, he carried takeout from a Chinese food restaurant. She held the door and then secured the bolt behind him. After joining him in the kitchen, she set the table while he shed his jacket and carried the food to the table.

He snagged both plates and apportioned the food.

Although the aroma was enticing, she was intimidated by the sheer volume of food on her plate. "I can't eat all this." *Why does my voice sound feeble?*

"You can and you will."

A mild and unhelpful reply.

"Now, be a good girl and eat up."

A good girl? "Sebastian, I'll get fat if I keep eating like this. Shrimp linguine, roast beef, now Chinese, it's too much."

"You won't get fat." His voice was sharp. "You need to put on eight pounds. We'll do it gradually and steadily. About two pounds a month."

Holy shit. "Who are you to judge what I should weigh? How do you know what I weigh?"

He named her weight and was off by one pound. She didn't have time to swallow her surprise before he spoke again.

"And the proper response is *thank you for your consideration of my health, Sir*."

Her eyes narrowed. "You expect me to say that?"

"And I expect you to mean it." His tone was icy. "So let's try it again. Say *thank you for your consideration of my health, Sir*."

She balked. "I can't say that and mean it because

you're being too intrusive."

"Eat up while I decide what your punishment for impudence will be."

"Punishment?"

"Eat your food before I get more annoyed."

Not daring to argue further, she sucked it up and ate as much as she could manage. At her annoyed glare, he simply raised an eyebrow. When he finished his meal, they both rose. She scraped the rest of her food into the garbage, then put the dishes into the dishwasher while he stowed the food. Upon finishing, she followed him into the living room.

"You were rude earlier. Now strip."

What the hell? "I'm sorry?"

"You aren't now, but you will be. Clothes. Off. Now."

What the fuck? "I'm sorry, but I don't think so."

"Don't push me any further, or there will be more serious consequences. Now, strip."

An icy dread overtook her. She wanted to argue this wasn't in the contract, but she knew that wouldn't be accurate. He had the right to tell her what to wear.

Or, in this case, what not to wear.

With great reluctance, she pulled her sweater over her head. Taking her time, she folded it and let it fall to the sofa. Unbearably shy in her bra, she silently pleaded with him, but his expression brooked no opposition.

Off came the jeans and socks.

"I'm undressed."

Sebastian chuckled sardonically. "I said *strip*. That means everything. Each time you disobey me, you earn another punishment."

Off came the bra and the panties. When she tried to

cover herself, he took her hands and placed them at her side.

"You need to learn how to present yourself. You stand with your feet together, your spine straight, your knees slightly bent, and your gaze toward the floor. You answer all direct questions, ending your answers with *Sir*, and you don't offer an opinion or suggestion unless asked for one." He provided her with a moment to reflect. "Are we clear?"

She gaped. *He expects me to do that?*

"I'm sorry."

Clearly, he wasn't.

"I wasn't specific enough. I expect you to do those things right now."

Reviewing the instructions in her head, she set to work. Feet together, spine straight…damn, what was the rest of it? She should've been paying attention, but she was still so shocked at having her clothes taken away. While she searched the recesses of her mind, he stepped behind her, stooped down, and pressed a hand to the back of her knee.

"Hey!"

"Knees slightly bent and head bowed. Really, Tarah, they were simple instructions."

Now she saw red. "I thought you said this wasn't about sex."

"Have I done anything overtly or covertly sexual?"

"Well, isn't being naked part of sex?"

He stepped in front of her. "Look at me."

In response, her gaze shot up.

"You have yet to address me as *Sir*. I'll let that lapse go for now. To answer your question, yes, being naked while having sex is normal. But nudity is much more than that. You have inhibitions holding you back from exploring your inner self. I'm here to change how you perceive both the world and yourself."

"By forcing me into submission?"

"No one's forcing you, Tarah. You read the contract. Would you like me to get it for you?"

"No." She quickly added, "Sir." A quirk of his eyebrow told her he was aware of the lag time.

"Now we'll watch a hockey game. For your lapse of memory, you can join me, but you'll have to sit on the floor."

She goggled. "But the floor is cold."

"And you'll remember to address me as *Sir* and present yourself properly next time, won't you?"

Gulping, she eyed the floor. "May I at least have a mat?"

Sebastian sighed. "Get a towel from the bathroom. I wouldn't want you making a mess on my floor."

Making a beeline for the bathroom, she didn't ask what he meant.

****

When the game went into overtime, Tarah barely suppressed a groan. She was stiff, uncomfortable, and cold. She'd been allowed to lean against Sebastian's thigh, and he'd pet her hair occasionally, as he might a dog.

One hundred and seventy-seven days.

When the Canucks won the game, she let out a sigh of relief.

"I heard that."

"Sorry, Sir, it won't happen again."

He rose from the couch and offered her his hand.

She needed it because her muscles were cramped

and screamed in protest.

"You may go to the bathroom and go to bed. I'll see you in the morning."

She merely bobbed her head and fled the room.

Chapter Five

Saturday morning Tarah made sure she was up, showered, dressed, and was prepared to make him whatever he wanted for breakfast.

Turned out he was happy with scrambled eggs and toast. After they cleaned up, he led her to the couch.

"I have two gifts for you, Tarah."

She was afraid to ask.

"First, your own credit card."

When he told her the credit limit, she almost fell off the couch. She couldn't even fathom what could be purchased with that kind of money. Before she recovered, he spoke again.

"Second, I bought you this."

She'd seen him come in last night with a parcel wrapped in brown paper but hadn't given it much thought. Now she took it in her hands and eyed it with some wariness. "Thank you, Sir?"

"Open it."

She was careful with the wrapping, curiosity warring with dread. When she had removed the brown paper, she read the name of the store on the box. No wonder he'd chosen plain brown paper. After she opened the box, she started. Hesitantly, she reached out a hand.

"It's not going to bite you, Tarah."

"Maybe not, but I'm still scared."

He took the box from her arms. "Stand up."

The command was soft, but she leapt to her feet.

He took the leather bustier from the box and held it up to her. The garment was black with deep-purple piping and ties.

She held it to her as he pulled out a black leather skirt. She shouldn't have been surprised at the shortness of it, but to be honest, she was shocked. Would it even cover her ass?

"And before you ask, no underwear."

She barely suppressed the urge to roll her eyes. "Dare I ask why you purchased me this lovely outfit?"

"Watch the sarcasm, Tarah."

The rebuke was mild, but she recognized it as a warning.

"And you haven't seen the pièce de résistance." He held out a large velvet jeweler's box.

Tarah laid the outfit on the couch and opened the box.

A beautiful jewel-encrusted mask, which was all black except for the purple feathers, and the eyes were surrounded by…

"Are those diamonds?"

"Of course."

Said lightly as if of no consequence. *Sheesh.* "So I guess we're going out tonight."

"Give the girl a gold star."

She didn't miss the sarcasm.

"We're going to Club Kink tonight."

She tried to swallow, but this time she couldn't get the saliva past the lump in her throat. "Club Kink?"

"You've heard of it, of course."

As she closed the jeweler's box, wariness abounded. "That's Smith MacLean's club."

"Yes, but he won't be there. He might own it, but he doesn't frequent it anymore. He and Alessandra have gone... Well, to the outside world, they're vanilla."

"But they're kinky?"

Sebastian chuckled. "Unabashedly so. Now, I have a few hours of work to do." He pointed to his home office, then pulled out his wallet and handed her a pile of bills. "Why don't you go grocery shopping?"

"How do I know what you like?"

"Anything will be fine."

With that, he was gone, leaving a wave of uneasiness in his wake.

Gingerly, she picked up the outfit and took it to her room, paying special care to the mask. She didn't even want to think how much it had cost. He was being considerate of her—likely aware she'd never be comfortable stepping into a club like Kink without a mask.

Oh, who was she kidding? Nothing would make her comfortable with this plan. She was undeniably naïve. Of course she'd heard of Kink. She'd even suspected Rielle and Gage, then Smith and Alessandra, had frequented the club.

She ran her hand down the outfit again. Now she understood why a long trench coat had been among the new items bestowed upon her. Whoever was working the security desk tonight would see the trench coat and might surmise what was—or wasn't—beneath it.

****

Grocery shopping, preparing lunch, and reading another third of the book were pleasurable distractions, but lurking just below the surface was an unbelievable bundle of nerves. Sebastian asked her to prepare a simple

66

pasta dish, so she made spaghetti and meatballs with garlic bread and salad. He was appreciative and kind in his praise, giving her a moment's peace. It ended abruptly when he told her to be ready to go at nine o'clock. Tonight was a special night, and they'd want to get there early.

She was ready with ten minutes to spare and spent the time trying to stretch the skirt so it'd cover more of her nether regions. She wouldn't be bending over in this getup.

"Stop fidgeting." His admonishment was stern as he helped her into the trench coat. "Not that such things matter, but it's soft calf's leather. You'll damage it."

"A baby cow died so I could wear this?"

He rolled his eyes. "The calf died so it could become veal. His hide being retrieved was a side benefit."

I'm going to be sick.

Sensing her mood, he stepped forward. He took her hands in his and pressed a kiss to her forehead. "I'll make a donation to a calf-rescue organization if it'll appease your sensibilities."

Despite her discomfort, she laughed. "Make a donation to the aquarium, and I'll be happy."

"You like the aquarium?"

"I love the aquarium, but it's expensive to go." *Please let him not see my desperation.* "I don't get to go often." *Like, never.*

"If you do well tonight, we'll go tomorrow."

"Just like that?"

He pressed a kiss to her nose. "Just like that."

She took a deep steadying breath as he put on her mask, taking a moment to adjust the strap.

"Ready?"

"Of course." She put far more bravado into it than she felt, but the thought of going to the aquarium tomorrow buoyed her. She could handle this.

Twenty minutes later, in Club Kink, when he attached a bejeweled leather collar to her neck and snapped on a leash, she rethought that assertion.

Immediately, she put her fingers under the collar and tugged. "What the hell?"

He gave her a look that issued a clear warning. *Behave, or there will be consequences.*

She wanted to say the collar chafed, but given the lining was rabbit's fur and soft against her skin, the argument carried little weight. Some bunny had given up its life so she could be comfortable.

"It's fake rabbit fur, and stop fidgeting. Your name, in case anyone asks, is Anastasia. That should suit your sensibilities."

It eased her nervousness a bit. She despaired at being recognized even though about a zero chance of that happening existed. Still, she dreamed of being an elementary school teacher, and it wouldn't do to be seen in a fetish club. The mask she wore also provided her with a cloak of anonymity—good thing because she'd reluctantly relinquished her trench coat upon entry. The damn leather skirt barely covered the globes of her ass, and since she wore no underwear, an actual breeze passed up her legs and into her nether regions. Maybe just her imagination, but that didn't improve the situation.

She hadn't gotten a good look at the dog collar, but it'd been black with deep-purple accents and shiny jewels. Probably diamonds to match the ones on her mask. Sebastian didn't do anything by half measures, so they were likely real and obscenely expensive. She tried not to obsess about how many homeless people could be fed off what he'd spent to mark her as his own. He might as well have peed on her, as she was now clearly marked as his property.

She stuck to him like glue because he had a tight grasp on the leash, and because she was afraid of tripping over her own feet. She was wearing ridiculously high stiletto heels. Sebastian knew she wasn't used to them but didn't seem to care.

Already, numerous people milled about, and he'd said tonight was a special night—whatever that meant.

He led her up the stairs to the balcony where they stood, leaning against the railing. She was positioned between Sebastian and the wall, leaving her between a rock and a hard place.

"Sir?" She strained to be heard over the steady beat of the house music.

"Yes?"

"Permission to remove my shoes?"

He rolled his eyes but gave his assent. She stepped out of them and immediately dropped three inches in height, but she didn't give a shit. The solid concrete floor was heaven, and the cold seeped into her feet, bringing needed relief. If she had to wear those spiky things the rest of the time they were here, the night was going to be very long.

Unbidden, his promise came to her. If she was well behaved tonight, he'd take her to the aquarium tomorrow. She loved the Point and watching the African penguins. They were oddly majestic, even when they waddled. She tamped down the excitement and anticipation of tomorrow and focused on the main stage below.

She didn't have long to wait as a young woman was led to the stage.

In front of the crowd, two hooded men stripped her naked.

Sebastian's hand rested lightly on hers as it gripped the railing.

Once the last of the blonde's clothes were shed, they rotated her around, finally leading her to some contraption in the middle of the stage.

"That's a St. Andrew's Cross."

Sebastian's whisper tickled her ear. Okay. An interesting tidbit, but not all that informative. She'd glimpsed one in his condo before he bought it, but she'd no idea if he still had it. She'd been living with him for four days and, although filled with curiosity, hadn't ventured into the space.

Curiosity had killed that cat, and she was not a feline with nine lives.

The hooded men attached the woman to the cross, using manacles at her ankles and wrists.

It must have been uncomfortable for her, but Tarah found something erotic about watching a naked woman undulating her hips. The bound female seemed to seek relief, but from what?

A murmur rippled through the crowd as a man with a whip stepped on stage.

She did a double take. She'd met that man. Over a year ago he'd brought Rielle home. Tarah'd been working security that night and had been concerned for her friend. The man with spiky hair, lots of earrings, nipple rings, and covered in tattoos, had intimidated her, but he'd also reappeared about ten minutes after he arrived. Tarah had known Gage was upstairs waiting for Rielle, so she convinced herself everything would be okay. And okay it had been. Rielle had moved in with Gage—they'd married and now had a baby.

Still, Tarah was leery of the man who was stripped to the waist, his chest slicked with some kind of oil. His good looks didn't diminish her unease. Silently, she admired the tiger tattoo on his back, as well as the coil of interconnected whips making up the tattoo circling his biceps.

"Remember, she wants this. Spike's a genius at what he does," Sebastian whispered in her ear as the first crack of the whip was let loose.

The woman screamed, the crowd cheered, and Tarah jumped about two feet into the air. Sebastian's arm went around her waist, and he held her tightly against him so she couldn't move. That should've panicked her, but calm descended. The uniquely Sebastian scent enveloped her, bringing peace. Which was good because as the whipping continued, she cringed at each lash, but she held herself steady. In some perverse way, she was curious. What would make a woman want to be whipped? What was the blonde getting out of this?

Even from the balcony, the lash marks were visible. The red welts crisscrossed the woman's back and ass. It had to be painful, and she expected the woman to ask the man to stop, but she didn't. Hell, Tarah wanted to stop him, but the unwritten rules were clear, and Sebastian had explained them meticulously. Dungeon monitors could stop a scene if they had concerns over safety, but since everyone was a consenting adult, interference from voyeurs wasn't appreciated.

Spike let loose one final snap and coiled his whip.

The crowd erupted in applause and dispersed as they found other places in the play area and were off in search of the next show.

"Put your shoes back on, Mia—we're going to go mingle."

Mia.

Mine.

And she admitted she belonged to Sebastian. Or at least her body did. He'd proved this point effectively last night when he took away her clothes for insubordination. She put on her shoes with all due haste and prepared to mingle.

He hadn't worn a mask, obviously unconcerned about recognition.

And after twenty minutes of mingling, she saw why.

Even in the sea of good-looking people, he stood out. Over six feet tall, lean and trim, he commanded attention in his black silk shirt and black pants.

She knew from experience his eyes would be black in the low lighting of the club.

Hard to read, he garnered plenty of appreciative looks from other club goers. More from the submissives than the Dominants, but a close call.

She was getting better at spotting the difference. Dress wasn't always the best indicator, but behavior usually was. The submissives sought permission or approval from their Dominants, preening under praise and… What would she call it when a submissive didn't please her Dominant? Or his Dominant. More than a few men wearing dog collars. A few were even naked and crawling on the ground behind their mistresses or masters. Tarah had to be careful where she stepped. It wouldn't do to grind her stiletto into someone's instep.

"Bastian!"

She whirled, but he turned with more dignity.

"Master Dante." He held out his hand to meet the other man's. Their shake was firm.

She scrutinized the other man from under her lashes and decided masculine was an apt description.

Almost as tall as Sebastian, the man was as light as Sebastian was dark. Blond shaggy hair, light-hazel eyes, and a deep, appreciative smile.

"And who is this beguiling creature?"

Sebastian positioned himself between Tarah and Dante. "Master Dante, this is Anastasia, my submissive. Anastasia, this is Master Dante."

"Nice to meet you." Tarah offered a returning smile and held out her hand. A tug on her collar had her turning to Sebastian. "What did I do?"

"It's what you didn't do. You don't touch another Dominant without my express permission, as he would respect that boundary."

Master Dante chuckled. "A new submissive?"

"Very new." His eyebrow cocked in disapproval. "I should've spent more time explaining protocol."

She bristled. Since he had spent no time explaining protocol, she could hardly be faulted if she didn't know better.

Another tug on her collar.

Shit.

"I'm sorry, Sir—did you ask me something?"

"Master Dante was asking you if you might be interested in partaking in a scene."

She frantically searched the surrounding area. A man being flogged by a woman, another woman spread across a bench being spanked with a paddle, a woman suspended in ropes, and another woman doing some bizarre things to a man with an enormous cock.

No, she definitely did not want to participate in a scene.

The men chuckled at her bewilderment. Sebastian petted her hair like he might a dog as if he were trying to be soothing. Nothing, however, would calm her pounding heart and racing panicked mind.

"We'll pass this time, Master Dante, but thank you for the offer. Perhaps another night?"

Tarah didn't think either man could hear the *never* she grumbled under her breath, but a tug on the collar told her she should've kept her unruly mouth shut.

The two men exchanged handshakes, and she hurried to follow so the leash wasn't pulled taut again. She tried to tamp down the growing frustration and humiliation. Coming here hadn't been her choice on how to spend a Saturday night.

Relief flooded through her when they made their way to the coat check and retrieved their coats. After slipping into the trench coat, she buttoned it quickly and belted it as tightly as possible. She waited for Sebastian to remove the leash and collar, but he didn't, instead choosing to lead her outside and hailing a cab.

"Please, Sebastian." She looked around, desperate. "Please take the collar off." She'd do it herself, but she'd been surprised when he clipped it on and hadn't noted the locking mechanism. She clawed, fingers desperately searching for the buckle.

"Stop that." Anger in his voice. "I choose when I put the collar on and when I take it off."

He held the cab door open for her, then unceremoniously pushed her to the next seat.

Panic set in. The new security guard would be working. He was the man who'd replaced her, because a week ago she'd been a lowly concierge working the graveyard shift. Now she was being trained by a very rich man who had no compunctions of putting her in her place.

Unbidden, tears filled her eyes. The humiliation she faced was too much to bear.

And just like that, the collar was eased from her neck and tucked into a jacket pocket. Instead of the relief she was expecting, a rush of unease enveloped her. This was going to cost her. This entire night had just been one clusterfuck of mistakes on her part. Ignorance wasn't really a good excuse, but she planned to try.

A handkerchief pressed into her hand. "Clean yourself up—we're almost home."

Home.

His home. Certainly not hers. She didn't have a home. She'd agreed to live with him for six months, but that didn't give her claim to that most treasured of words. She'd grown up in a typical suburban home. When she was sixteen, her father had been diagnosed with cancer, and by the time she was eighteen, her family had been on the verge of losing their house. Her parents had sold the home and bought a one-bedroom condo. No longer having room for their adult daughter, they'd let her go to make her own way in the world.

She'd lived in a series of two-bedroom apartments of questionable quality in questionable neighborhoods and sometimes with questionable people. Her last roommate had been a student, and the apartment hadn't been all that bad.

But it hadn't been home.

She didn't have a home. She wasn't homeless, though. She was rootless.

One hundred and seventy-five days.

All she had to do was survive the next six months, and all her dreams would come true. If she had to be paraded around half naked in a club full of strangers and tugged around like a dog, she'd do it.

She dabbed at her running mascara. "I'm sorry, Sir. I didn't mean to make you unhappy."

"Although your apology is appreciated, Mia, your lack of trust in me is disturbing. I will always take care of you. My goal is to train you, not to humiliate you. Do you see the difference?"

Did she? Did it matter? Subdued, she twisted the tissue in her hands. "Yes, Sir."

"You're lying, but I'll let that slide." As the cab pulled up to the building, he handed over some bills to the driver and ordered her, "Wait until I come around to get you."

He exited, and she studiously avoided looking up. No sense showing her misery to the cab driver. The mask might give her anonymity, but it wouldn't hide her suffering.

As the cab door opened, she took the proffered hand. She leaned on Sebastian as he guided her into the building. He held the door for her and placed his arm over her shoulder.

The man at the security desk stood and stepped forward. "Good evening, folks. I'm Gus."

In her estimation the man was in his midsixties. He'd once been attractive, but age had taken a toll. Still, he held himself upright, and he extended his hand.

Sebastian took it and shook it firmly. "My name is

Sebastian Merrick, and this is Tarah Peters." He gently squeezed her hand. "Tarah, take off your mask."

Her cheeks flared, but she removed the mask. When Gus extended his hand to her, she surreptitiously looked for Sebastian's permission before she gave her hand.

"It's a pleasure to meet you, Miss Peters. Everyone has been wondering what happened to you." He looked back and forth between the couple. "Is there something I can say to them?"

"You may tell them she took a position as my personal assistant so she can dedicate more time to her schooling." Sebastian's expression was open. "You have a good evening, now."

"You too, Mr. Merrick, Miss Peters." Gus tipped his cap.

She felt his gaze on her as they walked to the elevator.

How smoothly the lies rolled off Sebastian's tongue. Except not quite a lie, more like stretching the truth. Still, no one in the building wouldn't speculate what *personal assistant* was euphemistic for. The entire building would think they were having sex and she was using him rather than the other way around. Except wasn't she using him? She couldn't say she wasn't getting something out of this because she was.

Were they just using each other?

As soon as they crossed the threshold, she rounded on him. "What are you really getting out of this? And don't give me some bullshit story about a companion for various functions. You didn't need me tonight. In fact, given the way some women were looking at you, I was more of a hindrance than a help. I even recognized a few of those women. You've brought them here before, haven't you?"

"Jealous?"

"Of those—" She wanted to call the women *tramps*, but that likely wouldn't go over well. "—those women?" God, she was sputtering.

"You *were* watching me."

"My job, Sebastian." Was he really this dense? "I was just doing my job."

He shook his head. "I told you not to lie to me. How many different women has Howard Walters brought back here over the past six months?"

"I…" She barely knew who Howard Walters was. She knew him by sight, of course. She knew most of the residents. But his companions? Not so much.

"What does Millicent Olivetti's boyfriend look like?"

"Well, he's…" Again, she had no snappy answer.

"How many different women have I brought back here since I moved in?"

"Eight in eight weeks." The words slipped out. "And since you've been here about two months, how do you know so much about everyone else's business?"

"I told you I'm acquainted with Jürgen Joseph. His wife has been happy to fill me in on all the gossip."

"Nosy Nettie."

Sebastian chuckled but inclined his head. "I'm sure you never called her that to her face."

Shit. "And I shouldn't have said anything now. I'm not jealous…"

"Just observant. So you've said." He shook his head. "I told you not to lie to me. That's the first rule, Tarah."

"Are these rules written?"

He appeared to consider and gave her a wicked grin.

"They aren't written, and I'll share them as needed. You're always free to write them down if that will improve your disposition."

"I'm going to run and do that right now."

"Include *no sarcasm* on your list while you're at it. Go." He waved her off dismissively. "Get changed. Come back out wearing the pale-blue silk robe and nothing else."

Of course.

"May I go to the bathroom?" Shit, was that sarcasm? Not likely to go over well. "I apologize, Sir."

He simply shook his head and made the shooing motion again.

Tarah took a deep breath and endeavored to follow his directions as best as she could.

Almost twenty minutes elapsed by the time she removed her makeup, managed to get out of the outfit, and put on the robe. It barely skimmed her thighs, and the slightest breeze would leave her completely exposed. Still, a sight better than last night when she'd been naked.

As she entered the living room, she tried not to count how many transgressions she'd made tonight.

"Did you write those rules down?"

Was she supposed to? "Um, no." She tried to smile. "I wanted to get back here as quickly as I could."

He scrutinized her. "Now, I'm of two minds. One way to train a submissive is to break her down and rebuild her. The other way is to praise and encourage."

"I like the praise-and-encourage method." *I can hope, right?*

He inclined his head. "Somehow, I'm not surprised. Let's be honest, Mia—you have a strong will. You've been independent with only yourself to rely on for many years now. It's hardly a surprise submission is not coming naturally to you."

"It's been three days." *Cut me some slack.*

"You did read the contract."

"Sure, but—"

"I don't like the word *but*. It's always followed by an excuse. Try again."

She took a deep breath. "I did read the contract, Sir—" How to express herself respectfully? "—and I have tried my best. I want to please you, but—"

Shit.

"Tell me what to do, Sebastian. Just tell me what to do, and I'll do it. If you'll just dictate the rules, I'll write them down and follow them." She wasn't above begging at this point.

He appeared to consider her plea. "It's not about rules—it's about behavior. It's about mindset, it's about spirit, and it's about intent."

Well, the writing's on the wall. "You're going to punish me, aren't you?"

"Correct you." His shrug was anything but lackadaisical. "You'll need it, and you'll thank me at the end."

"Do I have a choice?"

"Not this time, Mia. Actions and words have consequences."

He reached for her hand, and she gave it to him, albeit reluctantly. When he pulled her toward his bedroom, she balked.

"Really, Sir, I'm more than willing to take my punishment right here. There's nothing wrong with the living room."

He held tight, persuading rather than dragging. "It's

not like you haven't been dying of curiosity. It's not like you haven't been in there before."

"Not since I moved in. I only saw it once when Rielle lived here. Even then I didn't really look around."

He halted, and she barreled into him.

His expression was thunderous. "What did I say to you about lying?"

No way could he know how long she'd spent in the room. How she'd examined every implement. How she'd been dying of curiosity, but she'd never ask. How she'd been tempted to do searches on the internet but had been too busy.

He was bluffing. *No* way could he know.

And yet he did.

"Okay." *Damn it.* "I was curious."

"And…"

She huffed out a breath. "And I'm still curious. I've wanted to go in, but I've been good and resisted the urge. Give me credit for that at least."

"You see—the truth doesn't hurt—it sets you free."

He led her again, but this time she resisted. "Do you believe that? If people are just honest about everything, the world would be a better place?"

"Well, I can tell you one thing, Tarah." He stared her down, probably making sure he had her full and undivided attention. "The sooner you admit you're a born submissive, the easier this will be."

She was so stunned by his pronouncement she let him pull her into the dungeon. He flipped on the lights and closed the door, shutting out her last hope of escape.

The dungeon was every bit as scary as it had been the first time she stepped into it. Medieval torches were strategically placed around the room, giving off a low level of light. A St. Andrew's Cross in one corner, some kind of chair in another. It didn't look like any chair she'd be comfortable sitting in. A cage, as there had been when Rielle lived here.

The wall was still adorned with a wide variety of implements. She recognized the whip. Also several dildos, handcuffs, and a bunch of things she didn't recognize. Something told her she was going to become intimately acquainted with some of these items in the not-so-distant future. A set of shackles against one wall and when she glanced up, she spotted a set of manacles that could be lowered into the middle of the room.

Finally…the bed.

Huge. Massive. Bigger than any bed she'd ever seen before.

"Made to order, in case you're wondering. A specialized store that caters to…more discerning clients."

A fancy way of saying the rich and powerful.

"We're not…" She gestured vaguely in the bed's direction.

"I told you this isn't sexual."

"And I told you not wearing clothes in the presence of others is always sexual."

His gaze was penetrative. "You witnessed naked people there tonight. The woman on stage was naked. Was that all sexual?"

Don't lie. "Not all of it. Some of it involved power."

"Right answer. There is something called a total power exchange. That's a twenty-four-seven lifestyle where the submissive surrenders to the Dominant, trusting that person to care for them. Trusting the Dominant knows what's best."

"Sounds exploitative to me."

"In the wrong circumstances, any relationship can become abusive. But these people exchange power because they want to, not because they have to."

That caught her attention. "What did you mean when you said I was a born submissive?"

He drew a finger along her cheek. "It's not something I can define. You've been so strong for so long you don't possess the ability to give in."

"And you'll teach me how, right?"

"Mia, it's more complicated than that. Before we can exchange power, we need to exchange trust."

Yeah, right. "If there are arbitrary rules and punishments to be meted out on a whim, how am I supposed to trust?"

"Never on a whim. Every correction has a purpose." He let his words sink in. "Now, you need to give me your safeword."

"My what?"

"Your safeword. The word you'll use when you can't take any more."

"How about *stop*?"

Sebastian chuckled. "Oh, you'll be begging me to stop, but I'm talking about beyond that. You need to trust I won't push you past the breaking point, but I might miscalculate."

That was reassuring.

"Pick a word. A word you don't use every day. A word you'll only ever use in this room when you can't take any more."

"Rhetoric."

A pause. "An odd choice, I admit. I also need a word for when you need me to slow down. For when you can probably take more but need a break."

A break? How long were these sessions?

"Penguin."

Another chuckle. "You never cease to surprise me, my Mia. Now, let's be very clear—use either of these words carelessly, and there'll be consequences. Trust I know what's best and what you can endure."

Resignation seeped into her bones. "Why don't we just get this over with?"

"Again, Mia, you're looking at this from the wrong perspective. Take this correction as a time to surrender some of that control."

What do I have to lose? "Okay, show me."

"Such enthusiasm," he intoned. "Well, since enthusiasm is missing, we'll soldier on. You'll need to remove your robe."

Well, that was nicer than being ordered to strip. She unbelted the robe and shrugged out of it before carefully placing it on the back of a chair. Before she realized it consciously, she was presenting herself.

"You learned yesterday's lesson well, Mia. I have every faith tonight will go well."

He snagged her hands hanging loosely by her sides. After letting herself be guided over to the wall, she yielded when he leaned her chest against the wall. She let him press her against the cold and bumpy surface. She gave in when he guided her to turn her head and lay her cheek against the wall. She put up no protest when he placed her hands on the surface, each at the level of her ears.

Closing her eyes, she waited for what was yet to come.

"Anticipation is not always pleasant, is it?"

Tarah squeezed her eyes together even tighter. *Just get it over with.*

"You also need to know I'm always aware of what you will be feeling—physically anyway. I'm not doing anything to you I haven't done to myself."

Oh, for God's sake. "Please, just get on with it." She believed herself prepared. She'd seen the line of instruments of torture.

She had been dead wrong.

The wallop was so hard and jarring she slammed against the wall. Using her hands, she pushed away from the wall and rounded on him. "What the fuck was that?"

He stood, looking every inch the Dominant he claimed to be. The sleeves of his silk shirt were rolled up, and he held a paddle in his hand. Instead of responding, he pointed to the wall.

She received the unspoken message. Even so, she hesitated. "You expect me to turn my back to you, place myself against the wall, and wait for you to hit me again? It's fucking abuse."

"Those people you saw tonight, did they look like they were being abused? The woman on the stage, did she look unhappy at the end?"

"Well, no." *This is confusing.* The truth was people had appeared serene as they were being hit. Who was sicker—them for enjoying it or her for noticing?

"I'll only do as many as you can handle. But here's where the trust comes in, Mia. Relax your body. Let my hand's energy go through the paddle and then to you."

She eyed him warily. "Sounds Buddhist."

"Energy transference is also a concept in physics." He gave her a benevolent smile. "Try to let go. Try to trust."

Against her better judgment—and all things sane—she turned back to the wall. She placed her hands by her head, pressed her cheek to the wall, and waited.

This time she didn't have long to wait. Amazingly, it didn't hurt as much as the first time. Maybe he'd pulled the second one. Apparently, because the third wallop caused her to go up on the balls of her feet. Her heels were barely back to the ground when he let another one rip.

Let go. Let go. Let...

She let go. She stopped counting, stopped trying to judge if one was harder or lighter than the others. She gave in to the tears. She gave in to the pain. She surrendered herself.

His hands enveloped hers, gently uncurling the clenched fists.

"It's over, Mia."

The whisper was soft in her ear. In relief, she sagged back against him. "Over?" Her voice sounded breathy, even to her own ears. "No more?"

"No more." He turned her and pulled her into his arms.

She pressed her cheek to his chest as she had to the wall and found the same solidity. She wrapped her arms around his waist and clung on as if her life depended on it.

Maybe it did.

He scooped her into his arms and strode to the bed. He laid her down, making sure her head was on the pillow. A blanket was pulled over her. Warm. She felt warm. Like being in a womb.

And safe.

That was her last conscious thought.

Chapter Six

Consciousness crept across her like the sun burning off fog. Her eyes fluttered open to find Sebastian gazing at her.

He sat on a chair, casual, as if he always watched her while she lay naked in his bed.

"What time is it?"

"Four." Without looking at his watch.

"Clockwork."

His brow furrowed. "Clockwork?"

"They always leave at four in the morning. Like clockwork."

A slow and knowing smile spread across his face. "And you tried to tell me you weren't observant."

She rubbed her eyes with her fists. "Did you wake me?"

He shook his head.

"Then how do you get the timing so perfect?"

He shrugged. "It takes time for the sub to come down. Every time is different. Plus, it's not like I'm going to dress you and shove you out the door, so your empirical four a.m. theory has holes in it."

Now it was her turn to shrug and raise an eyebrow. "Come down? Did you drug me?"

"No, I didn't drug you. You were on a natural high from endorphins. I'll be honest—I was surprised how quickly you…gave in."

His perception of her was uncanny, because that was exactly what she'd done.

She shivered, pulling the blankets a little closer. "I'm scared."

"A natural reaction. I pushed you but not too hard."

Her eyes shut, and she winced. "It gets harder?"

"I've only begun to fuck with both your mind and body."

Hearing an expletive come from him sounded weird, but she understood his need to get his point across. His delivery was highly effective and the message clearly received.

"I suppose you want your bed back."

His brow arched, and she was afraid he was going to be intransigent.

He said, "You have three choices."

Her eyes widened, and she snickered. "I thought submissives didn't get choices."

"Do you want to go another round?"

"No." *Oh hell, no.* "You were saying something about choices…"

"You can go back to your bed, you can stay where you are and I take your bed, or we can share my bed."

She was up like a shot, the blankets falling away. Belatedly, she tried to pull them against her. She pointed toward the back of the chair. "Could you bring me my robe?"

With evident amusement, he snagged the robe and handed it to her.

She made a quick circular motion with her hand.

"What was that?"

"I'm asking you to turn around." She tried to keep the exasperation from her tone, but her cheeks were aflame.

His smile was that given to a petulant child who was demanding her own way but wasn't going to get it.

So Tarah did her best to hold the blanket against her while slipping into the robe. In the end, she got tangled up and had to get out of bed buck naked.

The whole time he continued to watch her with his indulgently curled lips. She wanted to scratch his eyes out but kept that particular sentiment to herself.

"I can see what you're thinking." The observation was offered casually.

"So now you're going to hold me responsible for what I think? Sounds unfair to me."

Shrugging, he rose with her. He walked over to the door and paused before opening it. He gazed down into her eyes.

"You'll learn to control your thoughts." His dark eyes flashed heat. "I can see the doubt, but you need to trust me."

That pesky word again. *Trust.* Hard to earn, easy to lose. Would she ever truly trust him? Would she ever truly trust herself? When he opened the door, she slipped through on a sigh.

****

Tarah had shut off the alarm when she'd crawled into her bed at the ungodly hour of four. The last coherent thought she remembered was amazement it'd only been seven days since Sebastian propositioned her.

Now, as she squinted her eyes to read the clock, she was shocked to see noon was nearly upon her. Eight straight hours of sleep. Decadence had a whole new meaning, and its name was sleep.

Still, her body was making demands on her, a full

bladder the most pressing one. After slipping into an oversized terry-cloth robe, she secured the belt tightly before venturing into the living room.

Sebastian sat on the couch, poring over a newspaper. "Good morning, Mia. Did you sleep well?"

"Actually, yes, I did."

"Glad to hear it. I made pancakes—they're warming in the oven. You had better hurry—those penguins aren't going to wait all day."

Penguins? "Oh, the aquarium." Joy burst through. "I'll just be a minute."

Taking the quickest shower on record, she then yanked her wet hair into a ponytail, then threw on jeans, a sweater, and brand-new hiking boots.

"I'm ready."

"You haven't eaten yet."

Well, duh. "I don't need to eat. I want to get going as soon as we can."

"And the sooner you eat, the sooner we can leave."

He still hadn't glanced up from his newspaper.

Having a hissy fit wouldn't get her far, so she went to the kitchen. Using the oven mitts, she pulled out the pancakes. Taking a plate, she then forked one over and began to eat.

"What the fuck?"

She jumped and nearly knocked over the plate.

"When I say you will eat, that means sitting at the table like a civilized human being. Stop stuffing yourself—it's bad for your digestive system." He snatched the plate away from her and headed to the dining room.

She rolled her eyes.

"I can see that."

Did he have eyes in the back of his head, or was she that predictable? Childish, if she was honest. He was being generous and treating her to a visit to the aquarium. The least she could do was be respectful. She sat where he indicated. "Thank you for showing me how to eat properly, Sir."

He frowned as if he couldn't quite figure out if she was being sarcastic or sincere.

She'd put in her best effort, but no fooling him. She ducked her head in shame.

Sitting down next to her, he placed his hand over hers. "Trust, remember? You need to trust I have your best interests at heart."

Tears burned the backs of her eyes. "Why is it so hard?"

"Because you're wound so tightly you don't know which way is up and which is down. All you know is survival. I'm trying to show you there's more to life."

"Why me?" Now she met his gaze. "There are thousands of women out there living on the edge—why pick me?"

"For the same reason you said *yes*. This is one of those things meant to be. Don't fight it, Mia."

His gaze was so intense it went straight to her core and skittered downward. She squeezed his hand, begging him to understand.

"You have to tell me what you want."

"I thought you could read minds." She managed a sniffle.

"Okay, I know what you want. But this is one of those times where you're going to have to ask."

And she couldn't. She offered a smile and asked for the next best thing. "Can we go see the penguins?"

****

She wanted to be suave and sophisticated, wandering from exhibit to exhibit as if she did this every day.

In the end it proved impossible because her enthusiasm overwhelmed. She and her father used to visit the aquarium once a year and had done so until he got cancer. It'd been nine years since she visited, and much had changed in that time. She wanted to explore everything at the same time.

Sebastian was both indulgent and patient, for which she was grateful. They stayed right until closing since she wanted to soak in every new piece of information she could. When they finished, he suggested a nice French restaurant, and she was amenable.

He ordered her food with a glass of wine, and she said nothing.

The food was, of course, delicious, but she struggled to come up with topics of conversation. She was out of practice with the intricacies of human interaction. Her weekly conversations with her mother were the longest she had, but even those were short. Tarah would say things were going great—even if they weren't—and her mother would say her father was doing well—even if he wasn't.

When something went wrong in her life, she had no one in whom she could confide. Her deepest and darkest secrets were hers alone. She made no secret of her dream to be a teacher, but that was as far as she was willing to go when it came to sharing.

And her inability to open up went hand in hand with the fact people didn't share with her. Tarah's demeanor didn't encourage others to open up about their problems or even their triumphs.

"What's wrong, Mia?" His tone was gentle, entreating.

She'd hardly eaten any food and hadn't been paying attention to what was going on around her. "I apologize." She offered her best smile, but it still was fake. "I'm not the best dinner companion."

He pointed to her food. "Have you finished eating?"

Afraid to speak, she nodded.

He waved for the check and paid the bill while she examined her hands. A glance at his plate assured her at least one of them had enjoyed their meal.

Stepping out of the restaurant into the inky blackness of night, she unconsciously pulled up the lapels of her new wool coat.

"Put on your gloves, Mia. It's just a few blocks to home, so I thought we'd walk."

Obediently, she donned the new leather gloves, reminding herself the cows were destined for dinner tables anyway, so nothing else to do with their hides but make leather products. Still, she was seriously contemplating becoming a vegetarian.

They walked two blocks in silence, and she assumed it would be the same for the last four when he spoke.

"You're introspective tonight. You had a good time today, but you lost focus over dinner. Tell me why."

Not a request, but a command. It never occurred to her to lie. "I don't make a pleasant companion, Sebastian. I don't know things. I'm out of step with the urbane. I work for them—I'm not one of them."

"Worked." The correction was mild. "And it's silly of you to claim you don't know things. Everyone doesn't know things. That's part of life. We ask questions. We strive to learn. We work to better ourselves." They stopped at a light, and he turned to her. "How do you expect to be a teacher if you're ignorant?"

"That's why I want to work with ten-year-olds. I can teach them what they need to survive and even thrive in the world. I can handle that level of education."

"That's breathtakingly simplistic, Tarah."

She started at his use of her name.

"Those kids will be worldlier. Just because they're young doesn't mean they'll have lived sheltered lives. You need to be prepared to deal with a lot more than just the third-grade curriculum." He took her arm and led her through the intersection. "For you to think otherwise is naïve."

"I don't agree. I don't need to be witty or charming with a ten-year-old. I just have to be familiar with the learning material inside and out. I need to answer their questions intelligently." She tried to extricate her arm but found she was unable because his grip was tight. Not painful, but disconcerting. "I find adults intimidating. I can handle the banalities of *how was your evening* or *how are you feeling*, but the rest eludes me. I can't remember the last time I sat and had a genuine conversation with someone."

He stopped mid-stride, forcing her to do the same. She gazed up at him, but his face was hidden as they were halfway between two streetlamps. They were in the shadows.

"What about your roommate? What about your fellow students?"

She tried to yank away, to pull back from the intensity radiating from him. A futile effort. "Ainsley was nice but always at her boyfriend's place when she wasn't in the lab or going to class. Each semester I take two courses at a time in two different departments. I've never been in a class with the same person twice."

"Coworkers?"

She scoffed. "I say hello and goodbye. It's a solitary job. My only interaction is with the people who live in the building." Her fingers clenched into fists because of her impotence in the face of such frustration.

"What about your work at the daycare center?"

"Almost everyone who worked there had kids of their own, so they'd socialize around their kids. And besides, I was asleep when they were awake and awake when they were asleep. Let's face it—as an adult, I'm a bust." She looked down the street, trying to get away from his intense and all-seeing eyes.

"What about boyfriends?"

"What about them?" *Watch yourself.*

"Surely, you had adult conversations with them."

Ducking her head, she studied the crack in the sidewalk. "Sure, I meant aside from my boyfriends."

"Were they too busy getting in your pants to have an adult conversation?"

Her cheeks heated, but she refused to meet his gaze. "Yeah, something like that."

"Something like that or exactly like that?"

She didn't answer, but he likely hadn't expected her to. With a slight jerk, they resumed their walk. She fought the tears as valiantly as she could, trying to hold them at bay.

At the building, Sebastian held the door for her.

Gareth was on the desk, and he gave them a broad smile. "Mr. Merrick." He inclined his head to her. "Tarah, it's nice to see you."

Gareth appeared pleased to see her, but she sensed the unease. Under normal circumstances, she'd be showing up in a few hours to relieve him. With a start, she realized she didn't know a single thing about Gareth. He was in his thirties, but that was it. Did he have a family? What did he do when he wasn't working? Was this a career or a stepping-stone for him? Hell, she didn't even know his last name.

Maybe she'd fool everyone if she plastered on a smile. "It's nice to see you too, Gareth. I hope you're doing well."

"It's been a quiet shift."

He hadn't answered her question, but she hadn't expected him to. Whenever tenants had inquired about her, she'd always be general and talk about how quiet things had been.

Sebastian spoke next. "Well, Gareth, we're grateful you're here. I'm going to take Miss Peters upstairs now."

"Yes, sir. I hope you both have a nice evening."

Finally, a moment of relief from the tension when she stepped into the elevator.

"He likes you."

She gaped at Sebastian. "What are you talking about? We used to work together."

"But he'd look at you. Linger at shift change. He was trying to get up the courage to ask you out, but your haughty demeanor scared him off."

When the elevator opened on the third floor, she leapt out ahead of him and whirled on him. "What the hell are you talking about? How could you possibly know that?"

Grabbing her by the elbow, he then propelled her down the hallway. "I'll thank you to keep your voice down. We don't need the neighbors hearing us argue."

He was right, but that didn't make it easier to swallow. She held her tongue until the front door was closed, then rounded on him. "Now, explain yourself. How could you possibly know those things?"

"I am under no obligation to explain anything to you." An edge to his voice.

Bewildered, she fought to make him understand. Her heart hammered. "You're awfully familiar with me, and yet I know virtually nothing about you."

His lips curled upward, and a moment's fear unfurled in her stomach.

"Do you honestly think I'd invite you here, to be my submissive, without having done my due diligence? That I'd allow you access to everything I have without having checked you out thoroughly?"

Swallowing convulsively, she shrank back. He still had a good grip on her elbow, and she wasn't going anywhere anytime soon. "I—" She faltered. "—I never thought about it, I guess. Did you interrogate the people around me?"

Oh God, what did he find out?

He let out a low rumble resembling a chuckle. "I was far more subtle. If you must know, I hired a private investigator. Would you like to see the report?"

Jesus Fucking Christ. "You are one sick son of a bitch."

He released her arm suddenly, and she almost hit the wall, only catching her balance at the last moment.

"Go to bed, Tarah. I don't want to see you until morning."

She balked. He was telling her to go to bed? What was she, a child?

"I told you once, and I won't tell you again. Go to the bathroom and then go to bed." He removed his coat and put it in the front hall closet, as if he had all the time in the world.

Mechanically, she did the same thing, keeping a wary eye on him. She no longer trusted him not to retaliate.

As he spun away, she whispered, "You're angry with me."

"Disappointed," he corrected but kept his back to her. "Your lack of faith is distasteful."

"And your lack of trust is as repulsive. You had me investigated, Sebastian. Would you tolerate it if someone did that to you?"

His shoulders straightened, but he still didn't face her. "If you had the sense God gave you, Tarah, you would've thought this through more carefully."

Now her anger bubbled up. "You gave me fourteen hours in which to make a monumental decision. Apparently, a monumental mistake."

"Go to bed."

He walked away, leaving her standing in the middle of the front hall, unsure of what to do next.

****

After six years of having lived a reverse life to most people, Tarah found mornings the most challenging. Normally, while others were waking up, she was preparing for bed. Six years of graveyard shifts made her body have trouble adapting to normal sleep patterns.

She was still wide awake at two in the morning. Not a big surprise. Why hadn't she eaten more of her dinner? Then she wouldn't be so hungry. Realizing breakfast was still six hours away intensified the pangs.

Mind over matter.

Until her stomach rumbled.

Hadn't he said the dungeon was soundproof? That worked both ways, right? If she couldn't hear him, he wouldn't be able to hear her. Anyway, he'd said he didn't want to see her until morning, and morning had come.

God, she sounded like a two-year-old. If she was hungry, then she'd get food, and that was an end to it. Still, she crept as quietly as she could to the kitchen. As she wouldn't find any junk food, she settled for crackers, cheese, and a yellow bell pepper she cut into thin slices. After pouring a glass of water, she sat at the kitchen table.

As she munched on the peppers, she tried to figure out what the next move was.

One hundred and… She had to stop, because if she didn't, she was liable to go crazy. Tomorrow her textbooks would arrive, and she could focus on her studies. Christmas was coming. As always, she'd spend Christmas Day with her parents. Arrive early afternoon and leave right after dinner. She had no idea what to get as gifts, but that was nothing new. She'd figure it out as she always did.

The manila folder dropping on the table in front of her startled a scream from her. Holding a hand to her heart, she tried to steady her breathing as Sebastian took the seat across from her. "Jesus, you almost gave me a heart attack."

"I wasn't trying to be quiet—you were the one who was eating with her mouth open." No amusement in the reproach.

She bristled, but yeah, he was probably correct. When she checked her plate, most of the crackers and peppers were gone. All the crunchy foods had been consumed, leaving only the soft cheese. Her mouth went a little dry when she looked across the table. Sebastian wore a bathrobe, belted low, giving her a glimpse of his wide chest. Trying to tame her errant thoughts, she eyed the folder warily. "What's that?"

"The investigator's report."

That she probably could have guessed.

"Look at it."

She waved it off. "Not necessary."

"I said look at it."

Her gaze shot up and met his. He was serious, and this was an argument best avoided, so she picked up the folder and opened it. The report was two pages. She scanned it quickly and put it down. "Didn't get your money's worth, did you?"

"Toby Driscoll is one of the best investigators in the city. He found little because little existed to find. Age twenty-five. Parents are Lawrence and Lynette Peters, married thirty-one years. No other siblings and no living grandparents. Graduated from high school at eighteen in the top fifth percentile. Three months later obtained a security position at Crystal Tower. Works five days a week, fifty-two weeks a year and takes a payout annually instead of a vacation. Missed three days of work in six years.

"No known substance abuse issues, and no arrests or convictions. Four apartments in six years with various roommates, including one currently in jail on an assault charge. Real charmer, that one, by the way. No signs he ever assaulted Miss Peters—"

"He didn't—"

But he continued on as if she hadn't spoken. "Part-time student at Simon Fraser University with decent, but not exceptional, grades. Used to volunteer at Charmers Preschool until this past September. Left because she was replaced by the owner's daughter."

That had hurt.

"On the whole, unremarkable. No close friends, no boyfriends, no enemies. Current roommate Ainsley Kincaid. One coworker, Gareth Stanton, wants a romantic relationship but feels Miss Peters is unapproachable."

Ouch.

"Most people remember her but cannot give specifics. Highly reliable and dependable."

Double ouch.

"If she has a social life, this investigator cannot locate it." His gaze settled on her. A brow arched. "And since Toby is the best, I'm confident to say you don't have one."

Closing her eyes, Tarah battled a pile of emotions all at once—embarrassment, humiliation, anger, sadness, and—above all else—regret. She'd lived on this planet for twenty-five years, and no one would really miss her if she disappeared. Her parents might notice, but it'd take them a while.

"If you had the report and you knew all that, why did you ask me about my relationships with other people? Earlier, I mean, when we were on the street. Were you trying to humiliate me or just reinforce how alone I am?" The penny dropped. "That's why you chose me, isn't it? Because I'm isolated. I'm an easy mark."

When her questions were met with silence, she opened her eyes.

Sebastian leaned forward with his elbows on the

table. "The reason I chose you is because of your unrealized potential and not just as a submissive. Being submissive to someone does not preclude success and achievement in other realms." His gaze bore into her. "Let me show you all you can be."

"That's awfully arrogant of you." She tried but couldn't put the sarcasm behind the statement. Part of her was intrigued, and part of her was scared. She took a breath. "Who is it you think I can become?"

He appeared to consider her question. "A young woman of poise and composure whose self-esteem carries her through life. Whether in the classroom or the ballroom, she has confidence and grace."

She was having an out-of-body experience because no way was he talking about her. No way could she be any of those things.

"Look, Tarah, you said you wanted to know what the rules are, and I was unfair not to be more specific. I'd thought they were explicit in the contract, but I was mistaken."

"It said I had to behave appropriately or there'd be punishments and consequences. I get that, but the rules elude me." Seeking the right words, she continued, "I thought because I've always followed laws, and not made any major mistakes in life, I'd be able to handle your rules. Maybe I was too hasty."

Sebastian shook his head. "On the contrary, Mia, you're more than capable. First, there's communication. I need you to listen to me as I will listen to you. But you also need to be aware of visual cues and body language to supplement the obvious oral cues."

"Do you mean I have to focus on you all the time?"

"Well, that's one way to look at it. Obviously, if

we're in public—when we're vanilla—you don't have to be so attentive."

"Vanilla?"

"You remember when we went to Club Kink?"

She inclined her head, making sure she understood.

"That would be the opposite of vanilla. Today, when we were out, we were vanilla. We were on even ground and treated each other as such."

"I enjoyed it, but I was worried about doing something wrong."

He tisked. "When you do something incorrect while we're vanilla, I'm far more lenient unless it brings shame to either of us. I've cultivated a reputation, and I expect my companion to add culture and elegance to that impression."

"Impression or illusion?"

He inclined his head, giving her a long look. "Are you saying I'm not a gentleman of good breeding? A man known for his charitable endeavors as much as his business acumen?"

"Is that what I am, a charitable endeavor?" She needed to ask, even though she dreaded the answer.

"I could've written you a check, but that wouldn't have helped you in the long run. I'm offering you an opportunity to learn how to interact with people. What I can give you is the confidence to be more than a greeter to the rich and powerful."

"Security guard." She didn't put much effort into the correction. Was she really that easy to read? Did she wear her loneliness and isolation on her sleeve?

He leaned forward. "I saw the longing, Tarah. I saw the vulnerability as well as the barely leashed desire. I could tell you wanted to be one of those women."

"That's awfully arrogant of you—presuming I wanted you that way. That I want you that way."

He chuckled. "I've only begun to show you what you want. Lucky for you, I can give it to you. I can help you explore the sensual side of life. I can help you expand your horizons."

She was white-knuckling through this conversation. He was right when he called it barely leashed desire. She wanted it so much her body and soul ached from the longing. "I want to have faith in you." Did she? Or was her desperation making her reckless? "But I'm scared."

"Of the journey or the destination?"

I can't lie. "Both. You intimidate me."

"A little intimidation isn't a terrible thing. But I don't want you to fear me. I want you to see that by serving me, you'll bring pleasure to yourself. I'm big on praise and rewards, when appropriate, but I can only do so much. One rule is you examine your own life and look for places and ways where you can improve upon it. It's a two-way street, Tarah."

A little impish grin spread across her face. "You mean I can give you feedback? Let you know when you get it wrong?"

Another chuckle. "A good Dominant is always open to constructive comments, but always consider them very carefully."

The grin diminished. "Because if I get it wrong, there'll be consequences."

"Criticism can be disrespectful if not given with great care. When I correct you, I never do it in anger. I do it with deliberate consideration." He let that sink in. "What's really on your mind?"

"Why do I sometimes misbehave even though I

know better?"

"That, my dear, is the question you must ask yourself. Are you doing it to get my attention? Are you doing it because you're seeking punishment?"

She was stunned both by the suggestions and by the insights. Dare she respond honestly? "Maybe a bit of both." God, that admission hurt. "I'm not used to having anyone pay attention to me. It never occurred to me I might do things wrong so you'll notice me."

"Let me make you a promise, Mia. You will always have my attention. Other people and matters might take some of the focus, but you'll never leave my mind."

That gave her a moment's pause.

"Let's try an experiment."

She eyed him warily but nodded.

"You'll come into my room every morning, and I'm going to mark my name somewhere on your body. So you remember me during your day."

The casual suggestion brought with it more anxiety. *As if I could forget.*

"I'll also be selecting your clothes because, in all honesty, you're not great at it."

She wanted to argue, really, she did, but he was right. She had no sense of personal style, no idea how people dressed from day to day in Sebastian's world. But was she really part of his world? One charity event did not mean—

"We're going to a business dinner on Tuesday and the opera on Thursday."

Her unspoken question answered.

"I'll print out some information about the opera and leave you a CD so you'll be familiar with it before we go." He held up a hand before she could speak. "No one expects you to be an expert. I don't want you to feel uneducated. Look at the material, don't look at the material—it's completely up to you."

She intended to spend hours poring over it.

"Saturday night is the office Christmas party. I have someone who oversees everything. My role is to show up, make an appearance, then slip out."

"That's it?" Sounded too easy.

"Well, it's a family event. Kids and such. Since I don't have any of my own, it makes little sense for me to stick around."

She giggled. "You own a chain of family restaurants, and you're uncomfortable around kids?"

His chin rose a notch. "I never said I was uncomfortable around them. I don't see how my presence contributes to the event."

His words were bluster, and her curiosity was piqued. He really *was* intimidated. "What are you going to do with your own children?"

For a moment, just a moment, he appeared…sad. Fleeting was the look, and she fought to hold on to the impression. Just as quickly, the implacable mask was back.

"I don't intend to have children."

Something stirred within her. "You're, what, thirty-five—"

"Thirty-eight." His correction was mild, but underlying tension prevailed.

"You're still young enough to change your mind. I mean, maybe you haven't met the right woman. Having kids is an enormous commitment, but it's the most rewarding experience in the world."

"And you know that how?" His voice dripped with

sarcasm, and it hit the mark.

Her hands twisted in her lap, knuckles white. "Not from personal experience, if that's what you're alluding to. Kids are a ton of work and commitment, but they are also worth the effort. We share ourselves with our children to make a better world."

"If you knew the real me, you'd be confident I am not father material."

His tone was so icy a shiver ran down her spine. She didn't look up. "I'm sorry you believe that. I want to be a mother, but as your investigator eloquently pointed out, as I have no social life, it's highly unlikely it'll ever happen."

"You might meet someone at teacher's college."

She tilted her chin. "As you've also pointed out, I'm shy. Dinner the other night involved me using every ounce of strength just to survive."

"The next time, it will be easier." His gaze bore into her. "Why do you think I chose you, Tarah? If you work with me, I can give you everything you've ever wanted."

Her eyes stung with unshed tears. "I need to go to bed."

"That's your prerogative. I expect you in my room at half past six. I'll mark you and select your clothes for the day. Your textbooks will arrive by midmorning, and that'll give you something to occupy your time. I'll have the information about the opera, and you might want to take a swim."

His speech had given her enough time to check her tears. "You're going to mark me and expect me to go swimming?"

"I'm sorry—I wasn't specific, was I? I expect you to be naked when you come to see me. Now go to bed,

Mia—morning will be here shortly. After I've taken care of you for the day, you can always go back to bed. You're having trouble adapting to true circadian rhythms."

Circa whats?

"We're programmed to sleep when it's dark and be awake while it's light. Your body has been living in an artificial environment for too long. Shift workers have a higher incidence of cancer and cardiovascular problems."

"You make it sound like I had a choice."

"Oh, you did what you had to do to survive. Now, Mia, I can help you thrive. Give yourself a week of regimentation—of waking and going to sleep at the same time—and you'll be fine."

She wanted to believe him. She wanted no more tête-à-têtes in the middle of the night. She rose to take her plate to the kitchen. When she returned, he still sat where he was.

"Thank you, Sir, for your consideration of me."

He rose, taking her hands in his. If he noticed hers were blocks of ice, he didn't show it. Instead, he pressed a kiss to her forehead. "You are important to me, Mia—don't ever forget that." He gently steered her toward her bedroom.

She went without question. As she settled down to sleep, his parting words repeated in her head.

You are important to me, Mia—don't ever forget that.

Chapter Seven

At the prescribed hour, suffering from the mother of all hangovers without having enjoyed the alcohol, Tarah knocked on the dungeon door. She shivered and wasn't sure whether from cold, fear, or anticipation. She didn't have to wait long as Sebastian opened the door. He was dressed for the day, and as always, she couldn't help but admire the picture he presented.

"Glad to see you, Mia. Come in." He stood aside, allowing her to enter the dungeon. The bed was made, and the room was as neat as a pin. He moved into the space, encouraging her to follow. When he sat on a chair, he indicated she come and stand between his thighs. She obeyed, curiosity and dread warring within her at the same time.

Sebastian removed a magic marker from his jacket pocket. "Now, this only comes off with soap, so the water in the pool won't remove it. You do not have permission to remove it. I will examine it tonight, and if I'm in the mood, I will let you wash it off." His gaze was dark and inscrutable.

"Thank you, Sir." *Was that the correct response?*

She watched with fascination as he uncapped the marker and took her breast in his hand. The touch was unexpected. She stepped back and away from him.

"Let's try again, Mia. The first time, you get a pass. Balk again during this ritual, and there'll be consequences."

Stepping forward, this time she closed her eyes. She didn't want to see the intimacy. When he took her breast lightly in his hand, she fought the instinct of self-preservation. After a long moment, however, she fluttered her eyes open. She followed his gaze as it settled on her nipple, and something heretofore unknown rocketed through her. The nipple hardened and distended under his attention, and she blushed.

"Your reaction is perfectly normal. Whether or not you're turned on, it's normal for a nipple to pebble." A light chuckle. "This turns you on."

She was about to speak, but his hand tightened slightly.

"I can tell when you're lying to me."

As if he needed to remind her. That threat was always there, just out of reach, ominously omnipresent.

She swallowed. "I...I like it when you touch me, Sir." Next, the marker gently pressed to her skin. The smell was noxious, but she bore it well. When he finished, he released her. She had nice breasts, not too big and not too small, but to have them under scrutiny was another matter.

"You may open your eyes."

She obeyed—meeting eyes black in the low light of the room.

"There are a few more rules you should know, so pay close attention. You may not masturbate without my permission. You may not orgasm without my permission. From now on, you sleep naked, and you never hide from me. I expect you to confess any rule breaking that occurs while I'm away." He gave her his all-knowing smirk. "Your guilty conscience will weigh on you, so consider carefully before you break a rule."

"Yes, Sir." That was the only response she could manage. When he indicated she could leave, she fled. She crossed the condo, went into her room, and closed the door.

Masturbate? Orgasm?

Hadn't he said this was to be a nonsexual agreement?

Yet when he had touched her… Oh God, what had she gotten herself into?

****

She emerged from sleep a few hours later, amazed she'd slept at all. She'd closed off her mind and given her body permission to do whatever it wanted. Sleep had been what the muscles and bones demanded, so she'd given in.

Ten thirty. Her bedroom here was similar to her bedroom at her old apartment only where before she had blackout blinds, now she was in a room with no natural light. The dungeon was the same way.

What was it with these people and an aversion to natural light? Well, that wasn't quite fair. Sebastian had enjoyed their trip to the aquarium, and that'd been made in daylight. Since he hadn't shriveled up, she assumed he wasn't a vampire. Plus, he ran a business demanding his attention.

Let me make you a promise, Mia. You will always have my attention. Other people and matters might take some of the focus, but you'll never leave my mind.

Was he thinking about her right now as she was him? She liked it when he touched her. Flipping on the light, she let the blanket fall from her chest.

He'd signed his name as opposed to printing it, and

she noted the strong flourish he gave his signature. With reverence, she touched her hand to the mark. Territorial and effective. The bathing suit would easily cover it, but she'd be conscious of it the whole time.

After slipping from the bed, she trod to the bathroom and put on the suit. It had a swimmer's cut but high in the thigh. Although the suit was plain black and un-sexy, when she glanced herself in the mirror, she was anything but. High firm breasts, a trim waist, and solid thighs. Hours of walking each week earned her a lovely body.

And now it belonged to Sebastian. The knowledge gave her a secret thrill she couldn't deny.

She slipped into the terry-cloth robe and flip-flop sandals and grabbed a towel. After locking up, she secured the spare key into the pocket. She'd take the stairs to the pool, avoiding the security desk. It shouldn't matter what her former coworkers thought, but it did. They'd see her as using Sebastian. It'd never occur to them it was the other way around.

Or maybe they were using each other.

She tried to reconcile that thought as she walked down the three flights of stairs. The pool area was, as with everything else in this building, elegant. Her focus, though, was the empty pool. She shed her robe and shoes, then slipped into the water. When she was a child, her favorite time of summer had been swimming lessons at the local outdoor pool. Nothing better than gliding through the water, the resistance against her muscles, and the burn in her lungs when she held her breath.

Length after length, she pushed herself—punished herself. Sought some kind of peace that'd eluded her since she agreed to Sebastian's bargain. Seeking the oblivion necessary to bank the sexual attraction and desire he elicited from her. Sure, she'd seen him as attractive. Might've fantasized about being one of those women he took up to the dungeon. But she'd never dared to hope she might be one of them.

Well, she wasn't really. Theirs was a platonic relationship, with no real kinship or a friendship yet. Might those feelings come? Or would her reliance on him always be a barrier between them? She had nothing to offer a man like Sebastian.

Except her submission.

She pulled up to the side of the pool and let the thought sit.

How could she demonstrate the devotion she owed him? Maybe if she acted like she wanted to submit to him, it might come more naturally. How hard could it be?

****

Four hours later, she was more confused than ever. Going online and googling submission only increased her befuddlement. Some of the information was pretty tame and logical. Keep a good house, cook his favorite meals, anticipate his needs, and fulfill them.

So much of the literature, however, involved intimate actions. Not all sexual, but definitely intimate. Nudity was an important element as she was expected to be open and honest. Apparently, clothes were a barrier. Some websites also suggested she was supposed to shave *all* her body hair. Again, so nothing would be hidden. She wasn't sure about that one.

Some websites went even further, talking about slavery. Not just sexual slavery, but actual slavery. It returned to the power exchange he'd talked about. He hadn't asked her to be his slave, but he'd put a collar on her to claim her as his own. But that'd only been at the club and had, according to him, been a way to protect her. The word was weighted with so much historical context that it felt wrong using it. Yet that was the word used in the lifestyle.

She could keep a decent house, especially with a cleaning lady coming every two weeks. And she could probably keep them fed with decent food, but the rest? How could she be a good submissive without submitting sexually? He wasn't likely to be celibate for the next six months. How would she endure it if he brought women home to have sex with? What if he met someone, and they became involved? How would he explain having Tarah living in the condo?

She was borrowing trouble. He'd made no promises, and she'd asked for none. Funny how he intuited she wasn't going to have any male suitors for the foreseeable future. What would he have done if she had a boyfriend stashed away somewhere?

Of course he'd known. The private investigator had been damn thorough. And accurate. She didn't have a love life, and that wasn't going to change any time soon.

Sebastian said she might meet someone, but she knew better. She had nothing to offer someone except herself. Would it ever be enough?

The condo buzzer sounding pulled her from her reverie. The courier with her parcel. Banking her excitement, she went downstairs to sign for it. Normally, she relished the tactility of a book, the scent, especially a new one. Whenever possible, she bought used textbooks. This time, though, she'd splurged on new. When she removed the shrink wrapping, she felt nothing but guilt. She hadn't bought this. Like the clothes she wore, his purchasing this for her would come at a cost. Was she strong enough to pay it?

****

Dinner was an unmitigated disaster. Why she'd possibly thought she could cook chicken teriyaki was beyond her. The chicken had burned to the pan thoroughly, and she needed a metal spatula to pry it loose. She tried a piece. Dry as the Sahara.

While all that was going on, she'd shut off the burner under the rice but had forgotten about it. Now the stuff was mush. The vegetables might've been the saving grace except the water had boiled off. The smell of burning corn was the last straw. She verged on collapsing in a puddle of tears when the key in the lock startled her.

Since Sebastian liked to be greeted at the front door, she stepped into the hallway. Some websites suggested not looking at the Dominant until being told to. She seized on that and lowered her gaze to his feet when he stepped into the condo.

"What the hell is that smell?"

She flinched but didn't look up. "I tried to cook, Sir. I…" She faltered. If she spoke further, she was going to embarrass herself. *Don't cry. Just…don't cry.*

When Sebastian tucked his finger under her chin and tilted her head upward, she closed her eyes. Unbidden, a tear slipped out.

He sighed. "Open your eyes, Mia."

With great reluctance, but powerless to do otherwise, she obeyed.

"Did I ask you to cook for me?"

Confused, she shook her head. "I thought you'd like…"

He pressed a kiss to her nose. "Although considerate

of you, I cook. I enjoy the relaxation that comes with it. It's my way to unwind." He took her by the hand and led her to the kitchen. "Now, tell me what happened."

In short, jerky spurts, she explained how she'd turned a pristine kitchen into a disaster area.

"Well, since I was planning to cook chicken tonight and there's none left, why don't I just call for a pizza?"

She gaped at him with something short of amazement. "You're not going to punish me?"

"For trying to be helpful? No. I should have been more explicit in my directions and expectations. Let me do so now. We're going out Tuesday and Thursday this week. I'm making baked wild salmon on Wednesday, and depending on how my week goes, we'll probably do takeout on Friday. Saturday night is the Christmas party.

"I expect you to eat oatmeal or toast with fruit every morning. For lunch, I expect you to have a balance of protein, carbohydrates, and vegetables. You may have yogurt and fruit for dessert." His expression lightened. "I expect some form of exercise three times a week. Is any of this unreasonable?"

She quickly shook her head. It all seemed reasonable.

"Now, I'm sending you for cooking lessons, but that's for your personal growth as opposed to for my benefit."

Absorbing his words, she smiled shyly. "But Sir will let me try out my new recipes?"

"Yes, Mia, if I'm working late, you may cook. But only after your studies, okay?"

Relief flooded her. What had seemed simple apparently wasn't. But he wasn't irate. Disappointed? Yes. Angry? No.

"We'll put these pots and pans in the sink to soak. Now, what do you want on your pizza?"

****

Pepperoni pizza with side Caesar salads arrived less than a half hour later. Tarah set the table while Sebastian went to his room to change into comfortable clothes. When he emerged in a T-shirt and jeans, her stomach did a little flip. God, but the man was gorgeous. She itched to touch and might've asked if the pizza hadn't arrived promptly.

Once they were settled, he leaned back. "And how was your day? What did you do?"

"I slept until ten thirty when I rose and went for a swim. I returned, did some surfing on the internet, and then my package arrived. I spent the rest of the day planning out my reading schedule for the next month."

"And what did you look for while on the internet?"

She'd rushed over that part, hoping he'd bypass it. Trust him to miss nothing.

"I…um…looked up submission. I searched for what my responsibilities would be." She couldn't meet his gaze, instead focusing away from the table. "I tried to figure out how to be the best submissive I can be."

"I'm pleased, Mia, but the internet can be a dangerous place if you're not careful. You read things disturbing to you, didn't you?"

Tread carefully. She knew she'd have to express herself clearly. "I also read about power exchanges. About twenty-four-seven power exchanges."

"And what did you think?"

"I think it'd have to be pretty deep between two people to do that. I mean, to give up one's identity to service someone else, that's deep shi…stuff."

117

His chuckle was sardonic. "It is deep shit. I'm acquainted with a few people who've chosen that lifestyle."

Her gaze snapped to his. "What's that like?"

"It's very intense for everyone involved. The question is whether someone can be totally dedicated to another while the other is totally in control. It's a two-way street. The submissive takes on the responsibility of pleasing her Master, and he takes on the responsibility of seeing to the slave's health and well-being."

"Isn't that sort of what we're doing right now?"

"Slavery is far deeper than what we have, and you should never step immediately into that role with anyone. Trust takes months to build. You can start with submission, but even that involves negotiations—trial and error. When you commit yourself fully to someone, it involves giving up a lot in the expectation of getting a lot." He paused. "One couple I know who do this are completely devoted to each other, to the exclusion of other people. They've opted not to have children, and she's chosen not to work outside of the home."

"Is she happy?" She had this perverse need to know. To comprehend. Because as abstract as these ideas were—and as foreign as they were to her—she could understand why someone might do this. How the call to service would be so strong as to give up everything for someone else. A special someone. Maybe a man like Sebastian.

He considered for a moment. "Can anyone be truly happy? She claims she's fulfilled, and this was the role she was always meant to play. He doesn't mind the responsibility and loves her. He takes care of her and has made sure she'll be cared for were anything ever to happen to him."

"Do I...might I know these people?"

He shook his head. "If you're thinking it might be Rielle and Gage or Alessandra and Smith, don't worry. Both those couples have love and devotion, but not a twenty-four-seven power exchange."

Relief flooded through her. "Just with Rielle...and that horrible man..."

"Carl Jergen?"

"Yeah, him. Rielle wasn't happy. He controlled her, and she never smiled. She was always sad, but I never knew what to say. With Gage, though, she's a different person."

"And although she's a submissive to him sometimes, she's not when the baby or other people are around. The submission is mostly kept to the bedroom."

TMI. "See and that's where I found another piece of information."

"The internet again, I assume."

Nodding, she sought the courage to go on. "Most of the submission websites talk about submission in the bedroom. I mean, for some couples—especially those with kids—the bedroom is the only place where submission can occur."

"What's your point?"

"That..." She faltered and took a fortifying breath. "I'm worried if I'm not providing you with sexual services, you won't be happy."

Sebastian's eyes narrowed. "I said this agreement was nonsexual, and I meant it."

"But what if you want sex? I mean, are you going to go somewhere else or bring someone here?"

He leaned forward, and she scooted back.

"What I do and who I do it with is none of your concern, Tarah. Are we clear?"

Her eyes widened at the use of her given name. He used it rarely, and this was one of those communication things he'd talked about. His voice was as cold as ice. "Yes, Sir. I was just trying to say I'm concerned."

"There is nothing for you to worry about." He pushed his plate away. "Go into the master bedroom, strip, and wait for inspection."

Words that should have thrilled—would have a few minutes ago—now brought dread. "Would Sir like me to do the dishes?"

"Sir has given you your instructions and would like you to follow them without question."

She leapt from her seat and left the room before she received another reprimand. She had to learn to keep her mouth shut. For a moment, she'd been lulled into believing they were on even ground—had let herself be comfortable with him. Too comfortable, apparently.

Fingers numb, she removed her sweater and jeans. She folded them neatly, then pulled off socks, underwear, and bra. She'd been forced to choose the outfit herself this morning as he hadn't told her what to wear. She'd been so desperate to escape after he'd marked her she hadn't gone back and asked. He had said nothing derogatory. Maybe she'd done okay.

She stood by the door and waited.

And waited.

She didn't have a watch so had no sense of passaging time, but over ten minutes had elapsed. She'd done exactly what she'd been asked, so what was taking so long? *Dishes.* He had to clean up the mess she'd made. She was willing to do it. He *should* have made her do it.

Too late now.

She shifted from one foot to the other. She was accustomed to spending a lot of time sitting—for work or class or studying. She walked for exercise and lay down for sleeping. What she wasn't used to was standing still for hours on end. Well, maybe not hours, but time was passing.

When the doorknob turned, relief surged through her. This would all be over soon.

Seemingly uninterested, Sebastian secured the door and faced her. His implacable mask was back. She squirmed under the scrutiny.

"Stop fidgeting."

Her hands dropped to her sides, and she hoped that was good enough. She held his gaze as he walked toward her and was mesmerized by the depths in those dark eyes. The flare of something in them did nothing to solve the enigma of Sebastian Merrick.

When he was a foot away from her, he broke eye contact. He gazed down at her breast, and his lips curled upward. "I like how you wear my brand, Mia—it suits you."

Despite herself, she preened under the praise. It took so little because she was like a child deprived of touch and love. Anything offered to her now was like balm to her wounded soul. "I was lucky Sir marked me." She gasped when he pressed his index finger to her breast, lightly tracing the path the marker had taken just that morning.

"Tomorrow after your swim, you have my permission to wash it off."

"What if I don't want to?"

He quirked an eyebrow. "Well, I'm marking another

part of you tomorrow morning, but if you don't mind two brands…"

"No, Sir." She tucked a lock of hair behind her ear. "I need you to use your power over me, and this is one way that you do. I remembered you every time I saw the mark."

"And when you couldn't see it?"

She met his gaze. "I thought about you then as well."

He was so close she could almost reach out and touch him. What would it be like? If he touched her in a more intimate way? A less clinical way?

He took a step back, and she was bereft.

"I have selected your clothes for tomorrow during the day and the outfit you're to wear tomorrow night. I'll be here to pick you up at six. I expect you to be ready as we have reservations for six thirty, and I detest being late."

He stepped back, clearing a path for her to the door.

Unlike this morning, however, she didn't feel the need to run. She stayed rooted to the ground.

"You've been dismissed, Mia. Do I have to be more direct, or are you going?"

She cleared her throat. "You said open communication was acceptable, yes?"

"You have something to say?"

Now she almost lost courage, but she fought valiantly to keep it. "Yes, Sir, I have something to say. I want more, tonight, than just to be dismissed."

He frowned, scrutinizing her. "Why?"

She wanted to wilt under the gaze but held herself erect. "I liked when you touched me." *Why does this have to be so hard?* "I wish you'd do it again."

His eyes narrowed. "You don't know what you're

asking."

"Just…no one touches me. You said it yourself—I'm alone."

"At the moment." His dark eyes flared again.

"At the moment." The confirmation hurt. "If Sir doesn't want to touch me, I'll accept your decision."

Please don't.

Please don't send me away.

I need this.

I need you.

He took a breath. "Any preference in how I touch you?"

Her cheeks flushed hot. "I hadn't…hadn't thought…" *Crap.* "I just meant if you wanted to touch me again the way you were. It felt nice."

"You have no idea what you're asking for."

Brow furrowed, she met his gaze. "Please, just for a minute. Just a touch. Is that so offensive?"

He barked out a laugh. "Offensive? No, Mia, not offensive. Just frustrating. You understand anatomy, right? If I touch you again, I might enjoy it. I might get aroused. I might—"

"Okay, I get it." She ducked her head. "I'll go—" But as she stepped away, he snagged her by the waist.

"I didn't say arousal was an unpleasant thing, but I wanted you to be prepared. I didn't want you to be uncomfortable with my potential reaction."

"But you might not get aroused, right?"

A low chuckle rumbled in his chest. "I'm a man, Mia. A flesh-and-blood man. You tempt me in ways that are completely inappropriate." He continued to meet her gaze. "Maybe there's a way for us to both get what we want."

Relief flooded her. He was going to touch her again. Her nipples tightened in anticipation.

"No, not that."

She tried to hide her disappointment but was unsuccessful, and he laughed.

"I can read all your thoughts. Now, be a good girl and go stand by the wall like you did the other night."

She obeyed with a loud exhalation. She hadn't meant the paddle, but it'd still be an extension of him, and she'd take anything that she could get. She held herself still, eyes shut tight.

The first connection shot through her like lightning. Not the paddle but his hand. First one cheek, then the other, he rained down blows upon her. She barely caught her breath when he'd hit her again. The pain was sharper than it'd been with the paddle, the sound more erotic.

God, was she getting turned on by this? What kind of sick person was she to get aroused?

Her mind flashed back to the websites. Those women had talked about being turned on while being punished. Was this any different? A hard blow had her gasping. Another couple and that was it. Or at least she thought he was finished.

Then the most extraordinary sensation. Sebastian placed his hands against her, cupping her ass and squeezing. Pain bloomed and diffused throughout her body. She shivered with need.

"Please. Please do something." She pressed into his palms and flexed her pelvis. Her body was demanding something, and she wasn't above begging. "Please." Might her pleas have some effect?

His release of her was sudden and violent, and only her hands on the wall prevented her body from slamming against it.

"Get out, Tarah, before I do something we'll both regret."

Terrified by his tone, she fled.

Chapter Eight

Waking up Tuesday morning was marginally easier than Monday because she'd fallen asleep just before midnight. She'd slept deeply and dreamlessly until the alarm buzzed.

When she knocked on the door, she endured a pause before it opened.

As always, Sebastian was completely put together. Not a single hair of that black mane was out of place. The style was longer than she would've thought proper for the president of a company, but seeing as he was in charge, he could do whatever he wanted.

"Right on time, Mia." He stood aside, and she entered the room. Without a word, she stood by the chair. She'd stolen a glance in the mirror, and yesterday's mark was still dark against her alabaster-white skin. Where would he mark her today?

He sat by the chair and beckoned her closer. She stepped between his thighs but didn't dare let her legs touch his. His hands were chilly when he put them on her hips, but she didn't start. Instead, she sucked in a breath. On the exhalation, he spun her so she faced into the room. She got a whiff of the uncapped marker before he pressed it against her left butt cheek, below the small of her back—the upper curve—then she felt the flourish. The cap snapped back into place, and she waited.

He pressed his hands against her ass. "Are we sore

this morning, Mia?"

"Yes, Sir, a little bit." She hesitated. "But it's a good sore."

"You enjoyed yourself last night, and that surprised you, didn't it?"

She pulled her lower lip through her teeth. *Honesty.* She at least owed him that much. "Yes, Sir, I enjoyed it." She let out a quick breath. "But you sent me away. Did I displease you?"

She didn't miss the sardonic chuckle she was becoming familiar with.

"You pleased me very much, be in no doubt. And I'd love to play with you again, Mia, but I have work to do. Eat breakfast and lunch, have a swim, do more studying, and, for God's sake, stay away from the internet. For today, at least. We can negotiate that later when I have more time."

Since she didn't normally spend any time on the internet, she wasn't going to be missing out. "I'll just read my book." She was a little disconcerted because his hands were still clutching her butt cheeks.

He withdrew them and gave her a playful swipe. "Get going and behave today."

She spun and offered him a smile. "Yes, Sir, I'll do my best." She did a little sashay and was rewarded with another chuckle. He seemed in good spirits today. Well, she'd do everything he asked her to do, and hopefully, that'd make him happy tonight.

As the day wore on, however, nerves set in. They were going out for dinner. A business dinner. What exactly did that mean, and what role was she supposed to play? Unable to concentrate on her reading and having already expended a lot of physical energy on her swim, she prowled the condo, caged. Would taking a nap help? No, she wouldn't be able to sleep.

Sebastian had left the door to the dungeon ajar, and she felt an irresistible pull toward the room of mystery. Figuring this would be an excellent way to kill a few minutes, she flipped on the lights. Even with daylight streaming in behind her, the room held an air of danger. The room was clever in both design and execution, and Tarah marveled at the ingenuity. Stepping toward a wall, she then pressed her fingers lightly to it. Not actual stone, of course, that'd be too heavy, but a solid material with stucco formed to make it look like blocks. Must've taken hours and hours of painstaking work to perfect the look. What had the workers thought when they put this room together? Probably, the rich had a weird way of spending their money.

The soundproofing must be good, because in all her years here, she was only aware of one call about a disturbance in the apartment. Rielle had dropped a glass and been cut by flying shards. Tarah shivered. Yeah, she'd probably have screamed as well.

Eyes now accustomed to the lower light, she stepped to the wall of implements. Since her search on the internet yesterday, she could recognize a few more of the toys. The women had looked happy being at the end of some of these…things…even so, she wondered.

"Curiosity killed the cat, you know."

She leapt a good three feet backward, then glared at Sebastian. "You said you wouldn't be home until six."

"And while the cat's away, the mice come out to play?"

"First you accuse me of being a cat, then you accuse me of being a mouse. Make up your bloody mind."

He chuckled. "I accuse you of snooping."

"You left the door open." A weak and lame excuse. "And I thought the room might need some cleaning."

"The room is, as you can see, perfectly clean. Gratzia does an excellent job."

"Your cleaning lady comes in here?" She knew, but it still blew her mind.

"Did you think I cleaned it? Gratzia started working here when Rielle owned the place. She worked for Smith, and I kept her on. Good and discreet help is hard to find. Why do you think the building pays its security guards so well?"

"Discretion." She couldn't argue. "We all know what a good gig this is and aren't willing to do anything to lose it."

Sebastian nodded his approval. "Now, what am I supposed to do with you, my bad girl?"

He sounded downright lascivious when he said the words *bad girl*.

No point pretending she didn't know exactly what was happening. "You're going to punish me. Is there any point in me trying to justify my actions?"

He met her with an arched eyebrow. "You can try, but even if you throw yourself on the mercy of the court, you're not likely to get leniency."

Worth a shot. "I'm nervous about tonight. I mean, you said a business dinner, and the outfit you chose is, well, businessy."

"Businessy is not a word, Tarah."

"But still, I started obsessing about all the things that could go wrong tonight, and I panicked."

His eyes softened from their usual hard flint. "I'm meeting with an advertising agency trying to woo me away from my current contract. They did their pitch today, and I have to say I'm impressed. Tonight will probably be a continuation of that conversation. I'm interested in your impressions, because they have some ideas of how to target the kids. A lot of our business is driven by children asking their parents to bring them in. We've always used the same themes, but this agency is pitching a whole new collection of ideas. You know kids, so I want your take."

Somehow, things didn't feel better. "I know preschoolers—that's far from knowing all kids."

"Tarah, I may run a chain of family restaurants, but that doesn't make me any more knowledgeable. When I bought my first restaurant, it was a strip club in an area undergoing gentrification. I saw the houses and condos being planned and knew the club's days were numbered. The owner had known it as well, and that's why I got such a good price. Six months I worked on that place while still working my construction job full time during the day. The manager stayed on with me, and, let me tell you, she knew what she was doing. She's been with me since the beginning and has been my touchstone."

"Get her opinion."

"She died of cancer last month."

Well, shit. She closed her eyes for a moment. "God, Sebastian, that was inconsiderate of me. I'm sorry—"

He held up his hand. "You had no way of knowing, and I shouldn't have put it so bluntly, but it's been tough. She was our vice president one minute, and the next she'd been given weeks to live. Bladder cancer. Truly awful, Tarah. She had three kids and six grandkids, but she never acted her age. She was one of those young-at-heart people."

Unbidden and on instinct, she placed a hand on his arm. "And you miss her."

He placed his hand over hers. "Yeah, I miss her. I would've left this whole advertising agency thing up to her. I probably should put this out so others can submit ideas, but this pitch enthralled me. It's a big change, though."

Somehow, as he spoke, he was calming. As if she were absorbing his stress. Her own waned as well.

"You don't have to decide tonight, Sebastian, so relax. Let them woo you, but you can still put it out to tender. They approached you because they saw an opportunity. The fact you're considering it means they've done something right."

"You're right, of course. I should be objective about this." He rubbed his hand across his chin. "But you're not getting out of your punishment so easily."

Well, worth a try. "I thought I provided more-than-adequate justification for why I wandered into forbidden territory although, in my defense, no one told me I wasn't allowed to come in here."

"I'll give you that, but common sense should have prevailed. I expect better of you, Mia."

Resigned, she pulled her lower lip through her teeth. "I'm hoping I'll like my punishment."

Sebastian let out an exasperated sigh. "The whole point of punishment is for you to learn."

"Oh, trust me, Sir, I've already learned my lesson. I'll never come in here again without an invitation."

"Fair enough. Still, punishment must be meted out."

"Do I have to strip?" The idea held a certain amount of appeal.

"Not today, Mia. Now, what's your safeword?"

"Rhetoric."

"And your slowdown word?"

"Penguin."

Again, he chuckled. "You have an odd sense of humor." He sobered. "I need you to understand it's acceptable to use these words, okay?"

"But only once I've hit the limit of what I can handle, right?"

"Correct." He led her over to the wall. When she started to turn to face it, he waylaid her. "Not this time. This time I want your back to the wall."

She obeyed, and he grasped her left arm.

"You need to relax it, Mia, or this will be hard on you."

Sure, just relax. When she had no idea what was about to happen to her?

Not likely.

Still, she put her mind to the task, and the muscles in her arm loosened. He guided it up to the manacle and secured her wrist. Knowing what came next, she relaxed her right arm, and soon he shackled it.

"Are you in pain?"

She shook her head.

"When I ask you a question in scene, I expect a verbal answer."

"No, Sir, I'm not in pain. It's uncomfortable, but I suspect that's what you want."

She was met with a quick and devastating grin.

"You're getting better at this. It will eventually hurt, but you need to work with the pain instead of against it."

Work with the pain? What kind of bullshit was that?

"Your doubts are written all over your face. You shouldn't doubt me, Mia. I know what I'm doing."

"Yes, Sir."

Next he moved over to the dresser, then opened one drawer. He pulled out one little item and one larger one. As soon as she recognized them, her stomach did an uncomfortable little flip. "I'm not sure about this."

"Do you trust me?"

"Yes." She said the words cautiously, all the while reining in her panic. "But that doesn't mean I have to like what you're about to do to me."

"Your safeword?"

She nodded, then caught herself. "Rhetoric." Her brow furrowed in concentration. "How are you going to hear me?"

"There are many forms of communication, but I'll be able to hear you, Mia. Just to be on the safe side, I'll give you a piece of cloth to hold in your hand. Dropping it will be the equivalent of saying your safeword." He stroked her cheek. "This is a way to broaden your horizons."

She almost laughed out loud but held herself in check.

"Now, the most important thing is to breathe naturally. Breathe too shallowly or too rapidly, and you might hyperventilate."

Again, she suppressed a nervous burst of laughter.

"Do you have questions?"

"Yes, Sir, how long is this punishment going to last?"

"As long as I deem it necessary."

Doesn't sound promising.

"Ready?"

She nodded, and he opened the little plastic package. *How hygienic.* She was getting her own pair of earplugs.

She could tell as soon as they went in that they were industrial-strength ones. She saw Sebastian speak but couldn't make out the words. Then she recognized what he was saying.

"Yes, Sir, I'm fine."

Weird to not be able to hear her own words.

When he lifted the hood with a question in his eyes, she simply inclined her head. He gave her what she thought was a look of approval, then slipped the hood over her face.

Her first thought was how dark it was, and she let out a nervous giggle. Of course it was dark. *Duh.* That was the whole point. She startled when his hand pressed to hers, but took the piece of cloth in her hand—clinging to it as if it were her lifeline. Her nonverbal safeword. That was more reassuring than anything else, because she wasn't convinced he'd hear her if she spoke. The heavy hood cinched at the base of her neck, so no light slid in. Even the dark rooms she slept in had clock radios. No such luck here. No way to tell the time, either. She could try counting, but it'd likely confuse her. The fabric was against her face, touching her lips. Oh God, what if she suffocated? Would he even know?

She sucked in a lungful of air and got a mouthful of leather. What had he said? Regular breathing? How was she supposed to do that? She took in another breath, but no give. She blew out as hard as she could and moved the fabric a few centimeters. But she let her guard down and was soon back in the same position.

Her nose. She should breathe through her nose. Except that didn't give her enough air. God, all she wanted was air. In and out. Regular breathing. Not too deep, not too shallow.

She took, by her estimation, about two minutes before she found a rhythm she could live with. In through her nose and out through her mouth seemed to work best.

Now her arms ached. Not just a dull ache, but a sharp pain, shooting from her shoulders up to her wrists. She tried to raise herself up on the balls of her feet to relieve some of the pull, but that was only marginally effective, and her calves cramped, so she had to go back down to her feet. Now her feet hurt.

How was she supposed to be her best tonight after enduring this? Oh, and he'd chosen high heels again. Not the same height as the ones she'd worn to Club Kink, but high enough to make her feet ache when she thought about wearing them. Again, she'd have to hold on to Sebastian for balance, but maybe that'd been the genesis for this diabolical plan. He seemed to like it when she was reliant on him.

Total power exchange.

Could she give him that much power over her? No, she couldn't. She needed to keep her own identity. But what was she doing right now? Handing him not just all the power but all the trust. He could do anything right now, and she'd never be aware. For all she knew, he might've gone to his home office. Or he might've left the condo.

Folly. Get over yourself. He'd said he'd hear her if she called out or see the cloth fall if she dropped it. But he hadn't specified how long it'd take him to react. She could drop the cloth now, but if he was in the bathroom, he might not see it for twenty minutes.

And the building could be on fire, and she'd never know.

Get a goddamn grip.

He'd asked for her trust, and she'd have to give it to him. Funny how he hadn't answered on how long he intended to keep her strung up. What time had it been when she came in here? After two, but before three. And they were going out at six, so she'd have to be free shortly after five to get ready. But if she stood like this for two hours, she'd be useless tonight.

She shifted her weight to her left leg, flexing her right foot. Less than two hours. She shifted her weight to her right leg. What was the longest she'd ever stood? Probably the day she'd waited in the snowstorm for a bus. An hour and a half, in the driving snow. She'd finished her shift, and the bed had been her sole focus. About a dozen times she'd almost drifted off to sleep while waiting for the damn bus. They didn't run often on Sunday mornings, and she'd wondered if the transit system had shut down without warning. She'd been about to get a cab, and drop money she could ill afford to spend, when the bus pulled up.

Yeah, about an hour and a half in the freezing cold. If she survived that, she could handle this. Except, that dark morning, she'd had options. She could've gone for the taxi at any point in time. Not calling for the cab had been sheer stubbornness and tightfistedness, and that'd kept her waiting while the snow piled all around her.

Did she have an out today? *Just let go, and all this will be over.* What had the bastard said? *You need to work with the pain instead of against it.* She'd called bullshit on it then and would call double bullshit now. She'd bet her last dime he'd never been hooded like this before. He asserted he'd experienced everything he was putting her through, but she couldn't envision him willingly submitting to anything—let alone this.

At least he'd let her keep her clothes.

Now her right hip was giving her problems. She flexed it, and her ass hit the wall. Her still-sore ass. Okay, wrong thought. Because last night she'd endured the pain, and he'd been pleased with her. Oh God, when he touched her, something had curled and unfurled inside her. What would she do to feel the pads of his fingers against her delicate skin one more time?

She'd endure one more minute of this. Just one more minute.

How many had it been?

Too many. She wasn't going with the pain—it invaded every muscle and bone in her body. Every tendon and nerve ending screamed in agony.

All she had to do was let go.

"Sebastian?"

She waited for what felt like an eternity.

"Um, Sebastian? I'm ready for you to let me down."

No answer. What if he had left?

"Okay, Sir, it's been long enough."

The leather pressed against her lips again, but she ruthlessly tamped down the panic.

What if she hadn't thought this out to its logical conclusion? What if he had no intention of letting her down until she surrendered? Until she safeworded?

Oh God.

Shit. Shit. Shit.

Think, goddamn it, think. No, he'd said he expected her there tonight to help vet the new agency. Ergo, he had to let her down. Unless he canceled the plans for tonight and left her stuck here.

Why was she desperate to please him? How did he know how much she could endure? He said he knew her intimately, and he'd proven he could read her mind, but still…

Breathe through the pain. She could do that. She bent her knees and let her wrists carry some of her weight. She was going to dislocate a shoulder, but at least her feet got a break.

She was going to dislocate *his* shoulder if he didn't let her down soon.

What would happen if she let go? Not of the fabric, but of the pain? Drift through it. Submerge herself in it. *Like swimming.* The water could hold her up. All she had to do was lie on her back, and she couldn't drown.

She let her head loll back, arching against the wall.

And let herself float away.

****

Awareness was sudden and abrupt. Her left wrist was released suddenly, and she pitched forward into something solid. Her right arm freed, she struggled to stay upright. Disoriented because of the hood, she feared landing face-first into the hardwood floor.

Sure, solid arms scooped her up and carried her.

She knew she was being laid on a bed because she was horizontal instead of vertical. Still, she could hear nothing, feel nothing, smell nothing, see nothing. *Relax.* She was no longer hanging, so it couldn't get worse.

Except she didn't have a muscle or bone in her body that didn't ache. She moved her fingers experimentally. No, her pinkie finger didn't hurt. Something tangible she could hold on to.

The hood was removed, but still no light. Shit, was she blind? In panic, she thrashed out her hands. And connected with something solid. She pulled her hands back and reached for the earplugs. When she tore them out, she was met with a stream of curses.

"Jesus Christ, Tarah, what the fuck?"

Well, served him right if she hit him in the balls. Small payback for what he'd put her through. She struggled to get up, but disorientation overwhelmed her. "Why can't I see?"

"Because you're in a dark room—there's no light."

"No light at all? None?" She fought the rising panic. She was back under the hood all over again. "Sebastian, please…"

"Close your eyes."

She obeyed. The click of the lamp yanked her out of her panic, and the light filtered through her closed eyelids. Relief flooded her system, robbing her of breath. A hand brushed her cheek.

"Breathe, Mia, breathe."

She gasped, air rushed in, and oxygen saturated her blood. Finally, she cracked open her eyes. He was crouched down next to her, his face level with hers. He held her hand in his, and his free hand stroked her hair. His eyes were, as always, dark and unreadable.

His face creased into a genuine smile. "How do you feel?"

Did he honestly want the answer to that? "How do you feel?" Churlish, but she didn't give a shit.

"Like I'll be singing soprano tonight."

"Serves you right." She spat the words out, but her tone lacked venom. "Seriously, Sebastian, are you okay?"

He leaned forward and placed a kiss to her brow. "I'm fine, Mia. Remind me to cheat right next time."

"As opposed to left?" She gazed at him intently, still seeking some equilibrium. "How long was I up there?"

"Thirty-seven minutes."

"No shit."

"Language, Mia. But, yes shit, you were up there for thirty-seven minutes. Thirty-five of which you struggled through. The last two were when you finally gave up the fight."

"You could tell that?"

"My eyes never left you, Mia, not for an instant. I saw every muscle twitch, every shift of foot, every cramp—"

She laughed. "I get your point. I don't want to relive it if that's okay with you."

"Okay."

"But…"

"But what?"

"When I called out to you, you didn't answer me."

His gaze was intense but with a hint of humor. "Well, actually, I did. You just couldn't hear me."

"Ha, ha, ha, Mr. Funny Man." She met his gaze. "Why didn't you let me down?"

His hand softly pushed her hair away from her brow. "Because I knew you could take more. And you did, my little warrior."

"Why? What was the point of the exercise?"

Without releasing his hold on her hand, he eased out of the crouch and sat on the bed.

She turned her head slightly to maintain eye contact, making certain her gaze never wavered. She wouldn't let him off easily.

"You've pushed yourself past the point of exhaustion every day since you turned eighteen. Today you had the whole day to do nothing, and you couldn't cope. You were lost. You always need to be in control and have a firm plan. I gave you a list of things to do, but still not enough. Do you want me to have to give you a minute-by-minute schedule to follow? Because if that's what you need, I'll do it."

Good God, no. "No, I don't need that. Is this because you caught me snooping?"

His face broke into a grin. "No, curiosity is healthy. What I saw when I came home, though, was a bundle of nerves. Even a long swim couldn't completely dissipate your excess energy. How are you now?"

"You mean aside from the pain?"

He nodded.

She took another inventory of her body. Sore, yes, but actual pain? Not so much anymore. "Actually, I'm okay. I can't believe I'm saying that."

"I promised you I wouldn't let you get hurt. I know your limits even if you don't."

She couldn't argue with his logic.

"Now, you close your eyes. I'm going to draw you a bath."

She closed her eyes and was a little bereft when he released his hold on her.

The outfit he'd chosen was a classic pencil skirt and jacket in a moss green. She wore two-inch cream-colored heels and pantyhose. She tried to replicate the makeup magic Kelci had taught her, and her hair was up in a fashionable chignon. After looking herself over in the mirror one last time, she left the safety of her room. Five minutes to spare, but Sebastian was waiting for her.

"You look lovely, Mia."

The admiration in his eyes was the only thing keeping her from looking down at herself and fidgeting. "When you say it like that, I almost believe you."

His brow furrowed. "I told you I'd only ever tell you the truth. You look elegant." He stepped over to the coffee table and picked up a jeweler's case.

"Another mask?"

He chuckled as he handed it to her.

She opened it, finding a string of pearls. She didn't have to ask if they were real. He took the necklace out of the case, and after she turned, he secured the clasp. After he took the case from her not-so-steady hands, he returned it to the coffee table and picked up another box.

Again, she opened the box to reveal matching earrings.

"Oh, my ears aren't pierced."

"I know." Quiet and sure. "They're clip on."

Her eyes watered, causing her to blink several times. He'd taken the time to notice she didn't have pierced ears. A little thing, but important. She took each earring and clipped it to her lobe.

"You ready?"

He was dapper in his dark suit and gray tie. "As I'll ever be." If her nerves didn't destroy her.

He led her to the front hall where he took out a long wool coat for her. "It will be chilly tonight. We'll take a cab."

She let him help her into the coat, noting when his hands lingered a moment longer than necessary. "Sounds fine. Is there anything else you can tell me about the people we're meeting?" She stepped out into the hallway, and he followed.

"Shelley and Mercy began their upstart advertising agency four years ago with one account. Now they have a staff of six with nineteen accounts and counting. Mercy's sister has kids, and one night they all went to one of my restaurants. The kids complained they were getting the same puzzles and games as they always did, and wouldn't it be nice if they had something different?"

Now they stepped from the elevator on the ground floor. Tarah waved to Carlos who tipped his hat at them. "So Shelley and Mercy had an idea."

"They worked out a whole new design and theme. It used to be castles, kings, and queens, but now they're suggesting create your own futuristic world."

Interesting. Tarah considered this as she folded herself into the taxi. She waited for Sebastian to come around to the other side.

"I can see where that could be interesting, but tried-and-true themes are that way because they work. On the other hand, our kids are a plugged-in generation."

"And that's where my hesitation is coming in. We're not known for innovation. If we make a change with the menu, it's after extensive consultation with our customers. Still, we hear about it if we remove someone's favorite item. We look at numbers, but that only tells part of the story. We tried to take clam chowder off the menu because the soup wasn't selling well. We thought we'd try varying the soup instead. What we didn't realize was we had a segment of regulars who came in solely for the clam chowder. They protested, and we listened. Clam chowder will always be on the menu." He paused. "And what do you mean *our children are a plugged-in generation*? You're a millennial, for crying out loud. You were born hooked up to a computer."

"Not quite, Sebastian. My parents were traditionalists. I was raised to read books, play outdoors, be a Girl Guide, and volunteer. I've never played a video game, and I only use a computer to complete homework assignments. As you well know, I don't even own a cell phone."

"Which was dangerous considering the hours you worked, Tarah." His tone was churlish.

At the use of her given name, she glanced at him, out the window, and back at him. She leaned toward him. "Vanilla, right?"

He pulled back and met her gaze. "Of course. Tonight we're equals."

A moment of relief followed by a brief pang. He wouldn't be calling her *Mia* tonight because she wasn't his. He scooped her hand and gave it a squeeze, providing silent comfort. He gave her confidence when she was with him, and that worried her, but she shelved the thought for another time.

When they arrived at the restaurant, she waited until he rounded to help her out of the cab. It threatened rain but hadn't yet started. She eyed her shoes and hoped they'd be sturdy enough to withstand a wet and rainy Vancouver night. When he offered her his arm, she took it, holding on tighter than might've been required.

Shelley and Mercy were already seated when they arrived. The women were in their late twenties and a study in contrasts. Shelley was an Indian woman with beautiful bronze skin. Deep-brown eyes matched her almost-black hair. Mercy was a tall and statuesque blonde with vivid green eyes. She was almost half a foot taller than her compatriot.

Tarah shook hands with the women, and an immediate connection formed. Warm and friendly with open smiles, the two women were relaxed. But when she scrutinized further, she noted an intensity she'd missed at first glance. These women had taken a hell of a risk approaching Sebastian. Now Tarah was expected to judge their ideas. *Hope I'm up for this.*

Sebastian alone ordered alcohol. After even this brief time with him, she felt disconcerted to be given a choice. She opted for diet soda because she wanted a clear head tonight. A bit of small talk passed before they placed their orders, but as soon as the waiter was gone, she looked back and forth between the two women.

"What's the pitch?"

If they were surprised, neither showed it. Mercy retrieved a tablet and pulled up some graphics. "Currently, there is only one scenario for the entire chain. If the kids come in once a week, they still get the same package. We're suggesting a different theme for each week of the month."

"And it would repeat once the month is over. Four sets in total?"

Shelley's eyes lit with pleasure. "We want to make it more interactive. Currently, the kids get a paper placemat with a puzzle, a word search, and a coloring section. Our focus groups tell us kids are savvier. We're suggesting a series of questions leading them on a quest."

"A physical quest or a metaphysical quest?"

The women laughed at Tarah's question. "We're not suggesting a treasure hunt in the restaurant—more of a question-and-answer situation. The kids are asked a series of questions and directed to the page most fitting their profile."

The digital mock-up was impressive. "The coloring placemat is a favorite with parents because they can converse with each other while the kids do the coloring. What you're proposing is interactive with the parents."

A conspiratorial look passed between the two

women. "That's the whole point." Mercy tapped a fingernail on the tablet. "Everyone is focused on their own devices these days, and they've forgotten what it's like to be a family unit. This encourages interaction between parents and children."

Tarah took a moment to consider what they were proposing. Ironic they were suggesting a futuristic theme while harking back to traditional family values. But Sebastian's chain was a throwback. They were places geared toward families. They had a special kids' menu with plenty of high chairs and booster seats at the ready. The one time Tarah had gone in, the place had a raucous and happy atmosphere. What she hadn't mentioned to Sebastian was she'd gone after she discovered he was president of the company. She'd sat in a corner and observed the interactions. The staff had been patient and obviously loved kids. She'd left with a new admiration for Sebastian as well as intense confusion. The man who owned a dungeon ran a chain of family restaurants. Incongruous. Of course Gage had been a high school principal and a Dominant while Rielle had been a lawyer and a submissive. How many people hid their kinky side from the world?

About to speak, she was prevented by the food arriving. The tablet was stowed, and everyone ate. She'd opted for the chicken teriyaki, and Sebastian had given her a wicked grin and ordered the same thing.

"So how did you ladies decide to start an advertising agency?"

Tarah didn't miss the look that passed between the two women. Oh, so *that* kind of partnership.

"I was working at a traditional advertising agency on an internship when we were contracted to do a website for The Nelson Group." Shelley held her fork aloft. "I wanted something more innovative than what our techs were coming up with. I put out the word on the local college campus."

"I'm a total geek." Mercy's grin lit the room. "I discovered this opportunity to design the site and knew I had to try it."

"Mercy submitted the site, and clearly the work was better than anything else on the table. But because she wasn't in-house, they decided against it." Shelley smirked. "I quit, hooked up with Mercy, and we pitched the site ourselves."

"Didn't they have a noncompete clause?"

Shelley beamed. "They do now. It never occurred to them an intern would have the gumption to do what I did. We landed the contract and haven't looked back. That was four years ago."

"Not to be judgmental, but you're both young. Not inexperienced." Tarah waved a hand in the air to clarify. "But young. Most women are your age before they consider having children. Your demographic is slightly older with at least one child."

Mercy nodded. "That's why we went the route of the focus groups."

"A large outlay and cost."

Shelley's gaze lingered on Mercy, moved to Sebastian, and finally, Tarah. "If we land the contract, it'll be time and money well spent."

"And if you don't? Will you take this to one of Sebastian's competitors?"

The hesitation was a fraction of a second but was there. "This was designed for Mr. Merrick's restaurants. If we were to pitch it somewhere else, we'd be starting from scratch." Shelley's answer was exactly what Tarah expected.

"In other words, you've put all your eggs in this basket."

Mercy held her gaze. "We're a company thriving on innovation and challenge. My niece and nephews were tiring of the same games at the restaurant and were pestering my sister with requests to go elsewhere. The thing is Mr. Merrick's restaurants are perfect for kids and families. Few sit-down restaurants are comparable. We want the company to succeed as much as you two do."

Tarah was momentarily disoriented by Mercy's assumption she had anything riding on the success of Sebastian's company.

Oh, the women thought she and Sebastian had *that* kind of relationship. Well, her own fault for not making things clear from the beginning.

Tarah pointed to the tablet as their dinner dishes were cleared. Shelley pulled it out and brought up the graphics again.

"I like the interaction part of it, and I love that it's gender neutral, but sometimes families are looking for a way to disconnect. The future is all about technology. What if you had weeks where the focus was the environment? Or history? Or world geography? You have a chance to teach without being preachy. That's a powerful tool and something not to be taken lightly."

She looked up uncertainly, not sure what the women's reactions would be.

An hour later, her head still spun. Both Mercy and Shelley had hugged her before they went off to their own taxi—still spitballing ideas back and forth. Tarah figured the hour of interaction at the table would've been sufficient, but apparently not. Only Sebastian's subtle urging had gotten them moving at all.

Letting herself be tucked into a cab, she then waited for Sebastian to come around and meet her. Finally, she chanced a glance at him. "I hope you don't mind I made the suggestion."

He chuckled. "You realize I now have to sign the contract?"

"Because of what I did?" *Damn.* She swallowed down the lump in her throat. "I mean, did I do something wrong?"

"Hell no, Mia. The problem is your idea is so good if they take it to a competitor, then I'm out of business."

"Well, that's an exaggeration—"

"It's not." His eyes were dark in the passing streetlamp. "Did you see the explosion of creativity? That's why I let them pitch me, and that's why I'll sign them. Many people would've balked at outside input and stuck to their original idea. You made valid points, and they were quick to incorporate them. But they didn't do it to suck up to me or even you. They did it because they were good ideas."

They made the rest of the taxi ride in silence, and slowly, the tension in her neck eased. His use of the term *Mia* helped her settle.

After they entered the condo, he eased her coat from her shoulders and hung it in the closet. "I liked them."

"I like them too."

After dropping to the couch, she kicked off her shoes. Damn, her feet hurt. Rubbing them helped. "They work well together."

Sebastian laughed. "And they play well together."

The penny dropped. "You met them through Kink?"

149

"No, but I wasn't surprised to find out they frequent the club. I did my due diligence—although I didn't go as far as hiring a private detective." He met her gaze and arched an eyebrow. "Did you notice the necklace Mercy wears?"

"It was exquisite, but I was afraid it'd be gauche if I mentioned it at a business dinner."

"Well, she would've loved you to mention it—it's her collar. She wears it all the time."

What? She was stunned. "It's a velvet Cameo choker with matching earrings, not a collar."

"Collars come in all forms. Mercy is Shelley's submissive in every way except at the office."

Holy cow. "I did not see that coming. Most people would never realize it."

"Mercy's standard response to queries about the necklace is that it's an heirloom from her relative."

"But Shelley's not a relative."

"In their world, the collaring was the equivalent of a marriage ceremony."

"But gay marriage is legal in Canada."

"And one day they may get married. For now they have a different way of expressing their love."

She idly fingered her own necklace. "You're not saying…"

The chuckle was a low rumble. "No, Mia, I wasn't marking you—I was giving you a gift."

"A gift?" Her eyes widened. "I thought the necklace was a loaner."

Now his eyes widened. "No, Mia, a gift. One you'll have occasion to wear again over the next few months. I hope you'll keep it, but that will be up to you."

"Why…what would I do with it?"

"Sell it or give it away."

Her grasp tightened. "It is a gift from you, Sir. I'd never get rid of it."

"I'm glad to hear it." He paused. "Would you like a nightcap?"

Not a chance. "After today's exertions, I'll sleep well tonight."

"Well, I'll leave the CD and the information about the opera for you."

"Please tell me I'm not going to have an endurance test again. I was a little sore through dinner." She might have sighed a bit on that thought.

"Uncomfortable or sore?"

She took a moment to consider, reviewing muscles and bones. "Uncomfortable."

"And what did you think at those times?"

"What a bastard Sir is."

A sardonic eyebrow rose. "But the point is you thought of me, and that calmed you. Mercy and Shelley would never have known how nervous you'd been earlier today."

"How did you know?"

"Know?"

"The exercise would calm me."

"More like help you focus, Mia." He met her gaze directly, his eyes sharp. "As your Dominant, it's up to me to guide you through your emotions. You've kept them bottled up for so long that when they overflow, they come out in a torrent."

"Does it really work like that? Suppress emotions, and they come back to bite you in the ass?"

"They've done studies demonstrating people who don't express their anger are more likely to have a heart attack."

She tilted her head slightly. "I wasn't aware." She paused. "You care about your employees."

Confusion clouded his features, and she was about to clarify when he smiled. "Yes, their health and well-being are important to me. Not just my head office staff. I care about the franchise owners, the managers, the waitstaff, the hosts, and the kitchen staff. They need to be treated with respect, or they'll leave. We have a lower turnover than the industry norm, and that's a good thing. When you spend time and money to train someone, you want to get your money's worth. We also have a policy of hiring people with disabilities because they have greater loyalty, are hard workers, and have a lower rate of absenteeism."

"Very generous of you."

He shook his head. "It might have started for altruistic reasons, but we immediately saw benefits. My managers are taught to keep an open mind when they hire." He paused, and his color heightened. "I'm often asked to speak at conferences about our policy and the benefits we've seen."

Well, well. She recognized his embarrassment, and she was pleased that he wasn't superhuman. He could, at times, be a regular guy.

As if sensing her emotions, he gave her a smile. "Time for inspection. This time, I want you naked and kneeling."

With a flush of excitement, she scurried to the dungeon. She took care with her clothes, borrowing an empty hanger from the walk-in closet so she wasn't having to fold the jacket and skirt. Pantyhose, underwear, and bra all made a nice neat pile on the bed.

Kneeling had her a little stumped. He'd instructed her how to present herself while she was standing, but he'd given her no such directions for when she knelt. Time was passing, so she picked a spot between the bed and the door and knelt. She put her hands on her thighs and downcast her eyes.

She didn't have long to wait before the door handle snicked. Sebastian's shoes were polished to a shine. As with everything else about his clothing, they spoke of quiet elegance and wealth. There to be seen, even though he never flaunted it.

"Good job, Mia. Now, spread your legs a little bit."

She placed her hands on the floor to balance herself and shifted so her thighs no longer touched. Her nether regions were more exposed. *That's the point.*

"Hands on your thighs."

She again obeyed, offering herself up for supplication. Opening herself up for him and only him.

"Excellent work. Now, I'm going to get you to stand, but I want you to do it without your hands touching the ground."

How was she supposed to do that? She rocked back, trying to get her feet under her. For her trouble, she fell back on her ass. "Shit."

"Language, Mia. There's a way to do this. Tomorrow I want you to go on the internet and find a video of a kneeling woman standing without using her hands. Then I want you to practice."

Eyes still downcast, she acknowledged the request. He wouldn't be asking this of her if it was impossible. For now, when he offered her his hand, she took it gratefully. She let him guide her over to the chair and waited for him to sit before he inspected her. Before her bath today, he'd instructed her to wash off the marks. The one on her breast had been a breeze, but the one on her ass had been a bit of a challenge. What if he put one on her back or lower on her butt? *Don't obsess about it.* He'd never present her with an impossible task. Tricky and creative? Yes. Impossible? No.

His face was an inch from her nipple, his moist breath against her breast.

"You did a good job, Mia. Now, turn."

She did with as much elegance as she could manage. Again, his breath was warm against her skin. She wanted nothing more than for him to press his lips to the place where he had branded her. She was his property. One touch, one caress. Something to show her she was special.

He placed his hands on her waist, pushed her away from him, and spun her so she faced him. His touch was clinical, no warmth from him. "You did well today—I'm proud of you. Go to bed and sleep naked." It appeared as if he were going to say something more, but he simply smiled. "Six thirty."

Being dismissed, she walked away, again distinctly unsatisfied.

Chapter Nine

When she presented herself Wednesday morning, she felt almost human.

Almost.

This time, he signed his name to her abdomen. This time, when he was done, his hands lingered a little longer. Unconsciously, she leaned forward into the smooth pads of his fingers. He might've once worked construction, but now he was a man of refinement. His hands were those of a gentleman—even if he was anything but.

"Have your swim and do some reading. You're almost finished with your first book, right?"

"Yes, Sir."

"Do you have your study plan?"

"Yes, Sir. By the beginning of the semester, I'll have all the literature read. The French class is more practical, so I'll need to wait until it starts. I'll also have about half of the required psychology reading done. I emailed the teacher to find out which chapters we're covering so I'm not doing anything needlessly."

"Good planning."

Her cheeks warmed under the praise. "I always email early so I have some of the reading done ahead of time. Basically, I write my final exams and immediately start in on the next semester's work."

His eyes crinkled when he offered a sympathetic

smile. "My Mia, always working very hard. Well, you'll take the week between Christmas and New Year's and enjoy yourself. I've been considering a trip somewhere warm."

Since no place in Canada could be considered *warm* in December, she had to speak up. "I don't have a passport."

He chuckled. "I assumed as much. Your task Monday is to go to the passport office and request an expedited passport. It'll cost more, but I can afford it."

She laughed, undoubtedly as he had intended.

"Now, you'll have to leave before I take the day off and spend it looking at you."

That lascivious tone again, and she responded. Her nipples tightened, and her face flushed. "What if I want Sir to spend the day looking at me?"

His eyes darkened. "Don't tempt me, Mia. Leave now."

His tone brooked no opposition, and she left.

****

Andrea Chénier was an opera based loosely on the life of a member of the French Revolution of the same name. A horribly depressing opera where the lovers wound up going to the guillotine together. Honestly, this close to Christmas and they couldn't find something more uplifting?

As she listened to the CD, however, Tarah was pulled in, understanding why it held such attraction. When she came to the solo of Maddalena singing about her mother's death, "La mamma morta," she didn't cry, but it was a close call. Sebastian had given her the old recording with Maria Callas singing the lead role. God, but the woman's voice was phenomenal. He'd provided a translation of the Italian to English so she understood the meaning to go with the emotion. Better to cry now, rather than tomorrow. To be on the safe side, though, she was going to take some tissues.

Study time over, she made herself a sandwich for lunch and prepared to finish her book. Next on her list was *The Diviners* by Margaret Laurence. This one held a bit of an appeal because fundamentalist Christians regularly tried to get the book banned. Another thick book. She downloaded it to her e-reader, which was turning out to be a handy little gadget.

She'd also read the instruction manual for the cell phone although she was confused about why she needed one. She'd gone twenty-five years without one—what was the big fuss now? She didn't have anyone to give the number to. She supposed she could give it to her parents, but that seemed silly. She'd given them Sebastian's home number when she moved in, and it ought to be good enough. She hadn't even called to relay the new number, opting instead to email her mother. Although she loved her parents, they were completely involved with each other, especially since her father's health scare. Lynette's life was work or taking care of Lawrence. Tarah was an afterthought.

She didn't mind, though. Her father's health, although frail, wasn't precarious. He'd never again be the hearty and healthy man from her childhood, but he was still alive, and that counted for something. She yearned to call him but couldn't. Her mother had to be there so she could gauge how much he could handle. Resignedly, she admitted she wouldn't call. Her visit at Christmas would have to suffice. When she went out on Monday, she'd select presents for her parents. What would it be like to not have to count out every penny? Not that she was going to take advantage of Sebastian's largesse. She still had her own savings she could dip into.

Mollified, she tucked away the opera material and continued reading about the political and cultural divide in Canada's two most populous provinces.

****

Sebastian baked wild salmon for dinner while she observed intently, staying out of his way. He made it look effortless, and she cringed. Surely, she could do this herself.

"I've hired Miguel Hernandez to come in on Thursdays to give you cooking lessons. That won't interfere with your classes, right?"

She considered, then shook her head. "No, Canadian Lit is Monday afternoons, Abnormal Psych is Wednesday mornings, and French is Wednesday afternoon. My Thursdays are free and clear." Her mind whirled. "Miguel Hernandez. I should know his name, shouldn't I?"

"He's the head chef at The Georgian."

Only one of the most exclusive restaurants in town.

"I'm sure he has better things to do with his time." Her stomach sank. "I'm sure there are cooking classes I can take."

Sebastian tisked. "Miguel started out as a cook in my first restaurant. I financed his training at Le Cordon Bleu in France. He still creates new recipes for me."

"I guess there isn't much of a conflict there, right? I mean The Georgian doesn't exactly cater to five-year-olds."

He burst out laughing. "That's accurate, Mia. I asked him if he could spare a sous-chef, but he insisted he'd do it as a favor to me. He promised he'd start out easy on you. Don't worry about being overwhelmed your first day."

"Oh, being taught by a Cordon Bleu chef can't possibly be intimidating."

"Sarcasm doesn't become you—now hand me the plates so I can dish out the salmon."

She did as bid and tried not to salivate over the aroma of food she carried to the table.

Their meal was half consumed before she ventured a question. "Did you meet with Shelley and Mercy today?"

Sebastian shook his head. "They want to work on mock-ups before we meet again. I told them if you liked what they did, the contract was theirs. They'll probably be contacting you at some point to get your input."

What the hell? "Me? You told them I have to be pleased? Oh, Sebastian, that's an awful lot of pressure—for me and for them."

Shrugging as if it were of no consequence, he forked in another mouthful of food, indicating to her he considered the matter closed. She wasn't sure she enjoyed being responsible for the success of two others, but parallels with the classroom existed. Wouldn't she be responsible for the welfare and success of twenty-five little ones? If she could do that, surely she could judge a presentation of mock-ups for children's entertainment.

Shelley and Mercy had also decided they would do two for each week—one for children under five and one for older children—which meant there would be eight projects. Sounded like an awful lot of work to her, but who was she to judge? They had a staff who'd dedicate themselves to this. Because Sebastian had alluded this contract would be lucrative for the agency, she understood why the women were willing to put all their proverbial eggs in the proverbial basket.

"Earth to Tarah."

She'd been caught navel-gazing. *Shit.* She shot her gaze to his. "I'm sorry, Sir—I was thinking about the project." She fingered her cloth napkin. "What were you asking me?"

"I asked if you wanted to watch television this evening or perhaps a movie. I have a library of discs in my office. Would you like to select one?"

She blew her bangs. "Look, Sir, I can count on one hand the movies I've seen in the past seven years, and most were on television. It's safe to say I have seen none of your films. I'd be more comfortable if you selected the movie."

His brow quirked as he considered her words. "And you have no preference?"

She quickly shook her head. "I'm not a fan of horror films, but otherwise, I'm good."

"While you clean up the dishes, I'll select three movies. You'll make the final decision, and I expect you to do it without guidance from me." He said this as an afterthought, likely knowing in advance she planned to do exactly that.

Drat.

She set about cleaning up. The man was efficient, and hardly any work was required. The dishwasher full, she spent about five minutes trying to decipher the settings before deciding which to select. If she got it wrong, then she'd run it again.

Stepping into the living room, she wasn't surprised to find him lounging on the couch, a drink in hand.

Several movie jewel cases were spread across the coffee table. An action adventure, a romantic comedy, and a science fiction flick. None of them would she have suspected him to have in his collection. She gave him a look. "How many movies do you own?"

He gave her a careless shrug.

I bet he knows the exact number.

"I love to relax and decompress while watching a movie." He offered the words genially. "If none of these appeal to you, I can pick another three, or you can select one yourself."

"No." *Stop stalling.* "These are appealing." She chose the science fiction film. "There are three, right?"

He nodded, warm approval in his eyes.

"Well, let's watch this one tonight and maybe the second one on Friday…"

"And the third on Sunday. Clever girl."

She basked in the praise because she wanted to please him—wanted him to be proud of her. He rose, took the disc from her, and put it in the entertainment system. Although she knew little about such things, she could spot quality when she saw it. The system must've cost a fortune.

Once the movie was loaded, he turned to her. "Do you want to join me on the couch or sit on the floor?"

"You're giving me a choice?" That brought her up short. She wasn't sure she wanted to decide.

"Why don't you sit on the floor? I think for tonight you might be more comfortable."

And she would be. She liked the idea of leaning against him. Something told her if they sat on the couch, there wouldn't be touching.

This time, he went to the closet and pulled out a

wool blanket. He folded it over twice and laid it at his feet.

"Thank you, Sir, that was considerate of you."

"I don't want you to get cold—hardwood floors can be uncomfortable."

She nodded, waited until he settled, then sat. She leaned against his thigh, and his hand stroked her hair several times before settling on the crown of her head. It gave her a warm and fuzzy feeling, accompanied by a sense of well-being. This was the way it was meant to be.

He sent her to bed right after the entertaining movie. Should she have misbehaved a bit to gain more attention? No, she wasn't a toddler—*no pouting*.

****

She lay in bed, naked and obsessing over Sebastian. He had muscles but not bulk. He must exercise in his day to keep his physique. How often had she wanted to reach out and touch? She was losing count. And that light smattering of chest hair she'd glimpsed during their late-night chat. Would it be coarse or soft?

Her cheeks flushed. *Knock it off.* She'd have to shelve those thoughts for tonight, or she was going to get herself into trouble. She flipped, punched the pillow, and recited the steps of childhood development.

Wasn't long before she slipped into sleep.

****

Sebastian examined his handiwork. "I forgot to look at this last night."

"You were distracted with the movie."

"Still, no excuse."

His finger traced the words drawn against her abdomen. God, if only those hands would explore her farther.

"How high is the cut of your bathing suit?"

Judging the place on her hip where it lay, she gave herself half-an-inch leeway. She was removing her hand when he placed his hand on it, trapping it between her skin and his fingers.

He uncapped the marker with his teeth and signed her hip, above her fingers. He recapped the marker and took a critical look. "I'm happy with that. You have the choice of what you want to do with yesterday's brand."

"Keep it, Sir." He seriously was asking? Her answer was always the same.

She could only see the top of his head, but he nodded his approval.

Just one touch…

His hand released hers, and he pushed her away from him. "Did you look over the material for the opera tonight?"

"I did, Sir, and I plan to look it over again. I also finished *Two Solitudes* and plan to start chapter one of my psychology textbook. It's the overview section."

"Outstanding work, Mia. We're having dinner with Lucille and Gordon Forbes. You remember them, right?"

"She's the writer for the *Vancouver Sun*."

Sebastian gave her a wide smile. "Exactly right, Mia. We're eating at The Georgian." He rose. "While you make yourself breakfast, I'll select your clothes for the day. You might also want to practice walking in the high heels I select. I like you leaning on me, but you also need to be independent. I can't take you to the bathroom."

She laughed. "No, I think Sir would create a stir if he went into the ladies' room. I'll practice. I also need to practice kneeling."

Unexpectedly, he leaned forward and pressed a kiss to her forehead. "That's my Mia." He grasped her lightly, propelling her toward the door. Before she was out of reach, he gave her a swat on the ass.

The sting carried her through her preparations of breakfast, flushing her with pleasure. She should've asked him if he'd wanted her to prepare something, but he would've told her if he did. He was like that. Everything he did had purpose and meaning. Their trip to the aquarium had been the only spontaneous thing he'd done since asking her to move in with him.

Did he ever lose control? No, not in his personality. Everything was regimented because that was how he wanted it. After laying down a towel, she sat on the chair at the dining room table. She'd learned her lesson and always ate at the table, even when she was alone. Eating naked ought to have been awkward but instead was natural.

"You make a lovely picture, my Mia."

She ducked her head shyly, heat blooming in her cheeks. "Sir makes me comfortable with my body."

"And a beautiful body it is."

Her flush deepened.

"Now, you need to be ready at five thirty since our reservations are for six. We need to be finished by seven fifteen so we can make the eight o'clock curtain. It's going to be a long night." He eyed her. "Consider having a quick nap this afternoon. Only an hour, though. You want to be refreshed, not groggy."

Was there anything he didn't know about her? Because that was exactly what happened if she slept too long during her *day*.

"Thank you for the suggestion, Sir. I'll set an alarm and be ready on time."

He took a step forward.

Was he going to... Despite her fervent wish he would, he nodded curtly and left. Swallowing her disappointment, she finished up her breakfast, even though she'd lost her appetite.

****

Tonight's gown was a plum-colored silk with a high neck and plunging back. No way to wear a bra. She was grateful for some...support...in the front. She'd spent a half an hour today walking through the condo with heels on. Lucky thing she wouldn't be bothering the neighbors below her. Then she'd practiced kneeling and getting up without the use of her hands. Doable, and she'd gotten progressively better but was far from graceful. More work would be needed, but she'd given up when her knees ached and her thighs quivered with the strain.

She'd be back at it again Monday morning.

She'd also trolled the internet, searching for articles by Lucille—specifically, ones involving Carl Jergen. The man was an egomaniacal sociopath who thought he could get away with anything. Insanity? He'd been deliberate and cold-blooded, and she firmly believed he shouldn't get off easy. He belonged in a prison, not a mental institution.

Lucille had written many exposés on politicians, businesspeople, real estate tycoons, and a few professional sports figures thrown into the mix. She must have unimpeachable sources, because people willing to be whistleblowers came to her in droves. The writing was tight and concise yet painted vivid pictures of her subjects. She'd also done a few profiles of people in power who kept their noses clean.

She located little about Gordon Forbes. He was a dentist, and aside from the practice's website, he didn't seem to have much of a digital footprint. Idly, she searched Sebastian again. Nothing since the last time she'd checked. Had she expected there to be anything? He was an intensely private man. In fact, she knew virtually nothing about his past. What had he said? He'd worked construction before buying a strip club and turning it into a family restaurant. It still made her chuckle. But he'd seen what others missed and continued to do so.

The key clicked in the lock, and she walked as quickly as she dared to the door. Eyes downcast, she watched his shiny shoes as he stepped forward.

"Eyes up, Mia."

She obeyed.

He leaned forward, checking her face. "You learned well from Kelci. I like the dark and smoky look. It makes your pale-blue eyes look exotic."

More flushing cheeks. "I'm happy Sir approves."

"We need to leave right away. Let's get you into your coat."

****

Throughout dinner, she endured a sense of unreality. Having breakfast here had been one thing, but she was now having a formal dinner in The Georgian. As Sebastian Merrick's date. If someone had told her two weeks ago she'd be doing this, she'd have laughed in their faces. She was little Tarah Peters. Shy and reserved Tarah Peters.

She was finishing dinner when a man approached in a white chef's outfit. Her stomach did a flip. God, the man was gorgeous. He had the same dark hair and eyes as Sebastian, but his skin was a dark tan because of his Latin heritage.

Women must fawn all over him.

Sebastian rose in greeting, and the two men hugged. Not an awkward, semi-hug and pat on the back, but a genuine hug with clear affection. He nodded to his guests. "Lucille and Gordon Forbes, this is Miguel Hernandez."

Lucille's eyebrow shot up, and Gordon extended his hand.

"A delicious meal, Mr. Hernandez," Lucille simpered.

Miguel ducked his head a little as if he were going to wave off the praise, but then he offered a smile. "I'm glad you enjoyed it. And, please, it's Miguel."

"Miguel." Lucille repeated the name, a gleam in her eyes. She offered her hand, clearly charmed when he pressed a kiss to her knuckles. "I've been trying to get an interview with you for ages." She withdrew a business card from her purse. "Please reconsider my offer. I can help your career."

He offered a courtly bow, taking the card. "Your offer, Mrs. Forbes, is appreciated. I think, however, my career is doing fine."

"But it would bring good publicity for The Georgian."

She had him there, and he waffled visibly.

Before the awkward silence continued, Sebastian placed his hand on Tarah's shoulder. "This is Tarah Peters."

Miguel's teeth gleamed in his wide grin. "Miss Peters, a pleasure."

She held out her hand, and he brushed a light kiss across her knuckles. Sebastian's brow furrowed, but she met Miguel's gaze. His eyes were blazing black.

"I'm looking forward to our lessons." He offered a look that took in the entire party. "If you'll excuse me—my kitchen awaits." With a slight bow, he stepped back and away.

Sebastian sat back down, and he and Gordon resumed their meals.

Lucille turned to Tarah. "Lessons? You're getting cooking lessons from Miguel Hernandez?"

Fighting to keep her features neutral, she answered, "Yes, Sebastian set it up for me. I confess my repertoire is a student's, and poor Sebastian has been subjected to more pasta than is healthy. He and Miguel are friends. I'm not sure of how it all worked out, but I start cooking lessons in the new year."

"Well, put in a good word for me. I really want to write about him. He's a bit of an enigma, you know?"

Tarah scrunched the bridge of her nose. "Actually, I know very little about him."

Lucille scrutinized her with sharp eyes. "You don't have that killer instinct, do you? That need to know everything. I don't like enigmas, and secrets drive me crazy."

"Aren't people entitled to some privacy?" Sebastian's private life flashed through her mind. He didn't hide the fact he frequented Club Kink, but he didn't advertise it either.

Lucille didn't miss a beat. "Privacy is an illusion. With electronic surveillance today, no one has secrets anymore. If someone doesn't want their conduct known, they shouldn't do things that wouldn't stand up to the harsh glare of the light of day."

"What about in their own homes?" She had to make the woman see reason. "Surely, it should be acceptable to have some measure of privacy at that point?"

After shaking her head, Lucille curled her lips upward but not in amusement. "Not in my book. If you can't do it in public, you shouldn't be doing it in private."

Such a black-and-white world. Good and evil. Right and wrong. Did people really see the world that way? Maybe because of what she'd seen—and the discretion expected of her—Tarah had a different perspective. What would Lucille think if she knew what Tarah and Sebastian did in the condo's privacy? Probably go wild at the thought of exposing the dungeon and all the things that might or might not go on in there.

Sebastian glanced at his watch. "We should be going."

The immediate sense of relief was disproportionate to the threat, but she was grateful when Sebastian pulled back her chair, helping her to her feet. "Thank you." Gratitude was easy.

"You're welcome."

She met his eyes, recognizing compassion. Was her distress so apparent?

He slipped her into her coat and pressed a light kiss to her temple. "You're exquisite."

Whether he intended to make her blush, she couldn't be sure, but she did. He was quick with his praise—clearly always heartfelt. He was a man who claimed he only spoke the truth, and she believed him. Ergo, she looked exquisite this evening.

Why complicate things with *what-ifs* and *maybes*? If Sebastian was comfortable with Lucille and Gordon, she would be as well.

The couples took separate taxis to the theater, but their seats were next to each other.

Tarah'd hoped for different arrangements but was seated between Sebastian and Lucille. Too cozy for comfort.

Once the opera began, however, her cares melted away. She was transported into another world. Amazing. How could such things exist and she'd never known? The majesty, the artistry, the talent. They all combined to take her away from her world and into another.

Going to the bathroom was an unwelcome interruption because she was so excited for the next act. Fortunately, the room was packed, and no opportunity presented itself for Lucille to talk to her. Suddenly, Tarah despaired of saying the wrong thing.

When they located the men, the time had come to go back inside. The show recommenced, and by the end, she was incredibly glad she'd brought tissues. Despite a valiant effort, the tears came when the lovers went to their deaths together.

She rose when the applause began, as did most of the audience.

Lucille was slower to get to her feet. When the final curtain lowered and the house lights flickered on, she placed a hand on Tarah's arm. "You seemed moved, my dear."

Unable to discern if the woman was being sincere or patronizing, Tarah opted for the former and smiled tentatively. "Beautifully tragic, I think. I'll admit this was my first opera."

Lucille seemed satisfied as she made no further comment. The two couples parted in the lobby, and

Tarah was surprised when Lucille gave her an air kiss.

"We should get together soon, my dear."

Despite wanting to shoot back she wasn't Lucille's *dear*, she held her tongue and instead simply inclined her head. "That would be lovely."

Then the Forbes were gone, and she took Sebastian's proffered arm, leaning on him just a little bit. Nothing wrong with that, right?

Just don't get used to it.

****

The cab ride was made in silence, but clearly, he had something on his mind. When they were a few blocks from the condo, he directed the driver to pull to the curb. He tossed over several bills and made his way to her side.

She took his hand and stepped from the taxi. She wanted to point out they were still several blocks from the condo, but he obviously knew it.

"I hope you don't mind walking. I need the fresh air." Then he paused and glanced down at her shoes. "I'm sorry—that was thoughtless of me. I should've sent you home ahead of me."

"It's four blocks, Sebastian. As long as you don't mind me leaning on you, it's not a big deal."

His arm lifted, and she tucked hers under it, clasping tightly to the sleeve of the dark wool coat.

"I practiced today." *Lame.* "High heels and kneeling. I'm not graceful yet, but I'll keep at it."

"That's nice." His voice was distant, then he halted, turning her toward him and tipping up her chin. "What did Lucille say to you?"

Momentarily stunned as she hadn't expected this, she took a deep breath to steady herself. "She said people shouldn't do in private what they wouldn't do in public.

She made it clear she has the right to have her nose in everyone's business."

"And you don't believe that." His tone was mild, his thoughts indiscernible. Was he angry or amused?

"What we do…I'm not sure I'd want the universe to know about it. I mean, if people knew I wore a dog collar at a kink club, would the parents trust me with their kids? There are parents who still think a gay teacher isn't capable of being a good role model."

"Is that your only concern?"

What was he getting at? She wasn't good with word games. "No. I also thought about you. You run a chain of family restaurants. How would it look if people knew you kept a woman at your house who spends half of her time naked and who kneels at your feet?"

"Half of the population would be appalled, and half of the population would be secretly cheering."

"I'm sure there are some progressive men out there who'd question the ethics of what we're doing."

"And there would be women who'd cheer for us. I didn't say it'd be split along gender lines." He quirked a brow. "Mia, I don't give a fuck what people think. I live my life the way I want and don't apologize for my lifestyle."

She punched him in the arm. "How can you make light of this? Lucille is a junkyard dog with a bone. Aren't you worried? I mean, how can you be friends with her?"

"I met her through Gordon."

"Let me guess—he's your dentist."

"He is, but that's not how we met. Gordon and I went to grade school together. He knows more about me than most people."

"More than me." She tried to keep the hurt from her voice.

He stopped short. "Are you saying you want to know more about me?"

"Hell, yes." Was he really that dense? "We'll be living together for six months. I want to know more about you because it'd allow me to…" She broke off, looking around to see if anyone was close, relieved to find the street deserted. "Allow me to better serve you."

"Did it ever occur to you my past has no relevance of who I am today?"

Her eyes narrowed. "I call bullshit. Our pasts always shape who we are today. I think it's reasonable for me to know more about you."

He broke eye contact, looking out over her head. "And I haven't asked you the tough questions either. I thought I could go off what was in the report, and it'd be enough. It's not, is it?"

Now or never.

Yet, now the moment was here, she hesitated.

He snagged her chin between his thumb and index finger, tipping her face up so she met his gaze directly. "Stop stalling and say what's on your mind."

A touch of wry amusement in his voice. Would it be there once she propositioned him?

Now or never.

"What if I want to renegotiate our contract?"

"Specifics, Mia."

"You said this isn't about sex."

"It's not."

"But what if we want it to be about sex?"

If she'd shocked him, he hid it well. "Submission does not have to involve sex."

"But what if it did in this case?"

"Be careful what you ask for, Mia."

She raised her chin a notch. "Are you saying you don't want me?"

His chest rumbled with laughter. "Oh, I want you, Mia, have no doubt. But I'm a gentleman, and we have an ironclad contract."

"So you're saying sex is off the table."

He tilted his head. "I'm saying this would require a whole new contract. Like I said, be careful. This isn't an either/or proposition. It's an addendum."

"Meaning I can have dominance, or I can have sex and dominance, but I can't just have sex."

"You're a smart young woman."

"I'm not so young." Her hackles rose. "I'm twenty-five."

"Over ten years my junior. I have the power in this relationship."

She couldn't argue with that assertion. "But you also said I had to be willing to give it up. That this was an exchange. Well, I want to add sex to the contract. You said you wanted me." She diffidently stuck her nose in the air. "This shouldn't be an issue."

"All right, let's work this through. Let's say you become my submissive both in and out of the bedroom. There has to be delineation."

Her eyebrow rose in question.

"Times when you're not trying to please me. Times when you exist only for yourself."

"When we're vanilla." Was she understanding this? "Like when I'm at school? Like when I'm studying?"

"Yes, precisely. I'm concerned if you become my submissive in the bedroom as well, those lines might get blurred."

"One hundred and sixty-nine."

His brow furrowed. "I'm sorry…"

"The days remaining in our contract." She offered him her brightest smile. "I'm suggesting a way to help pass the time."

His gaze was intense, and the breath left her lungs in a rush.

"I warned you to watch what you wished for, Mia." He stepped back and took her hand in his again.

****

She changed into jeans and a turtleneck when they arrived home. The silk dress was hardly appropriate, and Sebastian made it clear she couldn't be naked either. He selected the outfit and left her to change while he disappeared into his home office.

Fifteen minutes later, she met him at the dining room table. Her face was scrubbed free of makeup, and she'd pulled her hair into a ponytail.

Sitting next to her, he scowled. "You look sixteen."

Don't pout. "Have you changed your mind?"

"I could ask you the same thing." He pulled papers from a manila folder. "This contract isn't like the last one."

"In what way?"

"It's revocable at any time. You say the word, and we tear it up. We go back to dominance and submission outside the bedroom only." He wasn't looking at her, instead studiously examining the contract.

She was accustomed to his penetrative gaze and was disconcerted without it. "If it's revocable at any time, why have it at all?"

Her nervousness increased as his gaze remained

impassive.

"This is called informed consent. The truth is we've done things already that should've been negotiated before we engaged in them."

"Like what?"

"The branding. The spanking. The hood."

She drummed her fingers on the table. "But you said they were part of the submission and dominance process. You made it seem like I didn't have a choice."

"Then I haven't done a good job, Tarah." He let out a long breath. "I thought I was clear with the conversation about safewords. There's nothing I can do to you without your permission."

Now she was confused. "But you said there'd be consequences..."

"And there will be if you don't do your best. But your best may mean something different to me than it means to you."

She pointed to the contract. "Stop procrastinating and show me the papers."

A ghost of a smile passed over his face. "Don't say I didn't warn you. This is a list." With great care, he placed the pile of papers in front of her. "At each item you say *yes*, *no*, or *maybe*. *No* means it's a hard limit, and we don't go there unless you change your mind. *Yes* means there's a green light. You then need to decide how much you want to try it. One means you're vaguely intrigued, and five means you can't wait to do it."

"This seems awfully complicated—"

He continued as if she hadn't spoken. "*Maybe* means it's a soft limit. I can try to convince you, and you're free to say no." Finally, he placed the contract and a pen in front of her. "If you don't know what something means, ask."

After a quick scan of the list, she squeaked.

He snatched the papers from her hand and started to rise.

"Wait."

Her tone obviously caught his attention, and he slowly sank back into the chair.

She held out her hand, and after a moment's hesitation, he returned the contract to her.

"You caught me off guard." She picked up the pen. "You said my choices are *yes*, *no*, and *maybe*, then I add a number to express my interest."

"When you say *yes*." His voice was church-mouse quiet. "If it's a *no* or a *maybe*, you don't need to assign it a numerical value."

"Okay." She was already formulating a plan in her mind. "And I ask if I don't know what it means."

"Yes. And for God's sake, Tarah, don't agree to something because you think I might want it. Safe, Sane, and Consensual."

"What does that mean?" This was so confusing.

"It's part of BDSM."

Her brow furrowed farther.

"Bondage, Discipline, Sadism, and Masochism."

She blinked.

He sighed.

Putting down the pen, she listened intently as he explained the intricacies of the lifestyle and the different roles. Some of this she'd been able to figure out on her own, but a lot of this was new information to her. He was patient with her, taking her through each item on the list, showing no more interest in one item than another. He was totally unreadable, and it was intentional.

For every item terrifying her, there'd be one piquing her curiosity. When they came to the end, she read the several paragraphs of disclaimer, which was clearly meant to enforce the Safe, Sane, and Consensual aspects of this lifestyle.

She was about to sign when he placed his hand over the line awaiting her signature. She met his gaze.

"I warned you to be careful what you wished for, Tarah."

She placed the pen down on the table. "What can I say to convince you I want this? What words of reassurance can I offer? I'm a grown woman. You might have a decade on me, but I've had to grow up fast. I've been independent for over seven years, Sebastian. I know my mind. You said yourself I use the safeword and everything stops. You said there'd be no recriminations or hurt feelings. You said this is revocable."

Nailed it. Using his own words, she was now so close she could taste it. So close she could reach out and touch it, as if it were a tangible thing.

Something she could do? She placed her hand on his. He was startled, likely because this was the first time she'd initiated skin-to-skin contact. She eased his hand from the page and interlocked their hands. Finally, she took the pen in her other hand and signed her name.

"Fine, Mia, you've gotten what you wanted. Now, go to bed. We have somewhere to go tomorrow before we seal the deal."

Intriguing. But maybe she didn't want to know.

Chapter Ten

The next day, she sat in the doctor's office. She should've listened to the warning bells in her head.

The door opened, and a nice older gentleman stepped in.

"Miss Peters?"

"Yes." She fingered the cloth gown.

"I'm Dr. Anthony. You're here for a physical."

She could only nod.

"Well, Sebastian suggested it might've been a while since you had a physical…"

"I can't remember the last time I had one." She almost never got sick so didn't frequent the doctor's office. Aside from a nasty bout of pneumonia last year, she could report she was healthy.

"So we'll do a full exam. When was your last pelvic exam and pap smear?"

"Um…never?"

"That's not what I want to hear. Let's get started."

The first part of the exam was normal. Dr. Anthony poked and prodded, asked questions, and made inarticulate sounds in response.

When he had Tarah lie with her feet in the stirrups, though, the nerves set in. "Is this really necessary? I mean, I'm healthy…"

A long silence.

Tarah's face flamed.

"Is Sebastian aware of this?"

Staring up at the ceiling, she swallowed convulsively, wishing the floor would swallow her up. "What do you think?" Had she injected enough sarcasm? A sudden thought occurred to her, and she bolted upright. "And you can't tell him, right? I mean patient confidentiality and all that."

The doctor nodded. "But even if Sebastian wasn't the most incisive man I know, I'd still say he'd notice this."

"Can we pretend this never happened?"

He raised an eyebrow. "Odd turn of phrase, but okay. I'll order the standard blood and urine tests including an STI panel."

"STI?"

"Sexually transmitted infections."

"Oh."

He cleared his throat. "You should know Sebastian is having all the same tests today. Well, obviously not the pelvic exam."

"Obviously." Her voice dripped with cynicism. "Just give me the paperwork."

After they had their blood drawn, Sebastian suggested a light lunch. Once they were settled and he ordered for both of them, he met her gaze directly.

"What's wrong, Tarah? You've been acting strangely since we left Anthony's office. Did something happen?"

"What if I wasn't completely up front and honest with you?"

"Did you lie to me?"

"Not so much of a lie. Maybe an omission?" She was hedging, but this was much harder than she'd imagined.

"Look, if this has to do with your past, I don't care. We'll both get our blood test results, and we can take this relationship to the next level."

She squirmed in her seat. Maybe telling the truth here, in public, was the best course of action. He couldn't get too angry, right? "What if I told you I already know what the results will be?"

"Well, I'd say…" His voice trailed off, then he clearly regrouped and leaned forward to afford them some privacy. "The only way to be one hundred percent sure you're clean is if you've never engaged in any sexual activity. None." His eyes narrowed. "Is that what you're telling me?"

She closed her eyes to break the contact, knowing the answer was written all over her face.

"One small omission." He didn't worry about hiding his derision. "Did you think I wouldn't notice?"

"I hoped…"

He made a scornful sound under his breath, telling her what he thought of the quaint notion.

"Does this really change anything?"

"This changes *everything*."

That she hadn't expected. "But it's not something I can do anything about. I mean unless you want me to go find some guy—"

"Hell, no."

Cold. Ice cold. Brook-no-opposition cold. "Well, what do you propose we do?"

"Not make any decisions while sitting here in a restaurant."

He blew out a breath and, for the first time in her memory, appeared uncertain.

"I have to go into the office this afternoon. I might be there for a while, so don't cook dinner or wait up for me."

Wow, that hurt. She sipped her water to cover up the lance of pain shooting through her.

"I didn't say it to wound you."

Lame offer at best.

"Not that I have to explain myself, or justify my actions, of course."

"Of course." What choice did she have?

"I hadn't planned on being out of the office this morning, and I need to get caught up."

"So it has nothing to do with what I said." She sought some confirmation she'd misunderstood.

"Exactly."

What would happen if she called bullshit? Probably nothing good, so she kept her mouth shut.

****

She shouldn't have told him the truth. Just because Dr. Anthony had confirmed she had an intact hymen didn't mean Sebastian would've noticed. *Yeah, right.* The doctor had called her on that one and had been correct to do so. Last night, during the renegotiations, she'd acted like it was no big deal she was agreeing to blow jobs and anal sex.

She dropped the textbook to the desk and flopped in the chair.

Maybe she should surf some porn sites and see what she was agreeing to.

Just as quickly, she shelved the idea.

No, if she was going to find out, she was going to find out firsthand.

She jumped from her chair and prowled through the

condo. There had to be a solution to this. Because she sure as shit wasn't going to give up a perfectly excellent opportunity to get rid of her virginity just because Sebastian Merrick had scruples. She'd seen the dungeon. She'd gone to Kink. She'd let him paddle and spank her. She'd let him touch her. She'd let him mark her.

A man who owned those things, enjoyed those things, did those things, couldn't turn around and be morally superior with her.

She picked up her phone and sent a text message to the number he'd given her in case of emergencies.

She hoped he'd be the only one to see it.

****

She'd left the door to the dungeon open so she'd hear when he arrived home. The sound of the key in the lock was muffled, but his footsteps weren't.

He entered the room and stalked over to her, then grabbed the toy from her hand. "I don't like being manipulated."

"And you didn't have to come right home, but you did." Amazing that he'd come as quickly as he had. It'd been an empty threat—to rid herself of her virginity with a dildo—but it obviously had the desired effect on him. But when he flopped to the bed and put his head in his hands, she pulled the covers over her, trying to hide her previously brazen nudity.

He let out a lengthy sigh. "I've never been with a virgin."

"Wait…what?"

"You heard me fine, and I'm not a fan of repeating myself." He finally met her gaze. "I know how to do a lot of things, but deflowering a woman isn't necessarily one of them."

"Deflowering? Who the hell talks like that?" She made a grab for the dildo, but he was faster. "Is it really such a chore?"

"More like an honor. Jesus, Tarah, you're twenty-five years old. Who the hell is still a virgin after a quarter century?"

"Me." A painful and quiet admission. "I am." She placed a tentative hand on his arm. "The question is, what are you going to do about it?"

His dark eyes were stormy. "I want to be in you. I want to feel you when it happens."

"That was the plan all along." She took some comfort in the fact he was willing to talk about this, although a little disappointed she couldn't jump his bones right this moment. As always, the snakes in her belly slithered in overdrive. She wanted him. Here. Now. Still, they were closer than they'd been five minutes ago. That was worth something. "We wait for your test results, and then we can do it."

"I have my test results."

She gaped. "That fast?"

A quick shake of the head. "They're from six months ago."

"Wait...what?" She shook her head—this time she was the one who wasn't comprehending. "All those women..."

"They came to play, Tarah, nothing more. It's been a long time since I met someone I wanted to be intimate with."

"Isn't playing a form of intimacy?"

Now he was surprised. "You felt it too?"

Oh God, I'm going to go there. "Not just that I wanted you—I needed you. Like I need you now." She let him sit with that. "You have me, Sebastian. There's a signed and sealed copy of the new contract in your office." She let the sheet fall, exposing her breasts. Under his gaze, her nipples tightened, and a frisson of desire traveled lazily up and down her spine.

Never breaking eye contact, he rose and unbuttoned his shirt.

Torn between watching those intoxicating eyes and checking out the flesh being unveiled when his shirt dropped to the ground, she was mesmerized. When his hands went to his belt, her gaze drifted downward. Great pecs? Check. Fabulous abs? Check. Big cock? Double check.

Christ, that was going to fit inside of her? Suddenly, she searched her memory, reaching back to her sex-ed classes in high school. Nope, nothing had prepared her for this.

As if sensing her apprehension, he held out his hands in the universal *I'm not going to hurt you* gesture. Since the next move was hers, she pulled the sheet completely off her, exposing herself to him.

The look of appreciation was something she'd never forget.

"I want you so much I think I'm going to go crazy."

Knowing how much the admission cost him, she held her arms open. "So let's go crazy together."

He took her up on her offer and climbed into bed with her. Instead of lying on her as she expected, he lay beside her.

"Patience, Mia. We have all the time in the world."

"Except now that it's going to happen, I want to get it over with."

His eyes lit with laughter. "You know how to make

me laugh. Now, first things first. We've never actually kissed." Leaning in, he slanted his mouth over hers and pressed his lips to hers.

She wanted to react—knew she should—but didn't know how to.

He pulled back, gazing into her eyes. "Have you never been kissed?"

Heat rose from the tips of her nipples to the roots of her hair. "Remember me? The one with no social life? Shy and introverted?" Making a joke while trying to make light of a situation that was horribly embarrassing.

"Oh, Mia." He said the words on a sigh. "This is something we have to rectify right away."

"What…what do I do?"

"You follow my lead. If you need to stop, we stop."

"And if I want more?"

Clearly she'd caught him off guard as he hesitated.

"Tug my earlobe."

He'd made her laugh. And while her mouth was open, he swept in for a kiss, easing his tongue into her mouth. She'd known, of course, this was what people did when they kissed. Despite that, it felt weird. He tasted like coffee and something she couldn't put her finger on.

He pulled back. "You're thinking too much, Mia. You need to relax and feel."

Well, duh. "Okay. Can we try again?"

"Of course." But where she expected him to thrust his tongue back in her mouth, he instead gently nipped her lower lip. What could've been just plain weird was weirdly erotic. This time, when he slid his tongue past her teeth, she was ready. Desire swirled as his kiss became more demanding. Experimentally, she lightly dragged her teeth along his tongue.

A sound rumbled deep in his chest.

Amusement or arousal? She wasn't sure.

Then he coaxed her tongue into his mouth, a kind of parrying back and forth. As it continued, he placed his finger on her jaw, then moved downward, stopping on her pulse point hammering out a tattoo. Her heart beat so fast it might come right out of her chest. His other fingers joined the first as they moved down the column of her neck. They rested on the hollow. He could easily press down and cut off her air supply.

That thought was a fleeting one as his hand moved down even farther. She believed she'd be prepared when his hand touched her breast, but had been mistaken. His fingers were electric as they worked her nipple into a peak. He cupped her, squeezed her. She arched her back, trying to get more of whatever magic he offered her.

Sebastian's mouth left hers and began the same downward trail as his fingers had made. When his mouth replaced his hand, something new and unknown unfurled in her belly. His lips teased. His teeth nipped. He created suction with his mouth that made her want even more.

When he moved back, she groaned.

"Open your eyes, Mia."

She obeyed, looking down at him through hooded lashes.

"Have you ever masturbated?"

She blinked. Well, not what she'd expected. Powerless to lie, she shook her head.

"So you've never had an orgasm?"

He phrased it as a question rather than a statement. She shook her head.

His features were, at first, unreadable. Then, slowly, they opened. He gave her a grin. "I'm going to give you your first orgasm."

"Okay." There had to be a catch.

"The first one will be with me touching you. It's going to take a bit of work for us to figure out what makes you tick, but we'll get there."

"And then?"

"We make love, and I give you your second orgasm."

She smiled faintly. "You seem awfully sure of yourself. What if I can't orgasm?"

"I've never met a woman who I haven't been able to coax an orgasm from."

"Maybe they were faking."

Now he smiled. "You can't get away with pretending. I'll feel you when you climax."

And again with another furious flush of heat.

"I'd accuse you of acting like a virgin, but we know how that one ends. Did you learn nothing in sex-ed?"

"Nothing I bothered to remember." And boy, did she wish she'd paid more attention. "I put it away in the *never going to happen* file." She swallowed hard. "I never expected this, Sebastian, so you're going to have to be patient with me."

"I told you we have all the time in the world and we stop when you say so."

"And we can speed up if I pull on your earlobe."

They both grinned.

"It's okay to have fun, Mia. There's nothing wrong with laughter." He snaked out his hand to grasp her breast.

Instantaneously, an odd languor snaked through her. Her eyes drifted shut, and she pulled her lower lip through her teeth.

His mouth did clever things with her breast as his hand meandered down even farther. He nudged her thighs apart.

Okay, relax. All of this was unfamiliar territory for her, but he'd guide her through it. His fingers made lazy circles around her knee, creeping ever higher. Every touch was electric, and she urged his hand up faster. Now that she knew what he was going to do, she wanted him to get on with it.

He parted her nether lips and eased his finger in until he pressed a—

"Holy shit."

He pulled back from her. "Did I hurt you?"

"No." Because he hadn't. "I just didn't expect that."

"It's your clitoris, and its sole purpose of existence is to bring you pleasure. I'm going to do nice things to it, and you will come."

Okay, that sounded reasonable.

His eyes flashed dark. "Now I'm going to say something very crass and very politically incorrect."

She quirked an eyebrow.

"Spread your legs, lie back, and enjoy it."

He was right, of course. A very crass and politically incorrect suggestion, and it made her as horny as hell.

She closed her eyes, and this time when he pressed his hand against her, she let the sensation wash over her. Little sparks flew from his fingers to her insides, saturating her with licks of fire. She stood too close to the flame and might spontaneously combust, but she didn't care. She'd gladly explode, as long as he kept that talented hand working its magic.

Something was building within her, and on an intellectual level, she understood it. But her mind still ruled.

"Let go, Mia."

His voice was a whisper into her ear, and his mouth breathed warm and wet against her skin. He bit her earlobe, and she was overwhelmed by sensation. Brief blasts of light exploded behind her lids, and her back arched, bowing off the bed.

He grabbed her hand and yanked it down, pressing her fingers intimately against herself. Her eyes flew open to meet his. "That's…" Words escaped her.

"An orgasm."

Nonchalant, as if her world hadn't shifted.

"That's your body contracting."

"Yeah." *Holy shit.*

"I can feel it as well, which is why I told you there's no point in trying to fake an orgasm."

She pulled her hand back and would've let it drop to the bed, but he encircled her wrist in his hand and guided her fingers to her nose.

"That's what arousal smells like, Mia." His grin was wolfish. "I've smelled it off you before, but I suspected you had no idea. Your body's been aching for this since the first time you stripped for me."

So that was the reason for the liquid pooling between her thighs. She'd been too embarrassed to ask lest he think her inexperienced. Now he was sharing his knowledge with her, and she'd be eternally grateful. "What happens now?"

The arrogant and Cheshire Cat grin slowly slipped away and disappeared completely. "Virgin territory for both of us. It might hurt, and the thought of bringing you pain makes me ache."

"You bring me pain all the time."

"But that pain I can control. I follow your cues and can stop any time it becomes too much. This is one of those things I have to see through to completion, no matter the cost to either of us."

His words were more touching than she could say, but impatience was pushing her to desperation. "Fewer words, Sebastian, more action."

His wolfish grin returned. "Yes, Mia." He swooped in and recaptured her mouth.

This time, she knew what to do. She was the one who nipped, teased, and tormented. This time, she was the aggressor. It changed the dynamic but for the best. In *this* moment, she needed some control.

Then the moment faded away, and Sebastian's hand repeated all those clever things he'd done before. Her body was revving up when he rolled on top of her, nudging her thighs wider apart and urging her hips higher.

He entered her.

He wasn't gentle, and in the moment she didn't want him to be. The pain inside her burned, and she gasped. Her first instinct was to push him off, but she wanted this part over with so they could get on to the good stuff.

So she rode the pain as best as she could. She took several deep breaths and opened her eyes. He was levered on his elbows, gazing down at her.

"It gets better. I promise you."

She wanted to ask how he knew, but it didn't matter because the pain had dissipated. "Show me." Her breath caught on the whisper. "Take me to that place again."

He began to move inside her, and the oddest sensations washed over her. He stretched her, filled her. He pulled back and then pressed forward. He was taking his time with her, languid in his movements, slow as if he had all the time in the world. His chest created friction against her already-sensitive breasts, and an ache built deep within her. She clawed at his back, trying to urge him on, but he continued a maddeningly slow pace.

She didn't need slow. She needed passion. She needed violence. She needed more than he was giving her. She levered herself up and bit his earlobe.

As if whatever control he'd been holding on to was shredded, he thrust into her with increasingly rapid movements. He ground his pelvis to hers, and she arched to meet him. That previously unknown—but quickly becoming familiar—sensation washed over her, and she gave in to it.

As she rode the waves, Sebastian thrust into her one last time and held himself in place. She opened her eyes and met a look of tortured anguish. Now she knew what she looked like when she orgasmed. Relief flooded her, and she closed her eyes as he collapsed.

Part of her regretted having waited twenty-five years for this, the rest of her glad Sebastian was her first.

Chapter Eleven

Eventually, he levered himself off her. Rolling over, he tugged her with him. Now their legs tangled, and her head was pillowed against his chest. Her hand rested against his abdomen, making absent circles.

His heartbeat was returning to normal, and hers was doing the same. He ran his hand against her, patting down her hair in the same soothing manner he'd used with her two nights ago. He knew just what to do at the right moment.

"I'm sorry I hurt you."

"Sebastian—"

"No, Mia, let me say it. I saw how much pain you were in, and I should've stopped."

She elbowed him in the ribs.

"Ow. What the hell was that for?"

"For being silly. Even I, in my horrifically naïve state, knew it might hurt. Did I expect that much pain? No. Did I survive because of you? Hell, yes." She resettled her head. "Now we're going to put that subject to bed."

A sardonic chuckle. "Okay, there we agree." He let out a long breath. "But when I say I'm honored, Mia, I mean it. I hope you don't come to regret…Jesus Christ, stop doing that!"

"If you keep making stupid comments, I'll keep elbowing you in the ribs. Your call, Sebastian."

"I yield to the fairer of the sexes." He ran his hand through his hair. "Would you have gone through with it?"

"Oh hell, no. That dildo isn't getting anywhere near me."

He cleared his throat. "Actually, it's probably a bit smaller than I am."

Turning her head to face him, she scrunched her nose. "And you're not getting back inside me for a day or two either. I'm sore."

"It's okay—there are other things we can do."

"Yeah, like, what, fifteen?"

"Eighteen, not counting your soft-limit list." His hand wrapped around her, and he pulled her closer. "You might see things a little differently now you've removed one of them from the list."

"How many more can we do today?"

He let out a deep laugh. "Let's just say we have one hundred and…"

"Sixty-eight."

"Right. One hundred and sixty-eight days. Plenty of time to get through the list. Who knows, we might even move on to things on your hard list."

"You are not putting needles through my nipples or peeing on me. There's a reason they're called hard limits."

Now the grin turned sardonic. "Six months is a long time." Then, as suddenly as the grin had appeared, it vanished. "Oh, fuck."

"I thought we just did."

"I didn't use a condom."

"Well, you said you wanted to feel it, and you said you're clean—"

"You might get pregnant." He sat up abruptly, sending her sprawling. "Fuck, fuck, fuck."

She reached for him even as he leapt from the bed.

"There's a morning-after pill, right? Is it too soon to take it?"

"Sebastian—"

"I'll call Anthony. He'll know."

"Sebastian—"

"Goddamn it, how could I be so careless?"

"Sebastian, shut the fuck up."

The vulgarity stopped his nervous pacing.

"I'm on the pill, for Christ's sake. Take a breath."

He eyed her warily. "You're on the pill? It's that simple?"

"Yup. Been on it for ten years now. I was having menstrual cramps so bad I was missing school. The doctor put me on the pill, and it lessened my flow, which lessened the pain. Despite the health risks of long-term use, I'm not willing to go off of it unless I want to get pregnant. Way too much pain."

He sank to the bed, his head dropping into his hands. "That was incredibly insensitive of me. It's just I've never had sex with a virgin before. I should've talked to you about birth control first."

She grinned. "You were a little busy with other things." She sobered. "I'm not stupid, Sebastian. I won't get pregnant with a man I barely know."

"But you'll have sex with a man you barely know." He still wouldn't meet her gaze.

"Not the same thing. One involves a commitment of about ten minutes, and the other involves lifelong attachment."

"Ten minutes? I have more stamina than that."

True, but her comment had the desired effect—he was no longer obsessing about potential unplanned pregnancies.

****

They showered together, and she let him lather her up, rub her down, and do a few other naughty things in between. When she tried to return the favor, however, he gave her ass a pat and sent her on her way.

Slightly disillusioned, and definitely annoyed, she dried herself off. When he stepped from the shower, she wrapped a dry towel around him. "Will you at least let me dry you off?"

"No, Mia, I can do that myself. You could help me by going to get me a pair of jeans and my black silk shirt."

"I can do that. What clothes should I put on?"

"Nothing. I want to spend the night watching your body."

His words gave her a little thrill, so she went to retrieve his jeans and shirt. He had several black silk shirts, so she picked one at random. His loss of composure over a potential pregnancy had knocked her for a bit of a loop. He was always controlled. Still, she was safe, and that was what mattered.

"I asked you to bring me the jeans and the shirt." His gaze raked over her. "Are you okay?"

His jeans were folded over her arm—she held his shirt against her chest. She'd lost focus, and time had slipped away. She let out a quick breath. "Sorry, Sir, I was replaying the earlier events. Kind of mind-blowing, eh?"

He eased the shirt from her and shrugged into it. Then he took the jeans and pulled them on, leaving the snap undone.

Even in the low light of the dungeon, she spotted his muscles rippling. She was now familiar with the chest hair that was neither coarse nor soft but somewhere in between. Even though she wasn't up for going another round, she itched to touch.

He tisked. "Keep looking at me like that, and we won't be having dinner." His grin was quick and easy. "How about Greek?"

"Sounds great. Do you want me to greet the delivery boy dressed like this?"

"Oh yeah, I forgot you'd know…whoever it is."

"His name is Ching."

His brow arched. "You're kidding. Ching delivers Greek food?"

"Now don't go being prejudiced. Ching is a good delivery person. And—don't laugh—Chong delivers the Chinese food."

"Ching and Chong?" As if he couldn't help himself, he laughed.

She nodded. "They're twins. The only way I can tell them apart is with their uniforms. And they're twenty, so I guess they're old enough to see a naked woman."

He shook his head. "I'll meet them while you set the table. In the meantime, could you start a load of laundry?"

"Afraid of running out of black silk shirts?"

He grabbed her arm, spun her around, and slapped her ass so hard she yelped.

"For being sassy."

"Laundry. Right away, Sir."

She scooped up the clothes he'd worn to work today and made her way to the laundry closet. She'd done laundry last weekend, so no big deal, right? Well, she hadn't been naked last weekend, so maybe this was a bigger deal. She giggled at the thought of greeting Ching without a stitch of clothing. He was such a polite young man—he'd probably look her in the eye and give her the change.

After setting the machine, she made her way into the living room. Daylight was a long-ago memory, and night was well and truly entrenched. How long had they been in the dungeon? Long enough she was no longer a virgin. She got a secret thrill out of that. She also enjoyed knowing, for one minute, she'd been a novelty to Sebastian as well.

"Food will be here in ten minutes." His gaze raked over her when they met up in the living room. "Now why don't you go find that sequel we talked about watching?"

She grinned like a loon. "Oh, that'll be cool." As she entered the office, she cringed at her choice of word. *Cool? Really?* Who the hell talked like that? What was she, ten?

Then she saw the movie collection, and her only thought was that cool was such a tame term. An entire wall full of media. He had to have at least three thousand discs, if not more. If he watched three movies a day, it'd still take him over three years to make it through the collection. Yet he didn't show off his wealth. He didn't rub people's noses in it and never acted like he was entitled to be treated differently, unlike some of his neighbors. Some people who lived in this building had treated her like a speck of dirt under their shoe. Now, as she witnessed the other side of the coin, she was more empathetic of her former colleagues. The one thing she wouldn't miss was the disrespect. Only a few tenants like that, but they were memorable.

She skimmed through the movies. Ah, they were in alphabetical order. Soon she located parts two and three of the trilogy and brought them with her to the living room. Since Sebastian was nowhere to be seen, she assumed he'd gone down to get the food. She set the table and pulled a bottle of wine from the fridge. Tonight was for celebrations.

The door opened and closed quickly, the aroma preceding him into the room. Her stomach rumbled, and after he dropped the containers on the counter, he pulled her back against him. His hands snaked around her waist and landed on her belly.

"Is someone hungry?"

His breath was warm against her ear. She pressed back against him, fitting her ass against his crotch. "Yeah, and for food."

In response, he tweaked one of her nipples. Hard.

"Ouch."

"What you get for being sassy."

"Well, the table's set. Why don't we dish up this food before it gets cold?"

He held her for another beat before releasing her. *Okay, foolish woman, don't go thinking it meant something. It didn't.*

They dished up the food in silence and made their way to the dining room.

She'd shoveled in several mouthfuls of food before realizing Sebastian hadn't started. The look on his face assured her she'd screwed up.

"Is it the wine? I thought it'd be nice—"

"It's not the wine."

"Was it my attitude? Because I was kidding—"

"It's not the attitude."

Crap.

"Maybe you could tell me what I did." Hopefully, the transgression wasn't too egregious.

"You should always wait for me to begin eating. I don't care how hungry you are—it's no excuse for bad manners."

Damn. She ducked her head. "Sorry, Sir, it won't happen again."

"See that it doesn't."

This time, she waited until he ate before she resumed—this time at a more sedate pace. After she finished, she pointed to the food. "This is good."

"Of course it is." His dark gaze met hers. "You should know."

Her brow furrowed in confusion. "I've never eaten there before."

"But it's around the corner."

"And expensive."

Now his brow furrowed.

"My budget didn't have any leeway for takeout meals. Mostly do-it-yourself."

"With your cooking abilities, it's a wonder you didn't starve."

She shrugged. "No talent involved in microwaving ramen noodles." She tried for nonchalance. "Simply Noodles and I are on intimate terms."

"What about fruits and vegetables?"

She placed her knife and fork in the five o'clock position. "Life's not that simple, Sir."

"Sebastian."

"I'm sorry?"

"We're vanilla right now, Tarah."

What the hell? She held her arms against her chest, hiding her naked breasts. "And how am I supposed to know that?"

"I guess it's not fair of me, but I hate to think of where you've come from. The condo board should pay a living wage to its employees."

"I was paid a decent salary, but Vancouver is prohibitively expensive, and school doesn't come cheap. I needed to save every penny for teacher's college because I didn't want to have to work for those eight months. I've been socking away everything I can for as long as I remember." She swallowed convulsively. "That's why I took you up on your offer. You read the report. I worked every shift I could." She ran her fingers along the edge of the table and met his gaze. "I'm not looking for sympathy, Sebastian, nor am I looking for charity. I'm getting paid to be here."

"You make it sound like prostitution."

Fuck, no. She shook her head emphatically because she was not going to let him go there. "No way. You said yourself they were two different issues. Those were your words." She pointed accusingly. "I'm being paid to be a submissive for six months. I added sex to the mix. I'm an adult and can make that kind of decision for myself."

His eyes narrowed. "But you were worried I might find someone else to supplant you."

Her lips pressed together in a thin line, and she wrapped her arms around her waist. "That occurred to me."

"Is that why you came to my bed?"

"No." She pushed back her chair. "I came because I wanted to. You gave me your word you'd take care of me, and I believed you. I wanted more. Is that so wrong?"

Now he rose to his feet. "Tarah, I want to make sure there are no misunderstandings. You get paid—whether or not we have sex again."

"I'm aware." Her tone was flat, her stomach in knots. "I'm going to clean up."

"No, you're not." Her temper rose, but he continued. "You go get dressed, and we'll watch the movie."

His words slapped her in the face. "Please, Sebastian, don't make me dress. I don't want to be vanilla. I want what we had before."

"You want to sit naked at my feet? On the floor?"

Relief flooded her system, and she nodded. "Yes, that's what I want." His gaze was penetrating, but she held firm, even tipping her chin up in defiance.

"Go get your blanket and wait for me. But watch the attitude, Mia."

She ducked her head. "I'll be waiting for you."

****

She was kneeling on her blanket when he entered the room.

He put his glass of wine on the coffee table and gave her a glass of water. The disc slid in, and when he sat, she laid her head against his thigh. Not until the third scene did he finally pet her. To that point, she'd been totally focused on waiting for him to touch her. She didn't even know what'd happened on screen. She needed the equilibrium coming from this dynamic. His reassurance was a balm to her weary soul.

"Let go, Mia," he crooned softly. "Let go."

Which was enough to open the floodgates. She hadn't realized she needed to cry until the tears streamed down her cheeks. She pressed her face into his jeans, letting him absorb her pain. When he bent down to scoop her up, she threw her arms around his neck, letting herself be settled into his lap.

"What's wrong with me?" she whispered brokenly.

"I confused you, and I'm sorry for that. I should never have switched to vanilla without first warning you."

"You don't have to apologize."

"I know." He pressed the corner of his sleeve to her cheek. "But I'm choosing to. Just, in that moment, I was appalled. I've lived a hardscrabble life, and I hated that I'd forgotten what that life can be like. I've been living a very privileged existence for ten years now. I donate to charities and make sure all my employees make a living wage, but I still forget sometimes how the other half lives."

"I think you mean the other ninety-nine percent." She hiccupped the words through her tears.

He chuckled softly. "Although I appreciate the vote of confidence, Mia, I'm not that rich."

"Top ten percent?"

He slapped her breast. "That's for impudence."

And the right thing to do because as suddenly as they'd started, her tears abated. She glanced over at the screen. Oh, he'd paused the movie. "I'm sorry I interrupted the film."

"Mia, neither of us has any idea what's happened. We'll have to restart it."

She laughed, nestling farther into his arms, laying her head against his chest. When she shifted again, his breath caught. She leaned back to look at his face. "Am I too heavy?"

His eyes were closed, and an odd expression passed

across his face. "No, Mia, you're not too heavy."

"Then what…" She gulped. "Oh, that."

"Yeah, that. Give me a minute or two, and it'll go away."

"Really?" She was intrigued.

His eyes remained shut. "Well, not really. But if you get off my lap and we go back to watching the movie, that should do the trick."

"Sounds deceptively easy."

"It's mind over matter." Finally, he opened his eyes and met hers. "Or I go to the bathroom and jerk off."

Instead of being embarrassed, she was fascinated. "What if I were to help you?"

Apparently, that got his attention. He eyed her speculatively. "What are you proposing?"

"Well, to be blunt, what are my options?"

He grinned devilishly. "Well, straight sex is off the table for tonight. That leaves hand jobs, blow jobs, and anal."

If he'd thought to shock her, it had the opposite effect.

"Do I get to choose?"

The grin slipped. "I was kidding."

"I'm not. I mean, I'm sure it's fun to jerk off in the bathroom…"

He pulled her roughly toward him and bit off her next thought with a searing kiss. To make sure they were on the same track, she rubbed her ass against his erection. His groan assured her he was as affected as she was. Her body was also making demands she didn't know how to quench.

He slid his hand from her hip to dip lower and delve between her thighs. "Open for me, Mia. Only for me."

Awkward, for sure, but she let one leg slide down his and leaned back, leaving her pussy exposed. This was supposed to be about him, wasn't it? But when he pressed his finger to her clit, the electric shock zinged through her. He kissed her as his fingers continued to do wonderful things. No room for modesty, she opened wider for him. She offered herself up, and she hoped desperately he liked what she was doing. God knew she was loving everything he was doing.

He urged her neck back as he broke the kiss. He nipped his way down her neck and seized her nipple in his mouth.

He bit hard, and the multiple sensations overloading her system proved too much. She screamed.

If his arm hadn't been supporting her back, she would've flown right off his lap. Never had she known such agony and ecstasy at the same time. Her body was awakening from a dormant state. Filled with verve, for the first time in her life, she was really alive. She threw her arms around his neck and cuddled into his chest, trying to catch her breath. "Is it always like that?"

He chuckled. "Actually, no."

A stab of disappointment.

"Sometimes, it's better."

She pulled back, meeting those fathomlessly dark eyes. "Better?"

Now his wolfish grin was back. "Once I get to know your body better, I'll teach you about multiple orgasms. Just as you've recovered from one, you start climbing toward the next." He placed a kiss to her nose. "There are also orgasms that, with proper coaxing, can go on and on and on."

Now she met his smile. "And let me guess, you're

very good at coaxing."

"I'd consider myself proficient, yes."

She placed a hand over her heart. "Now that I've had my fun, it's time for me to get down to work."

"You don't have—"

She silenced his protest by pressing her index finger to his lips. He nipped at it, and she laughed. "My choices are hand job, blow job, and anal. Do you have a preference?"

"I think anal might be a bit much for you to handle today. One virginity at a time."

"It'll have to be two." She made her point with a wicked grin. "Because I've never given a hand or a blow job." She gave him a mock stern look. "Pick."

Although he pretended to consider, she knew his mind was already made up.

"I'll take blow jobs for five hundred."

Puzzled, she frowned at him.

He laughed. "A reference to *Jeopardy*."

"The game show?"

"Yes, the game show. I'm a huge fan of trivia."

Leaving her at a disadvantage. Except maybe with psychological theories and eighteenth-century poetry.

Obviously sensing her distress, he pressed his thumb to her frown line. "Relax, Mia, there'll be no quizzes. I like you just the way you are."

His words gave her a measure of relief. Knowing the time for action had come, she rubbed her ass sinuously against his crotch.

His eyes closed, and his breath hitched.

After sliding down his lap, she knelt in front of him. She opened the snap of his jeans, then eased the zipper down. Eyes still closed, he lifted his hips from the couch so she could pull the jeans down. Because he hadn't bothered with briefs, she faced one enormous cock. Well, if he could fit it into her pussy, surely, she could take it in her mouth.

Uncertainly, she touched. His skin was soft and warm. In response to her fingers, his cock twitched, and he groaned.

"I'm, um, not sure what I should do."

His eyes opened, and he gazed down at her through hooded lashes. "Aside from biting me, everything you do will bring me pleasure."

"Like when you said it would take you time to find out how my body works? What makes me tick?"

"Pretty much. Explore. If I like something, I'll moan. If I don't like something, I'll let you know."

She had no doubt he would, but now regretted she hadn't surfed the internet on how to give a blow job. She giggled.

"What's so funny?"

"I was thinking I should've done my research."

He shook his head, his penetrating gaze meeting hers. "I like your naïveté, Mia. I like we're going on this journey together."

"Enough talk and more action, right?"

In response, he closed his eyes and flexed his hips so his cock was even closer to her. She angled herself so her lips touched the head. Figuring she had nothing to lose and everything to gain, she pulled it into her mouth.

And gagged.

He pulled back. "Take it slow, Mia. Work your way up to it. Let your jaw relax as it adjusts. Breathe through your nose. I don't expect you to deep throat me on the first try."

Deep throat?

Finding courage, she began more slowly. She swirled her tongue around him and tried to replicate the same suction he'd used on her breast. Inch by inch, she took him deeper into her mouth. He wasn't just long—he was thick. Her jaw flexed, and experimentally, she scraped her teeth lightly along his length.

He moaned.

She tried to replicate the thrusting motion he'd done earlier to her. She bobbed her head up and down his length. When his hands rested on the sides of her head, she had a moment's panic, but he was merely guiding her, so she relaxed into it.

He let out another groan and seemed to grow even bigger.

"I'm coming." A broken whisper. "Oh, Jesus, I'm coming. If you don't want to swallow…"

His words ended in a long groan, but she understood what he was saying.

She wanted to tell him to go ahead, but she also knew now was not the time to stop doing what she was doing. Instead, she increased her speed and sucked as hard as she could manage.

She was surprised when hot liquid hit the back of her throat, and she almost choked. *Swallow.* While it seemed to go on and on, she kept swallowing. It tasted salty and a little tangy. Remembering what he'd said about coaxing, she continued to suck, wanting to draw out every drop.

Finally, his cock was shrinking in her mouth. She let it go and laid her face against his pubic bone, nuzzling herself against his musky scent. It smelled similar to her own smell, but she discerned subtle differences. For as long as she lived, she'd never forget this scent.

He stroked her hair, and his praise seeped through the tips of his fingers and into her. When she sensed his scrutiny on her, she tipped her head up to meet his gaze. He looked deliciously sated. "How did I do, Sir?"

"That was incredible, Mia. Are you sure it was your first time?"

Her brow creased. "Of course."

"Well, I can say you have phenomenal instincts and a knack because it fucking rocked."

He reached down for her, and she reached up for him, and they met somewhere in the middle, her head on his chest, her hips against his, and her legs between his thighs. She fiddled idly with the buttons of his shirt, opening them one by one. When the final one was released, she pulled it back to reveal an expanse of rippling muscles. Experimentally, she pressed her hand to his male nipple.

"I enjoy having it sucked."

She moved her mouth to repeat the action, but he waylaid her.

"Not in the afterglow, Mia, but during the warm-up."

Ah. She simply laid her hand against his abdomen. "I get to experiment as well, right? Figure out what you like, what you don't."

"It's a journey of exploration as much as the destination."

"Destination?"

"Well, although orgasms are nice, there's something to be said for sensuality. Each have their place. You'll learn sometimes you want down and dirty and other times when you want slow and soothing."

"I like the sound of both."

He pressed a kiss to her forehead. "Somehow, I knew you were going to say that." He grabbed for the remote control and shut the system off. "I think we've both had a long day. Don't come to my room until nine, and I'll find a creative way to brand you."

She pushed off his chest in surprise. "But I thought…I mean…aren't we sleeping together?"

He eased her from him without meeting her gaze. "I don't sleep with anyone, Mia, not even you."

"So I'm lucky you're not shoving me out the door?"

He tisked. "Watch your tone with me. You'll find nothing in the contract about sleeping together. In fact, as you recall, I decide what you wear, and I decide where you sleep."

She couldn't help it—her face fell. "Is there no way…"

He cleared his throat. "There's a pallet on the far side of my bed on the floor. I suppose you could sleep there."

Her chest expanded in anticipation. "Then I'll be close in case you need anything."

"It won't be comfortable." His warning was ominous. "You may come to regret this."

"I want to be near you." Was he really this dense? After everything they'd shared today, she didn't want to be apart from him. He might have regrets. He might change his mind about their arrangement. If she was there, within his grasp, it'd be harder for him to back away. "I don't care how it happens as long as it does."

His grin was wry. "I can see you're going to be even more of a challenge than I'd initially thought. Go to the bathroom and clean yourself up. The green sheets on the top shelf of your closet will fit the pallet. Bring a comforter and pillow. I don't want you to suffer too much."

"But a little suffering is worth it if I make you happy." She pushed her hair back. Hmm, she needed to brush it. "And this would make you happy, right?"

He considered for so long she wondered if she'd miscalculated.

"Yes, Mia, this would make me happy. Now go do as you've been instructed. I'm going to have another shower."

She finished up quickly in the bathroom so he could have his shower. She located the sheets and brought them along with her pillow and blanket to the pallet. The contraption was a raised platform about six inches off the ground with a thin mattress lying across it. She touched it experimentally. Solid. No way around it—this wasn't going to be comfortable. But what did it matter? She was sleeping in Sebastian's room with him. Her status had just been elevated. Plus, this would be good for her back, wouldn't it?

She made the bed and debated. Was she supposed to lie down and go to sleep? Was she supposed to wait? *Better wait for him.* She knelt in her appointed place between the bed and the door. She didn't have long to wait as he strode into the room. Since her eyes were lowered, she could only see his feet and his calves, but she knew he was naked.

He stepped forward and gently laid his hand on the crown of her head. "You may rise, Mia."

With ease, she rose.

"You've been practicing." Warmth in his praise. "You please me very much."

She beamed at him.

"Have you made your bed?"

"Yes, Sir."

"You may go lie down."

She bobbed her head and made her way over to her makeshift bed. Lying down, she pulled the blankets over her. Eventually, she found a sweet spot and relaxed into the mattress.

He flipped off the lights, and she panicked momentarily. No way to get used to the darkness—it just was. She could fight against it, or she could let it be her protective blanket. Better to choose the latter. The dark was his warmth and strength enveloping her.

Within moments, she was gone.

Chapter Twelve

Awareness came slowly, and she suppressed a groan. She was almost as sore as she'd been after the standing exercise with the hood. Well, she didn't have the right to complain, and she certainly wasn't going back to her bedroom.

Without a watch, however, she had no sense of the time. She was well rested, though, so it must be morning. Should she go make coffee? How could she even find her way out of here in such darkness?

Sebastian groaned.

"Sir?"

This time he moaned.

"Sir?"

"Sir is busy, Mia."

Something in his tone gave her pause. "Would Sir like help?"

A low rumble of amusement filled the room. "Sir would not be averse to help."

Instantly, she pushed off her bed and sought his. After finding the blanket, she slid under it, and her hands groped until they connected with his hip and his cock. He was rock hard. Didn't men sometimes wake up in an aroused state? Apparently a big hard yes.

Without preliminaries, she took him in her mouth. She remembered all his instructions from the night before and worked in earnest to bring his release. Bring him to climax. His hips shifted as she sought purchase, and they quickly found a rhythm that worked for both of them.

Experimentally, she touched his balls. The skin was wrinkly and had a different texture than his cock, but it carried no less interest. Then his hand took hers, and he pressed her index finger to some spot just under his sac. She wiggled her finger a bit, and he stopped her motions with a grip on her wrist.

"Right there, Mia. Oh God, right there."

She stroked, seeking the right amount of pressure. When his hand released her wrist, she rejoiced in having found his sweet spot. She continued to bob her head, alternating sucking, grazing her teeth, and swirling her tongue.

His groan made desire pool in her belly. She never imagined pleasuring him would arouse her, but her body had a mind of its own.

He grasped her under her arms and hauled her up. He rolled on top of her and ruthlessly pressed her thighs wide and her hips up. Now he was the one acting without preliminaries.

He thrust in her with such violence it robbed her of breath. A ruthless assault on her senses. He rained kisses down her face. Plunged his tongue into her mouth. A hand slipped between their bodies, seeking her breast. Upon finding the intended target, he squeezed her nipple.

All the time, he continued to piston in and out of her. Her body stretched, accepted, and demanded more. She sought purchase on his sweat-slicked back and dug her nails into his skin to hang on. She rose to meet each demanding thrust—reveling in the ferocity of his action. God, she needed this like she needed her next breath.

The crest hit at once, and it hit hard. She grabbed his ass, trying to hold him as close as they could get. The waves of pleasure ripped through her, robbing her of all sense.

Without warning, he increased the assault. Now he moved his hand to between her thighs and ground his thumb against her clit.

"Again." A demand through gritted teeth.

She wanted to argue, but her body was already responding to the command. As if it had a mind of its own, it spiraled upward, peaked, and rapidly descended. Still, he kept withdrawing and pressing home. The friction was both delicious and intense. Every nerve ending in her vagina was being deluged. Arching her pelvis to meet his thrusts, he growled, ruthlessly pressing her to the mattress.

She swore she felt him emptying inside of her.

He collapsed on her even as she sought breath. A struggle, for sure, but she sucked much-needed oxygen into her lungs.

For a man who prided himself on self-control, he sure as shit knew how to take a woman and let her loose. She might've been embarrassed by her own reactions, but she was electrified. She'd made him lose control. Little Tarah Peters.

"I must be crushing you."

As he pulled away, she held on tighter. "Just give me another minute, Sir. Just one more second."

He chuckled and nuzzled her neck. He nipped her.

She sighed. "Is this the time when I tell you how good you were?"

Another chuckle. "A man likes to hear about his prowess, but I don't need you to stroke my ego. A word of thanks never goes amiss, however."

"Well, you have my everlasting gratitude." She swallowed convulsively. "If not for you, I never would've known."

He rolled off her, and a whoosh of cool air hit her heated skin, causing her to suck in a breath.

"It would've happened eventually, Tarah. You would've met the right man, and he would've shown you."

She placed her hand on his arm, but he shrugged it off.

The mattress dipped as he sat up and stood. "I think I've branded you enough for today. Go have a shower, and I'll pick out your clothes. You can study while I work in my home office. We can have sandwiches at noon, and you need to be ready to go by four."

The staff party. She'd forgotten. "What about breakfast?"

"I'll take my coffee into the office. You have fruit and toast with a half a cup of yogurt. Go have a shower and wash off all the brands. I want you unmarked when we go out today." He paused, then strode to the door and ruthlessly yanked it open.

She barely had time to marvel how he found it in the dark before the harsh light of day hit her eyes, and they watered.

He stalked out of the room.

She pulled the sheet up to her breasts, suddenly very exposed.

She waited until he finished with the bathroom and went into the kitchen, then she fled for the safety of the bathroom where she could lock the door. She had no idea what had just happened and probably wouldn't have understood it anyway.

****

He didn't even join her for lunch, simply taking his sandwich back into his office. She'd sworn she'd get studying done, but all she managed to do was lie on the bed and stare at the ceiling. There appeared to be something up there. Experimentally, she flipped off the lights. The ceiling glowed with a weird greenish-yellow light. Lying back onto the bed, she squinted up at the ceiling. Planets, moons, and even a shooting star decorated the night sky. Who had put up the children's stickers, and did Sebastian even knew about them? Probably not, seeing as he'd have no reason to sleep in here.

They brought a certain amount of comfort to her. Rielle must have put them up. Her friend had faced some horrendous nights in this condo, and sometimes Tarah got the creeps thinking about it. Then she'd remember Rielle was happily married with one adopted baby and another on the way—happy endings existed.

What was Tarah's destiny?

She was so focused on teaching nothing else ever entered her mind. Was he right? Might she meet someone?

Could she find someone who touched her the way he did?

She'd known adding sex to the mix would change the dynamic, but who could've predicted his mercurial moods that went along with it?

A knock on her door pulled her from her reverie.

"Come in." As if he needed permission.

He stepped in. "What are you doing in the dark? Are you napping?"

All or nothing.

"Close the door and come lie down with me."

"I don't think—"

"Please, Sebastian, just do it for me." She tried to keep the plaintive tone from her voice, but it seeped in.

Something must've touched him because he did exactly what she asked. He lay next to her, gazed up, and whistled. "This wasn't mentioned in the specs of the condo."

"But it's cool, right? I mean it's like looking up to see the stars. It's hard to see the stars in the city."

He rolled over and flipped on the bedside light. The constellations disappeared. "I need you to come with me."

She knew better than to question that tone. Getting up, she wiped sweaty palms on her jeans, then followed him from the room. She wasn't surprised when he led her to the dungeon.

"I need you to strip."

Need? He needed her to do something? Without hesitation, she pulled the sweater over her head. Jeans, socks, bra, and panties were quickly dispatched, and she presented herself as he'd taught her. His feet disappeared from view. Within a moment, they were back.

"I want you to present your breasts."

What?

"You put your hands under your breasts and hold them up so the nipples protrude."

Easy enough. She placed her hands under her breasts and held them up. They were a secure weight against her palms.

Sebastian held up two pieces of metal attached to a chain.

"These are called nipple clamps."

She frowned. When she agreed to this, she hadn't expected them to look so…menacing.

Sebastian tweaked her nipple, and unsurprisingly, it responded to the attention. He held it until he replaced it with the clamp.

"Son of a—" She cut off the curse word, but it was a near thing. "That hurts."

He didn't appear to hear her as he repeated the process.

"Is there a purpose to this?"

His eyes met hers.

A storm was brewing.

"Are you questioning me?"

"Of course not." She was quick to reply, even though that was exactly what she'd been doing.

"Now, go lie on the bed."

This sounded more promising. She lay on the bed, arms next to her sides and her thighs clamped shut. She lay staring at the ceiling, trying to ignore the pull of the clamps against her nipples.

"Bend your knees and pull your heels to your ass."

She obeyed.

"Now let your knees fall to the bed."

Shifting her hips took a bit of time, but she complied. She was completely exposed.

"Now, I want you to touch yourself."

Her eyes snapped from watching the ceiling to meet his gaze. "Sir?"

"You said you've never masturbated. Well, you're going to learn."

Oh. That. She moved her hand to her thighs.

"Not so fast, Mia. You need to explore your body.

Stroke the top of your breasts. Pull on the chain so your nipples tighten. Caress your belly. You need to sensitize your body so when you reach for your clit, it's ready—begging for attention. Now, close your eyes and try again."

She began with her breasts. Instead of trying to ignore the pain, she tried to push through it. She cupped her breast and squeezed, reveling in the pleasure shooting down to her core. She shifted her pelvis to relieve the ache. Her hand caressed the undersides of her breasts, a spot particularly sensitive. Her breath hitched.

"Excellent, Mia." His voice was soft.

That did crazy things in her belly.

"Reach out and embrace the pleasure."

His words didn't break the spell being woven—only intensified it. Her hand trailed down to her abdomen, and she let her index finger lazily circle her belly button. She squirmed and tried to bring her legs together.

"Apart, Mia."

She complied. Her hand moved down to the spot where her belly met her pubic hair, and she floundered. How could something so theoretically easy be so complicated? And why had she never tried this before?

"Use one hand to pull back your lips while the other reaches for your clit."

At first she was confused about his use of the word *lips*, but eventually, the light went on. With her right hand she pulled back her nether lips and searched with her left. She was already wet, and her fingers became slippery. How on earth was she supposed to find her clit? She had no awareness of her body. Of anatomy.

Then her hand brushed against a hard nub and a bolt shot through her. She scrunched her eyes, arched her hips, and rubbed mindlessly. God, she was getting wetter. She smelled herself, and instead of being embarrassed, she was aroused.

As her body tightened, she increased her pace. One pass, two passes, and an explosion. Her body rocked, and her back bowed off the bed. He grabbed and thrust her fingers into her core. She was too far gone to think of anything but how powerfully her fingers were being squeezed. She gasped for air as his hand made her fingers imitate the intimate act she'd been engaged in recently.

"Ride it, Mia." A command. "Feel it. Let it consume you."

She did, and then nothing.

****

Consciousness came in degrees. She was naked and covered by a blanket, but much beyond that seemed too far away. A hand rubbed up and down against her arm, and soothing words were being murmured, but they had no meaning. She was floating and never wanted to come down.

Cool lips pressed to her damp brow. "I'm very proud of you, Mia. For your first time, you did very well."

Praise from Sebastian. Was there anything better in the world? "Thank you." She cleared her throat. "Thank you for showing me how it could be. Sir was generous."

"And Sir expects something in return."

Her eyes cracked open. "A blow job or a hand job?"

He chuckled. "Neither, Mia, although it is a tempting offer. No, I'm going to give you an assignment. You will masturbate once a day, every weekday. After you've had your swim and your shower, you're going to go into your room, spread your legs, and do exactly what I taught you to do." He paused. "Do you think you can do that?"

"Of course." Finally, something easy. "All I have to do is think about Sir, and I get hot."

Another chuckled elicited.

Yes.

"Now lie on your back, Mia—we still have work to do."

She obeyed, and the blanket was pulled down, exposing her chest. Sebastian leaned down and released one clamp.

"Son of a—"

His mouth replaced the clamp, softly sucking, gently soothing. Encouraging the circulation to come back to her nipple.

The bite was less the second time because the pain was expected. She lifted her hands to run through his hair, encouraging his ministrations. The tenderness brought tears to her eyes, but she blinked them back. She didn't want him to see how deeply he affected her.

When he was finished, he pulled back and placed a gentle kiss to her lips. "Wash up, Mia. We need to leave in half an hour."

He left the room, and she took one precious moment to absorb the tenderness before she rose from the bed. She padded naked to the bathroom, performed the necessary ablutions, fixed her hair, and did her makeup. As instructed, she'd removed Sebastian's marks, but then she felt almost twitchy. She enjoyed knowing she belonged to him.

Tonight, though, he needed her to be vanilla. He'd chosen a simple wool cream-colored dress with a plain gold belt. He'd given her matching gold clip-on earrings and a simple gold-link chain necklace to go around her neck. It reminded her of the chain between the nipple clamps, and a warm sense of well-being encompassed her. He was marking her, just doing it more subtly.

Matching pumps and a gold-colored leather purse completed the ensemble. As always, when she stepped from her room, he waited for her.

He touched her hair that flowed loose, pulled back from her face by gold-colored clips. "I like your hair like this, Mia." His eyes changed from softness to something edgier. "I just want to put in an appearance and then hightail it out of there."

She stepped forward to brush a piece of lint from his navy-blue jacket. Handsome. And goddamned sexy. He wasn't wearing a tie, and the first two buttons of his shirt were undone.

"It's a casual affair."

"With kids around, it's a good idea." She nodded.

"The kids have been around for several hours now, playing games and…I don't know, other stuff. About now they're sitting on Santa's knee." He frowned. "Myself, I find that thought a little creepy."

"Did you never sit on Santa's lap?"

Something passed across his features but then was gone. "We didn't do that kind of thing."

Touchy subject. This was not the first time he'd put up a wall when she'd inquired about his past. She smiled up at him. "Let's enjoy ourselves."

She expected him to grumble, but he gave her a reticent smile.

"Okay. With you, it might be tolerable." He helped her into her coat, and they were on their way.

She was surprised when they descended to the garage level. Soon she was tucked into his sedan. Luxury without pretension. The inside had every amenity. She'd never been in anything but a used ten-year-old beater, so this was a treat.

"You're not drinking tonight?"

"Neither of us are—it's a dry event. Too much responsibility because if alcohol is served and someone drives drunk, the company can be held liable. Better to make it a family event with punch and pop. It's a buffet, so the parents can pick the foods their kids will eat without a fuss."

"Sounds like it's well planned."

"Sharon's doing. She's my personal assistant and has two children. She spends half the year planning this thing."

Tarah chuckled. "Dedication."

"She has help, but I leave the details up to her and sign the check at the end."

Strange. "You don't bill this as a corporate event?"

Sebastian shook his head. "No, but no one knows I foot the bill. I also pay for each restaurant to close on the same Monday night in December so they can have a Christmas party."

"I thought you were Scrooge." Here, she could tease him.

He scowled. "Not Scrooge." His brow furrowed. "I'm not a big fan of the silly season."

"Are you a purist?"

"What the hell is a purist?"

"Someone who sees Christmas as a religious holiday and cringes at the crass commercialism."

He barked out a laugh. "Tarah, I'm an atheist. I couldn't give a shit about the religious aspects of Christmas. I just don't like…well, tonight."

"It's the kids, isn't it?" She couldn't help herself—she smirked. "Sebastian, you run a chain of family restaurants. How could a bunch of munchkins scare you?"

"Yeah, well, *The Wizard of Oz* creeps me out almost as much as Santa Claus."

"Why don't you have any children's films in your collection?"

"Why would there be?"

"Because lots of the animated films are designed for the enjoyment of adults."

"Now you're being ridiculous."

She wanted to point out the movie with all the animated toys had been great, but decided silence was the better part of valor. She'd also treated herself to the DVD of another animated movie for kids when she had a terrible week at school. She'd loved it. She planned to download the soundtrack to her new MP3 as soon as she figured out how.

"You didn't have a good childhood, did you?" She was on thin ice, but something propelled her to push forward on this.

"Can we talk about this later? We're almost there."

"Do you promise we will? You know everything about me, and I know nothing about you."

"There's nothing to know." Still, a slight smile crept to his lips. "Plus, not everything. Toby's good, but he didn't know you were a virgin."

Because they were stopped for a light, she punched him in the shoulder. "A gentleman should never say such things to a lady."

"After the debauchery we've engaged in during the last twenty-four hours, you can hardly call yourself a lady."

Likely as he intended, she laughed. "Tell me there's more debauchery to come."

"Count on it." He made the promise with a lascivious grin. "We still have sixteen items on the list."

His comment had her squirming in her seat.

"Get your mind out of the gutter, or everyone will think we've just had sex."

She snorted. "Well, it'd liven up the party."

"And get me a reputation as a Lothario."

Giggling, she appreciated the reference. He knew *Don Quixote*, did he? What other little gems were being held in that steel trap? Observant and whip-smart, of course he excelled in business.

"Is this the first time you've brought a date, or has there been a different woman each year?"

Something in his demeanor changed. "I'm not Casanova either. I live an intensely private life. No one knows about Kink, and no one knows about my relationship with you."

"Aren't your employees curious?"

He pulled into a parking spot, killed the engine, and contemplated for a moment. "I let Sharon set me up on a blind date with her cousin because she'd pester me to death if I didn't agree." His smile was rueful. "The woman was a complete Domme at heart. I have no idea what Sharon was thinking. Maybe she thought it'd be good for me to let go of control sometimes."

Now Tarah barked a laugh. "She doesn't know you very well."

"Because I can't be my true self with them the way I can be with you." Not waiting for a response, he got out of the car.

Stunned, she waited for him to come around and open her door. A blast of icy air hit her. "Is it going to snow tonight?"

He shrugged. "I've been a little occupied and haven't checked the weather channel. I have winter tires on the car, so there's nothing to worry about."

She took his proffered arm. "I wasn't worried so much as making conversation because suddenly you're wound as tight as a top. I'll be your shield of armor. I promise."

Relief flickered in his eyes as he led her toward the door of the community center rented for the night. A coat check positioned to their left was there as soon as they entered. She handed over the beautiful wool coat to a young woman.

"Keep it near the front." Sebastian's tone was brusque. "We won't be here long."

Tarah offered the young woman a smile. "You put it in order like the others. I'm not in a rush."

He uttered something nasty under his breath, but she refused to acknowledge him. Instead she stepped into the room. The lights were low, strings of Christmas lights everywhere and a tree in the corner.

"We put angels on the tree with a wish from an underprivileged child, and each one of our kids fulfills the wish."

Despite his matter-of-fact tone, she blinked back tears. "So they learn about giving during this season."

"Yeah, I guess. Sharon came up with the idea several years ago. She and two of the other women deliver all the presents the day before Christmas. She tells me the families are grateful."

"And you do something for the parents." Not a

question.

"Christmas hampers with hams, if you must know."

"You're a gigantic pile of mush, you know?"

He grumbled something under his breath but quickly morphed the frown into a smile when a woman approached.

Tarah's first impression was of a bundle of energy in a compact package. No more than five feet tall, busty, and a little on the heavy side, the woman held out her arms, and to Tarah's shock, Sebastian stepped into her embrace. He held himself awkwardly, but he let her hold on for another moment.

He stepped away and put his hand on the small of Tarah's back, propelling her forward. "Sharon, this is Tarah. Tarah, this is the woman who keeps me on the straight and narrow."

Tarah held out her hand but was pulled into a hug.

Sharon released her and gave her a once-over. "Good choice, boss. Now, they've just put out the buffet." She leaned in conspiratorially to Tarah. "I don't know how he does it, but he always arrives just in time for the food." She took Tarah by the hands, pulling her away from the safety of Sebastian. "And he always leaves right afterward. This time, you get him to stay, okay?"

Laughing, Tarah offered her brightest smile. "I can try, but Mr. Merrick has a mind of his own."

The woman waved off her assertion. "Boss just needs a woman like you to put him in his place. He needs to learn to relax."

Boy, Sebastian had nailed it when he'd asserted Sharon was clueless to his true nature. No woman alive could put Sebastian in his place or lead him around by the nose.

Once they had their food, they searched for an empty table. Tarah spotted two places at a table full of kids and all but dragged Sebastian over. Bracketing the empty seats were an attractive-looking woman and a five-year-old. Sebastian didn't bother to be a gentleman and all but shoved her into the seat next to the child. If she hadn't known better, she might've thought he was interested in the woman with the low-cut dress whose skirt barely skimmed her thighs. But she did know better.

"Tarah, this is Mindy Khan. She's the company's corporate lawyer. Mindy, this is Tarah."

She noticed he didn't clarify her position. Probably self-explanatory.

Mindy reached across Sebastian and offered a perfectly manicured hand. "My brother works in procurement. He and his wife were planning to come together with the four children. Leslie and their youngest both have the flu, so Reuben asked me to come and help."

"Very considerate of you."

Mindy laughed. "You're wondering about the dress. I'm going to my boyfriend's Christmas party as soon as we're done here. He works for a brokerage firm. Needless to say, it won't be a dry event."

Perhaps a little rude to say in front of the boss, but Sebastian laughed. Tarah was searching to find something witty when someone tugged at her sleeve. She turned and smiled.

"My name's Geoff."

She offered her hand, and after a hesitation, he shook it.

"Well, Geoff, my name is Tarah."

Apparently satisfied, he pointed to the three-year-old next to him. "This is my little sister, Amy. She's a bit of a pain in the—"

"Geoffrey." The warning was clear.

Tarah smiled as she met the young woman's gaze. Then the woman turned to her son, narrowing her eyes.

"We only say nice things about other people."

Geoff nodded and turned back to Tarah. "Amy's potty-trained."

Tarah burst out laughing.

The woman across the way looked like she wanted to murder her firstborn but evidently gave up and chuckled. She nodded to Tarah. "My name is Ina. You've met my two children, I see."

"They're charming."

Ina offered a rueful expression. "They're three and five. Charming is not the word I'd use."

"I used to work at a preschool. I have to say these two are well behaved."

"It's an illusion. Normally, they're holy terrors." Her beatific smile belied her words.

"Hey." Geoff crossed his arms against his chest. "I thought we weren't supposed to say bad things about people."

Every adult at the table laughed. Except Sebastian. His right leg tapped rhythmically under the table, and a sheen of sweat broke out across his brow. Slipping her hand under the table, she gave his thigh a reassuring squeeze.

He glanced at her quizzically, and a ghost of a smile passed across his lips. He resumed his studious examination of the contents of his plate.

His pain and obvious discomfort washed over her,

and she hoped the others didn't notice. He was a proud man, and she marveled the chink in his armor would be a bunch of rug rats.

She felt another tugging, this one at her skirt. Little Amy was holding out her arms.

"Up! Up! Up!"

Without thought, she grasped the toddler under the arms and lifted her to her lap. Usually, children took a bit of time to open up, but clearly, Amy saw her as a kindred spirit. She pressed her nose to the toddler's hair, remembering the unique smell young children had. She'd missed this. Four painful months she'd been away from this.

Amy turned around and offered Tarah a grin. "Happy!"

"Oh, Amy."

Tarah looked up at Ina when the other woman gasped. Confused, she glanced down. And found two nice handprints of chocolate icing on her breasts. She couldn't help herself—she burst out laughing. Amy appeared a little stunned, but Tarah pressed a kiss to the little one's forehead. "Yes, Amy, I'm very happy."

At Ina's panicked expression, Tarah waved her off. "I know a good dry cleaner—no worries."

"I should pay—"

"Don't be silly, Ina." This was the first time Sebastian had spoken in some time, and everyone looked at him. Obviously realizing he was now the center of attention, he hesitated a fraction of a second. "Like Tarah said, we know a good dry cleaner. Kids do stuff like this, and it's no big deal. Our uniforms are black to hide the spills."

Everyone burst out laughing, and Ina appeared

marginally less stressed. Tarah winked at her and returned her attention to Amy who was babbling about Santa Claus.

****

More than an hour passed before they were able to leave. People kept dropping by the table to give Sebastian their thanks. He held up beautifully, though he clearly didn't want the gratitude. Finally, when the party started to break up, he stood and pulled out her chair.

Tarah waved goodbye to everyone at the table.

The line at the coat check clearly irked Sebastian, and he bristled when the young woman had to do a search for Tarah's coat.

When he wasn't looking, she left a hefty tip.

Just before she put the coat on, he inspected her dress. Then he returned to gentlemanly behavior and exchanged salutations with several people before they escaped. He helped her into the car.

She held her breath as he rounded the front.

He was silent as he pulled out of the parking lot, and they were halfway home before he finally spoke. "That's a nine-hundred-dollar dress."

"And the dry cleaners will get it clean."

"It's wool crepe. It needs special attention."

"Sebastian, your dry cleaner works in one of the richest areas of the city. I'm sure he can handle one dress." She refrained from pointing out he was the one who'd chosen the dress. "Now, why don't you tell me what this is really about?"

He didn't answer.

The silence spun out, and she assumed the rest of the ride would be made in silence until he spoke.

"I'd rather have stood naked in the middle of Club

Kink than go through tonight."

"Sebastian, if you stood naked in Kink, every submissive in the place would be kneeling at your feet. Probably a Domme or two as well."

"I wasn't fishing for compliments."

"Which is why you should be gracious when you get one. Didn't your mother teach you any manners?"

He didn't answer.

The quiet descending upon the car was oppressive. Had she crossed some arbitrary line he'd drawn? What had she told herself? *Don't talk about the past.* Sometimes she needed to listen to herself.

Sebastian was solicitous on the way back to the apartment, but she found no warmth in his gestures. When they were in the door, he took her coat and hung it up. "I need a drink."

"I can get you one."

"I need you naked."

"I can do that."

She was stepping away when he pushed her up against the wall. He slanted his mouth over hers.

When she gave him entry, he ruthlessly plundered. He was hot and demanding, giving nothing while taking everything. One hand grabbed her breast while the other yanked up her skirt. He put his thigh between hers, and she rubbed desperately up and down against him.

His erection was hard, unyielding against her hip. He grasped her nylons and ripped them. He was tugging at her underwear, but they weren't willing to give up the fight easily. She flicked the button of his pants open with one hand, pulled down his fly, and slipped her hand into his underwear.

He was still pulling at her clothes, all the while

pushing her higher and higher.

"Too many fucking clothes." He growled out the words.

As much as she wanted him in her, and as much as he wanted to be there, it'd take too fucking long. She dropped to her knees and took him in her mouth. None of the gentleness or finesse of the night before. This time he set an unrelenting pace. *Breathe through your nose.* The rest of the instructions went out the window.

She was offering relief the only way she knew how. She didn't know how to comfort an adult. She didn't know the right words or platitudes to give. All she could do was be a vessel for his pain.

Tears streamed down her face, but still she didn't pull back. She raked her teeth against him, and he bucked, flexing his hips and going in even deeper. She laved him with her tongue, and he pressed even farther into her. He hit the back of her throat, and still she sucked.

The first emotion when he climaxed was relief. Relief it was over and relief she'd given herself to him. Whatever else happened, she'd shared this with him.

Spent, he collapsed on the wall behind him, and she took stock. The nylons cut into her skin where there were runs, her dress was askew, one half hiked up over her hip, and her hair clips had been dislodged. Her makeup was likely running, and her face must be tear streaked.

Still, she didn't move. Was she supposed to go get herself cleaned up? He'd ordered her to get naked, but that was before he ravished her right here in the front hall. Was she supposed to wait until she was dismissed? He'd said he needed a drink. Was he going to get it now, or was she supposed to do it for him?

She simply didn't know the protocol for this particular situation.

"Get out of here."

His voice was preternaturally calm. Eerily calm. Terrifyingly calm.

She didn't even hesitate. She used her hands to push herself up from her kneeling position and ran to the bathroom.

Chapter Thirteen

Only when she was locked inside did she take a full and deep breath. She shook as she pulled off the dress. Her emotions had been so ferocious and visceral the neck of the dress was soaked in black mascara-laced tears. It went well with the chocolate handprints.

The first thing she did was take a brush to her hair. She tugged viciously until she removed all the tangles. She pulled it into a high ponytail and scrubbed off the makeup. The water was too hot, but she didn't care. All she wanted was to be clean.

Finally satisfied, she finished undressing. The bra and underwear went in the laundry hamper while the nylons went in the garbage. Deciding to take one last look at herself in the mirror, she was shocked to see the fingerprint bruises on the breast Sebastian had grabbed. She had no memory of it being painful, but she'd been a little occupied.

Nothing to be done about it now. She could hope Sebastian wouldn't notice—zero chance of that happening. He spent too much time examining her, scrutinizing her. Nothing was too small to escape his notice. The mirror showed a pale face, white skin across her collarbone, and red-rimmed eyes. He often gazed into her eyes as if they were the windows to her soul. What did he see? She'd convinced herself she was a person without depth. She'd cried twice in two days—a record for her.

Deciding she could no longer hide, she unlocked the door and walked across the condo. She was almost at the door to her room when a light flipped on in the previously dark living room. She stopped in her tracks.

"Look at me."

She pivoted slowly, holding the folded dress against her chest.

"Come here."

She advanced toward him.

He sat on the couch, shirt unbuttoned, a drink in hand. He looked…bleak.

Her first reaction was to reach out and comfort. She might not know how, but she was willing to give it everything she had.

"Closer."

She advanced until she stood between his open thighs. He was leaning back against the couch and looking up at her through hooded lashes. He held out his hand, and she didn't pretend she didn't know what he wanted. She handed him the dress, and he laid it down gently on the couch beside him.

He put his drink on the side table and pushed himself up to a properly seated position. His head moved, and he sat up. He wasn't touching, just looking.

His hand reached out, and she thought he'd touch her. Wanted him to touch her. His mouth was so close to her breast all she needed to do was sway forward, and lips would meet nipple.

His hand dropped to his knee, and he slumped back to the couch. He picked up his glass and took a sip. "I marked you."

So what? "You mark me all the time. This is no

different."

"It is, Tarah, and we both know it."

The use of her given name made her uncomfortable. As far as she was concerned, as soon as they'd stepped through the threshold of the condo tonight, she'd become Mia. She didn't want to be Tarah. She wanted to be his. "Sir, you didn't hurt me."

His lip curled. "It's Sebastian."

"What if I don't want it to be? What if I want it to be Sir? What if I want to be Mia? What if I want to kneel at your feet and sleep on the floor by your bed? What if I want to serve you? If I want those things, what does that make me?"

"A fool."

That hurt.

"You told me I was made for submission, Sir, and you were right." She dropped to her knees in front of him. "I'm an adult, and I make my own choices."

"But did you have a choice tonight? I practically raped you."

"Ravished, Sir, not raped. I didn't do anything I didn't want to. You didn't do anything to me that I didn't want to happen."

His eyes closed, and his head fell back against the back of the couch. "You make me feel things. Things I'd thought long suppressed."

How was she supposed to answer? "Can you tell me about it?"

"Get off your knees."

This time, she rose gracefully, without using her hands, for all the good it did. His eyes remained closed.

"Tarah, please go put on the flannel pajamas and a pair of thick socks. Then you may come back out."

Still confused, she reached for the dress, but he was quicker.

"Please, Tarah, go get dressed."

Please? The request, more than anything else, propelled her to her bedroom. The pajamas were white with little pink roses—almost virginal. She pulled on a pair of wool socks and padded back into the main room. The sole discernible difference was Sebastian held a bottle of water. He handed it to her and pointed to the opposite corner of the couch. She sat with her back to the armrest and her knees drawn up to her chin. She took a long pull of water, all the time watching him.

He sipped, then carefully placed the glass back on the table. "I don't like children because I grew up surrounded by them."

That she hadn't expected. Holding her breath, she waited for him to elucidate.

"I was the oldest of six boys and two girls. I was expected to help raise them. My father worked in the tar sands and came home just often enough to keep my mother knocked up and battered. My father wasn't just abusive—he was a mean drunk. I mean, any of us could be targets, but I made sure I was in the way the most so he'd take out his anger on me."

He paused. "At least he did until I became bigger than him and stood up to him. He stopped coming around as often. My mother had eight mouths to feed and no way to do it, so I dropped out of high school and went to work at the local lumber mill.

"I was working the overnight shift when an RCMP officer came to tell me my father had shown up and burned the house down. All the kids and my mom were home. I couldn't figure out how none of them got out, but when they did the autopsy, they found eight bodies with eight bullets to the head." He swallowed convulsively but still didn't look at her. "My father was found hanged in his cell a few weeks later, and the matter was closed, but rumor was he had help with the noose. Even criminals don't like family annihilators. My youngest sister was six months old.

"My name isn't Sebastian Merrick. I didn't want his name, and I didn't want a reminder of my life before that night. As soon as the funerals were over, I left that crappy shithole of a town and made my way to Vancouver."

He paused again. "I was good with wood, and soon I was working as a day laborer. The work was sporadic, and I was taking my high school equivalency at night. I pushed myself to the point of exhaustion every night so I wouldn't have to think about how my whole family was dead." His eyes closed. "Construction paid well back then, and I saved every penny I could. I worked seven days a week, knowing I wasn't meant to work with my hands for the rest of my life. One day I went into a strip club and noticed business was crappy. I asked the owner why, and he grumbled about the family homes being built up all around him. I put everything I owned into buying the place, and the rest is history."

Was this where she was supposed to speak? What was she supposed to say? She remained silent.

How had he reconciled himself to this? It'd been over twenty years, but from the look on his face, it might as well have happened yesterday. No wonder control was such an important thing to him. His entire childhood he'd had none. Now, as an adult, he could construct the life he wanted. Obviously, this was why he didn't want children. She'd bet her soul he'd loved each of his seven siblings.

The silence continued to spin out but not nerve-wracking. Nor was it companionable. It just…was.

Finally, he let out a long breath. "So now you know. Go to bed, Tarah. I'll see you in the morning."

"No."

His head turned sharply. "I'm sorry?"

"You can't tell me what to do, Sebastian. Not this time." False bravado, to be sure, but it still had to be done. "You can't tell me a story that horrific and expect me to turn my back and walk away. You can't expect me to fight this desire to soothe."

"What do you know about soothing? You hardly know how to interact with adults."

"You're upset, so I'll let that pass, but don't think you can lash out at me because you're hurting. I feel things too." She pounded her chest. "I ache for the young man who lost everything because of a monster. I rage against a man who could do such things, and am only comforted by the fact he's dead. I wish he'd suffered before he died. I'm frustrated you won't let me in." Her voice was stronger now, and she was shouting.

Sebastian looked like he was going to argue, but he closed his eyes. "I want the comfort you're offering, Tarah, but I don't know how to accept it. I'm the strong one. I'm the Dominant in this relationship."

"And I'm the submissive, but you were the one who talked about delineation. This is one of those times. One of those times when we're equals. You said yourself twenty-four seven is deep shit. Well, so is what we have. For tonight—just for tonight—let me be the strong one. You may not believe this, but I can withstand a lot."

He opened his eyes, and they softened. "You're a

warrior, Tarah. I've never met anyone who's worked as hard as you have to get what you want."

"Except you."

"Except me."

"Can't wounded warriors lean on each other?"

"What you're offering…it scares me."

"You're afraid if you let go of it, you'll never get it back. You're so self-reliant it'd never occur to you relationships are a two-way street."

"I dominate and you submit."

Sweet Jesus. God save me from stubborn men. "What if I want more?"

"Goddamn it, Tarah, you wanted more, and you got sex. How much more are you asking for?" His words were more teasing and bluster than actual exasperation.

She pushed herself up and off the couch. She walked toward him and offered him her hand. Seconds ticked by, and she started to falter. Had she gone too far? Was this a bridge he couldn't—or wouldn't—cross?

Please let him agree. I need to do this for him.

Please give me the strength to do it.

Please provide him the wisdom to accept it.

She was close to giving up when he grasped it.

"Just for tonight." His eyes were red, his expression bleary.

"Just for tonight." That assurance she could give.

He rose, still holding her hand.

Instead of leading him to the dungeon, she took him to the room of light. The room of purity. The room of hope. The room where the universe watched over those below.

She let go of his hand and stepped back. "Strip."

His eyebrow quirked, but he didn't move.

"I said strip."

"Tarah—"

"Do you trust me?"

Her words seemed to bring him up short.

"I said, do you trust me?"

He started to speak and then stopped. His mouth opened again and then closed. Finally, he shut his eyes. "Yes, Tarah, I trust you."

"Then take your clothes off, Sebastian." Her tone swung from authoritative to soothing and coaxing.

Without opening his eyes, he undid his belt, and his pants dropped to the floor. At some point he'd removed his shoes and socks, so it was just a matter of letting his pants fall.

When he stopped, she clicked her tongue. "You know the meaning of the word strip, Sebastian."

Thumbs hooked into briefs that soon joined the pile of clothes on the floor. This was the first time she'd seen him flaccid, and she had to hold back a giggle. How something so small could get to be so big was beyond her. Something about blood flowing to the penis... Should've paid more attention in sex-ed class.

"Tarah, I'm naked. Now what do you want to me to do?"

"Um, get into bed and lie on your side facing away from me."

His mouth was set in a grim line, but soon he pulled down the comforter and slid under it. As instructed, he lay on his side facing away from her. After she flipped off the lights, she wasted no time divesting herself of her own clothes. When she was naked, she slipped in behind him. She pressed her breasts against his back, fitted her hips to curve around his buttocks, and slid her thighs against his. She snaked her hand under his arm and laid it against his breastbone.

"I don't think—"

"Good, Sebastian, don't think. Just let go."

A long time passed before he did, finally.

When something solid connected with her jaw, Tarah saw stars, and they weren't the ones on the ceiling. A leg kicked out, and she barely pulled her knee out of the way in time. *What*... Her head finally cleared. Sebastian was thrashing about. Unlike her, however, he wasn't awake. She placed a hand on his shoulder.

"Sebastian."

His arm flew out, and she ducked.

"Sebastian!"

She kept stroking, kept soothing, kept praying she could pull him out of this before he really hurt her.

Then, as quickly as it had started, it ended. He let out a long sigh and rolled onto his back.

"Tarah?" His voice cracked, laced with confusion.

"I'm here, Sebastian." She placed a hand over his hammering heart. "I'm here. Relax. I'm right here."

He still shook but was calming. "I haven't...I was dreaming, wasn't I?"

"A nightmare, Sebastian. A bad one. You've had them before, haven't you?"

The silence was more telling than anything he could say.

Finally, he let out a long shudder. "It's been a while. It's always the same. I'm outside of the house, and it's on fire. I hear screams from inside, but the flames are too hot, and I can't get close. I'm willing to let myself burn, but my legs won't move."

She said nothing, just continued to stroke her hand

up and down his chest. Up and down and then along his collarbone. She was making the sign of the cross. Trying to absolve an atheist of sins he hadn't even committed.

He took her hand in his, pressing it to the left side of his chest, right above his heart. "I was raised in a strict Christian Fundamentalist home. No Santa Claus, no birthday parties, and no birth control." He sighed. "I didn't just walk away from that town that day—I walked away from my faith. I stopped believing in God."

"Whereas I was raised in a nonbelieving household. We never talked about God."

"And we did nothing but talk about God."

"Do you…" Damn, how should she say this? "Do you think if you went back to your faith, things might get better for you?"

He snickered. "Oh yeah, God would love to hear about how I tie up women and whip them. How I get them to suck my cock. How I stick my dick up their asses. You think there's redemption for someone like me?"

"The question is can you find it within you to forgive yourself? Because no one else is passing judgment on you, Sebastian."

"I baited him."

"What do you mean?"

"I baited him. The last time I saw him, I told him I was more of a father to those kids than he ever had been or ever would be. I told him we didn't need him and to not bother coming back." Sebastian shuddered. "He waited until I left for work. He made sure I wasn't there. He herded them all into one room and…well, you know the rest. He did it to spite me. To show me I was wrong. He did it to prove that by his hand and seed the kids had come into the world, and by that same hand, he could obliterate them."

No wonder he carried around such intense guilt.

"Help me forget, Tarah. Just this one night, help me forget."

"Of course." At least something she could try to do. She faltered. "But you'll have to show me, Sebastian. I don't know how."

He rolled onto his side and eased her onto her back. The constellations weren't as bright, and she couldn't see his face, but his breath was warm and moist against her skin. His mouth pressed to hers. Once. Twice. And again a third time. On the fourth pass, he ran his tongue along the seam of her lips. On a sigh, she opened to him. His tongue slid into her mouth, seeking rather than demanding. His hand pressed to her breast, asking rather than requiring. Whereas their coupling earlier tonight had been him taking and her giving, now it became a back and forth. Gentle touches and soft sighs. Fingers reaching instead of raking. A quest rather than a destination.

At last, he rolled on top of her, and she was ready. Her thighs opened invitingly, and when he hesitated, she guided him to her. He eased into her as if she were fine china that might break with the slightest tremor. No ardor, only tenderness. Each stroke, each moment of delicious friction intensified her need for him. She'd never get enough of him.

Then, measured in minutes and inches, he picked up the pace. They were both close, and his thrusts became more insistent. He made demands of her, and she was up to the challenge. She flexed her hips, taking him in to the hilt.

He arched back and let go. Moments later, she followed him over the precipice.

****

She wasn't surprised when she awoke alone but was disappointed. Her limbs were heavy, weighted down. Still, the clock read nine, and she had to pee. Slipping on her robe, she padded to the bathroom. On her way back, she detoured to the kitchen for a coffee and a cup of yogurt. She entered the dining room and found Sebastian reading the paper.

Sitting across from him, she took a greedy look. He wore a crimson silk shirt and black pants. As always, he was sexy as hell, but he hadn't shaved, and the stubble gave him an air of mystery.

He laid the paper on the table, then leaned forward. He pointed to her chin. "What's that?"

The question she'd dreaded. "It's nothing, Sebastian—it's not a big deal."

But didn't they both know it to be a lie? She had a nasty bruise where the heel of his hand had connected with her jaw last night. Even with concealer, the bruise was hideous.

"Eat your breakfast and get dressed. Jeans, turtleneck, and a warm sweater. You're going with Ina and the kids to the aquarium. Be ready to go in twenty minutes."

Without another word he took his coffee and went into his home office.

She swallowed twice to get down the mouthful of yogurt. She loved the aquarium, and the thought of spending the day with Amy and Geoff held a lot of appeal. *Pretend last night never happened.*

Hadn't that been the sound plan? She'd offered

247

comfort for one night, and he'd taken. Now they were back to a different dynamic. Something was off, though. She needed equilibrium. Maybe a day away from each other was needed.

When she was ready to go, Sebastian handed her some cash and sent her on her way.

The day was fun, but she couldn't rid herself of a persistent panic lying just below the surface. When Ina entreated her to join them for an early dinner, Tarah wanted to refuse but didn't. She did, however, wish she'd brought her cell phone so she could call Sebastian to tell him she would be late. Of course they hadn't settled on a time for her to come back, so what difference did it make?

When Ina drove back into the city, she took a different route.

"Oh, but Sebastian doesn't live this way."

"I know." Ina's mouth was in a tight line. "He told me to bring you to this building here." She pulled up in front of another tower of soaring concrete and steel.

"I don't…" Tarah's voice trailed off as she saw the solitary figure standing by the door.

Ina's brow furrowed. "Is everything okay, Tarah? I mean, Mr. Merrick was very specific—"

Tarah laid a hand on her new friend's arm. "It's fine, Ina. You brought me to the right place." She turned back to the kids and blew kisses, all the while fighting the tears. Without another word, she slipped from the minivan and stepped toward the building.

"Miss Peters, nice to see you again."

"Mme Veronique, I have to say this is unexpected."

The other woman's smile didn't diminish. "Mr. Merrick had me prepare everything for you." She led

Tarah through the lobby of the hotel to the elevators. "This is where I work." She held the elevator for Tarah, swiped a key fob, and pressed the twenty-sixth floor.

"Half of the building is hotel suites, and the rest is residential. Mr. Merrick purchased a suite in the residential section when we were under construction, but never moved in. We have been renting it temporarily for him since then, but it has been empty for a week." She held the elevator door and pointed down the hall. "You are in suite 2605. The kitchen is fully stocked, and all your belongings have been moved in." She used the key to open the door, and Tarah followed her instructions on how to disarm the alarm.

"We have a kitchen open all the time, so order food if you dislike cooking. I understand Miguel Hernandez will come on Thursdays in January to give you cooking lessons. I hope the kitchen will be up to his standards."

Tarah merely nodded because she neither knew, nor cared, what Miguel's standards were. At the moment, she didn't give a good goddamn about anything.

"All of your belongings were moved in earlier today." Mme Veronique handed her the key. "You have a three-year lease but are free to stay as long as you want. You have a ten-thousand-dollar monthly allowance and fifty thousand dollars to pay for your schooling. I have arranged for you to meet with a financial advisor at the credit union. She can set you up with a budget and a retirement plan."

Tarah couldn't help herself—she started laughing. Then once she started, she couldn't stop. She tried to suppress the waves, but she could do nothing about this situation. She laughed so hard her sides hurt.

"My dear—" The unflappable Mme Veronique

appeared flapped.

"So this is what submissive retirement looks like." She wiped the tears from her cheeks and let out another couple of chuckles. "So how many women have received the great kiss-off?"

As quickly as the laughter had come, the tears of pain began. When Mme Veronique guided her to the plush leather sofa, she dropped like a rock. She bent forward, pulling her arms tight around her waist. She tried to keep it in, but she was flying apart. How could she be in this much pain and still be alive?

Mme Veronique sat next to her and handed her a handkerchief. A real cloth handkerchief. This was as surreal as the rest of the situation. When Mme Veronique placed a soothing hand to Tarah's back, she fell into the woman's embrace.

For the first time in about twenty years, she needed someone to lean on.

A long time passed before she could pull away. She wiped furiously at the rivulets of tears. "I'm so sorry."

"No need, my dear." The older woman patted Tarah's hair. "Mr. Merrick has never let anyone close enough for him to have to give them an…exit strategy."

"So I should either feel honored or shafted."

"Or both," Mme Veronique offered primly. "Miss Peters—"

"Tarah."

"All right, Tarah." The woman seemed to have trouble getting the name past her lips. "This hurts. I know this hurts. I can offer no platitudes or pretty words to make the landing any softer. All I can say is if he really wanted to be rid of you, then he would not have put you up in his suite with an unlimited expense account. A quick check and the closest motel would have been far more expedient, but he would not know where you were or what you were doing."

Looking around the room with its luxurious appointments, Tarah laughed. "I'd be far more comfortable in a motel. Look, I can't stay here."

"Do it for me, if not for you."

"What?"

"If you will not do it for yourself, try thinking of other people. If you leave, I might lose a valuable customer, and I might get a poor reputation."

The thought was so ridiculous she laughed out loud. "I call bullshit."

A ghost of a smile crossed the normally prim Mme Veronique's lips. "If he knows you are here, he can come and get you when he is ready. If you leave, he might have to look."

"He's got a good private investigator."

"Yes, I was the one who gave him Toby Driscoll's name."

Tarah pulled back to look at the other woman's face. "Is there anything you don't know?"

"I am what is known as a *fixer*. I have a lot of fingers in a lot of pies. Some things need more fixing than others. Timmy Lister more than most."

"Who's Timmy Lister?"

"Oh, sorry, I meant Sebastian Merrick."

The penny dropped. "You know about his past."

"I do. You are too young, but the story was all over the news. I still remember the photo of the gangly teenager next to seven coffins."

"I thought there were seven siblings plus his mother."

"The baby was put in her mother's coffin."

Tarah's intake of breath was sharp. "Oh my God."

"A man has to run a long way before he can forget."

"And forgive…"

"And forgive." Veronique nodded. "And it takes a strong woman to stand by that man."

Well, she wasn't strong enough, was she? "I tried to show him, and I cared for him. For my trouble, he sent me away. You expect me to have faith he's coming back?"

Mme Veronique stood. "I cannot ask you to wait for him, but if you do and he comes back, you will know it is real."

She walked toward the door, and Tarah followed.

"And if you do not stay until the first of June, you are in breach of contract." She gave a curt nod and left.

Tarah slammed her fist into the closest wall.

Chapter Fourteen

If she was a drinker, she would've emptied the minibar. Since she wasn't, she settled for eating an entire pint of ice cream and crying at a sappy Christmas movie on the classics channel.

Monday morning she felt like she'd gone ten rounds with a heavyweight boxer and looked like it. Deep-mauve bruises under her eyes matched the purple contusion on her chin. Funny how both Ina and Mme Veronique had been circumspect. Had Sebastian offered an excuse, or did the two women think he'd hit her?

No, Mme Veronique definitely knew the truth. She'd never have coaxed Tarah to stay if she'd suspected an assault. Ina also didn't seem to be a pushover although whether she'd cross her employer was another story.

Still, after a shower and getting dressed, Tarah took a shot at trying to lessen the effect of the bruise. She'd enjoyed the fresh air yesterday and was planning another long walk today. She was rifling through the fridge when the phone rang.

Her heart leapt, and she ruthlessly tamped it back down. Sebastian Merrick did not stoop to calling.

Resignedly, she answered.

"Is this Miss Peters? Tarah Peters?"

"This is she."

"Miss Peters, my name is Noora. I work at Honeycomb Daycare. I got your name from Joyce at

Charmers Preschool. I'm hoping you can help. One of my workers got hired by the Mission City School Board unexpectedly. She started today, and I'm desperate. Might you be able to help?"

Rielle's husband, Gage Clayton, worked for the Mission City School Board, and they were friends of Sebastian's. But did it matter? She could be in a classroom by tomorrow morning.

"Of course I can help, Noora. When do you want me to start?"

"How is tomorrow morning? I secured a copy of your police background check from Joyce. There's no impediment to keep you from getting in with the kids tomorrow. Are you sure? I mean, do you need time to think about it?"

If I think about it, then I might back out.

"Tomorrow morning is perfect."

****

Christmas dawned as an unexpectedly sunny December day—the first time Tarah could remember there not being rain on the most special of special days. The bus ride to her parents' place took an hour, and she tried to concentrate on her latest novel, but it didn't work. More than a week had passed since she was summarily given the kiss-off, and the hurt hadn't lessened. She used all her willpower not to call Sebastian to wish him a Merry Christmas. She *knew* he was sitting in the dungeon all alone. Well, unless his latest conquest from Kink had stayed longer than the prescribed five hours.

Wrong thought.

She missed her stop and had to backtrack four blocks to get to her parents', which blackened her mood even further. With the size of her bank account, she could've taken a cab, but some habits died hard. When she knocked on her mother's door, she put on her bravest face.

Lynette Peters appeared older than her fifty-six years. Worry had aged her, and a pang of sympathy zinged through Tarah for the woman who used to be vivacious. Still, when her mother pulled her into an embrace, she sagged. Sharon, Veronique, and now her mother. She'd never been hugged this much in her life.

"Tarah." Her mother's voice was soft. Soothing. "I'll get you a cranberry juice. Why don't you join your father on the patio? Such a beautiful day, we're sitting in the sun."

The temperature outside was freezing cold, but her father was wrapped in several blankets. He sipped a cup of coffee and looked unbelievably frail. A bony hand brushed snowy-white hair from his brow.

"Are you sure you should be out here?"

"I'm not dead yet, Tarah, and I'm sick and tired of being cooped up in this place. I wanted fresh air, and I'm getting it."

Lynette bustled out with the cranberry juice and her own cup of tea.

"The most amazing thing happened, Tarah—you won't believe it."

"What, Mom?"

"Your father and I won a two-week vacation to Greece. We leave on New Year's Day."

"Mom, it's probably some kind of scam."

"Oh no, dear. My boss gave me the tickets himself. Said all the employees of the month were receiving a bonus this year. I was employee of the month for June, as you well remember."

"Of course, Mom, I'm very proud of you."

Her mother's boss was a good friend of Sebastian Merrick. Well, she couldn't take this away from her mother, but she could bloody well tell him what she thought of his interference.

Tarah tried not to stew through turkey dinner but was relieved when the time came to say goodbye. She loved her parents but had nothing to contribute to their lives. They were entirely wrapped up in each other, and she was an afterthought.

The bus ride back to the city seemed interminable, and until she walked through the lobby of Crystal Towers, she hadn't completely made up her mind on what she was going to do.

Gus sat at the desk. He rose.

"Pulling a double?"

He nodded. "Carlos wanted the day with his family, and seeing as I'm a widower, didn't mean much to me. Extra money always comes in handy. Are you here to see Mr. Merrick?"

"Yes, thanks. I know the way."

She was almost past him when he stepped out. "Is he expecting you?"

Holding up the key she'd taken with her when she'd gone to the aquarium, she gave him a charming smile. The key she'd never been asked to return. "I want to surprise him, but he knows I've got a key."

Indecision was written all over Gus' face, but his demeanor changed, and he smiled. "It'll be a nice present for him. He gave all of us huge Christmas bonuses. We figured you might be behind that."

Damn man. She shook her head. "I had nothing to do with Mr. Merrick's generosity. That was all him.

Have a Merry Christmas, Gus."

"Thanks, Miss Peters." He let her pass without another word.

When she stood outside of 313, however, her bravado proved false. At least half a dozen times, she raised her hand to knock and let it drop back to her side. Well, shit, if she left without trying, she'd never forgive herself. If he sent her away, she'd go for good, contract or no contract.

She lifted her hand and knocked on the door.

She waited.

She lifted her hand and knocked again.

And waited.

He was there, goddamn it—she *knew* it. This time, she pounded. "Sebastian Merrick, you open this"— *fucking*—"door."

At least she hadn't cursed out loud.

Still no answer.

Once more unto the breach, dear friends, once more.

If Henry the Fifth could talk his men into going to war, she could coax Sebastian Merrick out of his lair.

This time she used both fists. "Open the door, or I'll tell everyone you knocked me up and abandoned me."

A lock did click, and Mrs. Wannamaker stuck her head out.

"Hello, Mrs. Wannamaker." She offered her most cheerful smile. "Did you have a good Christmas?"

Another lock clicked, and air whooshed when the door to 313 flung open. Tarah barely had time to wave to the elderly woman before she was bodily seized and hauled inside. The door slammed shut, and she was dragged by the wrist into the living room.

"You're pregnant?" He seethed, nostrils flaring, dark eyes wide. "You fucking bitch. You told me that you were on the pill."

She dared to grin. "Actually, what I said was if you didn't open the door, I was going to *tell* everyone you knocked me up and abandoned me. Since you opened the door, I won't have to tell them because it isn't true."

His face twisted in mottled rage. "What kind of game is this? What part of *there's the door, and don't let it hit your ass on the way out* didn't you get?"

She should've been cowed. She should've been terrified. But no way would he get this worked up if she meant nothing to him.

She stuck out her finger. "You were the one who got me the job at Honeycomb, you're the one who's sending my parents to Greece, and you're the one who gave all the security staff huge Christmas bonuses."

He looked at her like she was crazy. His eyes were wide, and his brow furrowed in evident confusion. "Yes, I gave bonuses—I do that wherever I live. As for honey whatnots and Greece, I have no fucking clue what you're talking about."

"Noora said she lost Candice because she was hired by the Mission City School Board. Gage Clayton works for the Mission City School Board. Gage Clayton is a friend of yours." She let out a huff. "You're acquainted with Jürgen Joseph. He's my mother's boss. Suddenly, all the employees of the month are being given free trips."

He was still looking at her as if she'd lost her mind. "Gage Clayton is a high school principal in the district of Mission City, and he's a friend, yes, but I can't get him to hire someone. I had nothing to do with your mother being named employee of the month. If Joseph gave them a vacation, that's on him, not me."

"But I thought…" She faltered. "Oh, shit."

"Yes, shit. Goddamn it, Tarah, the whole fucking building heard you say you're pregnant with my child and I've abandoned you."

"Well, technically—"

"Don't fucking talk to me about semantics. You were wrong, and you know it. You know about discretion, and you bloody well know better. I live here, you little idiot. In a few minutes you'll be on your way, but the entire building now knows my business. Fuck, you might as well have put it on a billboard, because you know Mrs. Wannamaker will call the newspaper first thing in the morning."

"That's a bit of an exaggeration—"

"Shut the fuck up—I'm not finished."

He took a breath, but she didn't dare fill the silence.

"We had two weeks together, and you think that gives you some kind of claim on me? That's not just creepy—that's, like, stalking."

"Says the man who hired a private detective to have me investigated," she shot back. "Pot, kettle, kettle, pot. Black."

His brow furrowed in bafflement, and she knew she'd messed it up but also knew what she meant to say. She was about to speak when he resumed where he'd left off.

"And while we're at it, you were the one who asked me to divest you of your virginity, and I did—"

"Such a goddamn chore for you—"

"Yes, fucking hell, it was. I don't think I've ever been so nervous…"

His voice trailed off, and her stomach clenched. She waited. She was about to speak when he resumed his pacing and ranting.

"You asked for one night, and I gave you one night." He ran his hand through his hair. "I have nothing left to give, Tarah, don't you see?"

"No." Plain and simple. "I don't see."

"I hit you."

"You, wait...what?" She looked at him uncomprehendingly. "You didn't hit me. I'd remember if you hit me."

"Your jaw...I saw what I did."

"Fuck, you were having a nightmare. You didn't mean anything by it."

"But don't you see? That's why they never stay the night. That's why I never sleep with women. God, Tarah, I'm capable of such violence."

She was thunderstruck. "You think it's genetic, don't you? You think because he was violent and abusive, you will be as well? Goddamn it, Sebastian, you are one of the gentlest men I know."

"Then you mustn't know many men, because every time I was with you, I was brutal."

"There is a world of difference between enthusiastic and brutal. You're vigorous and a challenge to keep up with, but I love that about you. You pushed me to feel when no one else gave a damn if I crawled into a hole and stayed there for the rest of my life. Christ Jesus, Sebastian, you gave me a life when I never had one before. You can't show me what my life can be like and then yank it away from me. That's below the fucking belt."

His face had an odd look. "You love that I'm rough

with you?"

Trust him to have noticed *that* part of her diatribe. "Yes, I love it when you're rough with me. When you push me I'm alive. When I'm without you, I'm a hollow void. I don't care about school. I don't care about the kids. All I can do is obsess because I had it all and lost it because I asked you to trust me."

"To trust…"

"If I hadn't pushed you that night…if I hadn't comforted you, none of this would have happened." She was back to yelling. "I made you vulnerable, and you hated it. And you hated me for making you relive it."

"I don't hate you—"

She went right on as if he hadn't interrupted. "And I let you push me out of your life without a fight. I took the new condo and the bank account and didn't even send you a fucking thank-you card. Veronique told me I had to be patient and you'd be back, but I'm tired of being patient. I'm tired of being the good girl. We might've had fourteen days together, but you promised me one hundred and eighty. By my count, you owe me…"

Shit. Why hadn't she counted this out in advance?

"One hundred and sixty-six—" They spoke simultaneously. A look passed between them, and she fought for it.

"I want my days. I want what you promised. And then, Goddamn it, I want more."

"More?" Now *he* amped up the volume. "You want more from me? Fuck, Tarah, I gave you my heart—what more do you want? My soul? Well it's yours too. Everything I have and everything I am—I'm willing to give to you."

Surely, she'd misunderstood. She gaped like a

landed fish. She fought to unscramble her brain. "Wait, I have your heart and soul, and you sent me away? How the fuck does that work?"

"I only sent you away because I love you. I promised myself I'd never again hurt someone I love, and I'd never love someone who might hurt me. You're both. You can hurt me, and I love you."

"Then why did you send me away?"

"Because I couldn't bear to hurt you." His expression was pure anguish. He reached out for her chin but pulled back at the last moment. "And I wanted to know if you'd come back on your own. I wanted to know if you wanted me for the money or for me."

"I will give you back every single thing you've given to me and go back to my shithole apartment and crappy life if it'll prove to you that your money means nothing. It's empty, Sebastian. Without you, it's nothing." She blew out a long sigh. "I love you too, you know."

He rolled his eyes. "Well, when you say it like that, it makes me want to drop to my knees and propose."

"Or stick a collar around my neck." She offered the suggestion helpfully. This entire conversation was surreal, and her throat hurt. She swallowed painfully. "Can I get a glass of water?"

"I'll get it for you."

He left, sucking all the wind from her. How had she ever thought she could live without him? He was oxygen to her. She needed him to keep going, and that scared the shit out of her. But she was so close. She couldn't give up now.

She sensed Sebastian come up behind her. As she was turning, he reached around her neck and clicked the collar into place.

She should fight him. So much unsaid, so much unresolved…but none of that mattered. She wore his collar, and that meant everything.

He tugged on the collar and pulled her back against him. "You're wearing entirely too many clothes."

"Yes, Sir, I am." She smiled because he couldn't see her. "And what are you going to do about it?"

His hand threaded through her hair, and he yanked on it. Hard.

Liquid pooled between her thighs. God, how she'd missed this.

"Go strip. I want you ready for inspection."

"Yes, Sir." She practically ran to the dungeon.

He was hot on her heels but not fast enough.

When she flipped on the torch lights, her breath caught. Clothes strewn everywhere. Half the toys had been thrown around the room in what she'd guess had been a fit of anger.

The place was a mess.

And she couldn't have been happier.

She wasn't the only one who'd been suffering.

"You must clean this up." His whisper in her ear sent shivers up and down her spine.

"I'll do it on my hands and knees, Sir, and thank you for the pleasure."

Numb fingers dropped her purse and struggled to unbutton her coat. With deliberate care, she put it on the chair. She sat and began removing her boots.

"If you're not naked in the next thirty seconds, there are going to be consequences."

"You mean I might get punished?" She didn't hide the pleasure in her voice.

"Later, Mia." His eyes were black. "If I'm not in you inside the next minute, I think I'll die."

She pulled her sweater over her head and flicked open the button of her jeans. She paused and pointed. "I'm not the only one who's wearing too many clothes."

His eyebrow quirked, and he smirked. "I wasn't specific on which part of you I wanted to be in."

Grinning, she shed her clothes as quickly as possible. She liked how he thought. As soon as she was naked, she dropped to her knees.

"You may service me."

The order ricocheted through her, and she grew damp. Could he smell her? Did he know how much she needed this? Eager hands opened the button of his jeans. She slid down his fly and licked her lips when his cock sprang out. He'd gone commando today. Probably no clean underwear, if the mess in this place was any indication.

Leaning forward, she darted her tongue to touch the slit, lapping up a drop of pre-cum. The taste rolled over her tongue as she sized up how best to approach this rather enormous problem. Starting at the base, she lazily nibbled up toward the head. As she did, she took his balls in her hands. Gently, she rolled them, weighing them, honoring them, worshiping them. Remembering the special spot he'd shown her, she pressed her thumb behind his sac.

Now she took him into her mouth, inch by delicious inch. Her jaw flexed as she welcomed him into her. Swirling her tongue, she created gentle suction to draw him out.

"I can't take this anymore." His words were a hoarse and harsh whisper. He took her cheeks in his hands and thrust into her.

As he fucked her face, the secret thrill enveloped her because this was exactly what she'd wanted. Neither of them needed tenderness in this moment, and she reveled in the ferocity of his thrusts. Tears streamed down her face, and she struggled to breathe through her nose, but she was more alive in this moment than she'd been in weeks.

He shouted he was coming moments before his hot semen hit the back of her throat. *Mind over matter.* She swallowed eagerly and greedily because she appreciated the gift of being able to serve.

Pulling back from her mouth, he pressed a hand to the crown of her head. "Mia, you did wonderfully."

She tipped her head up and met his hooded gaze. "I'm honored you let me serve you, Sir."

His thumbs traced the tracks of her tears. "I think maybe it's time for me to turn the tables on you."

A frisson snaked up her spine. "I'm here for your pleasure, Sir."

"Lie on the middle of the bed."

Rising from her knees without using her hands, she made her way over to the bed. She scooted to the middle of the bed and laid her head on a pillow.

Watching him strip, she crossed her legs, attempting to tamp the need coursing through her.

"Have you been touching yourself?"

She met his eyes. "Every day." *Without fail.* "And cursing you."

"Mia, you surprise me. Why would you curse me?"

"Because I didn't want to touch myself. I had no desire, but I'd made a commitment to you." She shuddered. "Days passed when it'd take me forever to come. I'd be sore but would push through."

"Weren't you fantasizing about me?"

She snickered. "I was thinking about what I'd do to your balls if I ever got hold of them."

An eyebrow quirked. "You had hold of my balls just now."

"It's probably a good thing I've forgiven you for your deplorable treatment of me. Otherwise, you might've wound up singing soprano."

"Again."

"Again." Another glorious memory. "But tonight all I wanted was to forget what you put me through and show my gratitude."

"Well, you did an outstanding job, Mia. And I'm proud you followed my instructions even when you didn't have to."

She offered another shrug. "It never occurred to me to disobey. You told me I could learn more about myself if I did this. So I did it."

"And what did you learn about yourself?"

Well... "That I'm stronger than I thought. That if I have to do it alone, I can, but it's much more fun to share." She pulled her lower lip through her teeth. "Tell me I won't have to be alone again."

His look was deep and dark. "I can't be your everything. There will still be times when you'll need to be strong."

"And you've proven to me I can be strong. But you've also shown me what a life of submission looks like. What a life of fulfillment looks like." This conversation was taking a dark turn, and she needed to lighten things up. She licked her lips as she surveyed his naked form. "You were saying something about turning the tables on me?"

Stepping forward, he took one of her wrists in his hand. He secured her with the shackle attached to the bedpost. In response, she rubbed her thighs together, seeking to silence the urgent need flowing through her.

He tisked as he rounded the bed and repeated the process with her other arm.

She enjoyed this. As she settled back into the pillow and the mattress, the air had the slightest of chills that cooled her heated skin. God, but she wanted him, and now he was the one taking his time. Retribution for when she'd purposely dawdled earlier.

Sitting on the side of the bed, he snagged her ankles. Instead of shackling them, he urged her to bend her knees, bringing them to her ass. Then he urged her knees to float down to the mattress.

She flexed her hips to find a more comfortable position, and the chilled air touched her pussy. She sucked in a breath. He might be a sadist, but he wouldn't make her wait for too long.

He crawled onto the bed and placed himself between her thighs. He gave her a wicked grin and whispered, "Time to cross off another item from the list." He parted her nether lips.

She knew what he was going to do—he'd explained this when they'd been preparing the list—but the reality was much more than she could've expected. The first time he laved her, she nearly bucked him off. Since she was already sensitive, the friction from his tongue was almost unbearable.

As he pressed the tip of his tongue against her, he hit her clit. She offered a prayer to a deity when he sucked and nipped. Those little electrical shocks shot through her, leaving her gasping for air. Somehow, all those lonely days alone with just her hand for company didn't compare to his talented tongue. Nothing came close. It never would.

And then, with the slightest effort on his part, her body rose toward the climax she was familiar with. Heat suffused her body as she let go. Falling over was easy, so she did.

Waves of pleasure enveloped her, capturing her body in some vortex of bliss, and drifted away. The mattress dipped when he stood, and although disappointed, she was still grateful for the gift she'd been given.

"Thank you, Sir." Her whisper was reverential, her eyes still shut as if she could keep hold of this contentment.

When the mattress dipped again, signaling his return, her body hummed. She'd suspected they weren't finished. She opened her eyes and immediately widened them. "That's a…"

"Vibrator." His dark eyes shone with glee. "A small one, but in this case, size doesn't matter." He studied her. "You know, I think you'll enjoy this more if you can't move."

She yanked at the manacles. "I'd say I can't move."

He touched her knees, then rose. When he returned, he held two thick pieces of rubber.

She was intrigued as he tied her thigh to her calf. She tested it and found she couldn't move. When he repeated the process, she tested the bonds. "Sir knows how to tie a girl."

He quirked an eyebrow. "You may not be thanking me when we're done."

Not sure about that. She shook her head. "I will always thank Sir for his attentions."

"Was it so bad to be away? I mean, you had time to yourself…"

Don't cry. "I started working at a daycare. Two days a week, and it won't affect my studies—despite that, I thought I'd be happy. The kids were amazingly welcoming, and I told myself it'd be enough. It *should* have been enough. But I'd come home to an empty apartment, and no amount of exercise, studying, or reading could stop the memories." She sniffed, valiantly keeping the tears at bay. "That kind of hurt goes to the marrow, and it nearly broke me. There'll be times when I'll be alone, but I dread them."

He winced, his face contorting. "I thought I was doing what was best for you. I want you to achieve all your goals, and if you focused too much on serving me, I might hold you back."

God save me from stupid men. "I'm used to working full time, volunteering, and studying part time. The schedule you set up worked for me, even if it took me time to adapt to it. You showed me I can serve you at night while studying and volunteering during the day. It never occurred to me that you might keep me from achieving my goals." She paused. "Now, are you going to do something? Because my legs are aching, and my pussy is awfully exposed."

The glint was back in his eyes. "A little suffering is good for the soul."

Shit. Why hadn't she kept her mouth shut?

Yet even as she had the thought, he was back on the bed, positioning himself between her thighs. He crawled up her body, placing his thigh against her pussy and grinding. He took her breast in his mouth, and all rational thought fled.

He nibbled, nipped, sucked. He did all the things that elicited little sighs of pleasure. Making sure one breast didn't feel neglected, he moved to her other nipple. Already hardened into a peak, it appreciated the attention he paid it.

She tried to pull her thighs together, but he simply chuckled against her breast and bit. Her thighs immediately dropped back to the bed. Flexing her hips, she tried to find purchase against his thigh, but he held it just beyond the reach of her clit. She let out a breath of frustration as her body begged for a second release he was unwilling to give her. Would the feelings never cease? She took more deep breaths. *Mind over matter.*

With lightning speed, he removed his body from hers, and although she missed the contact, she enjoyed the cool air against her heated skin. Her relief was short lived as a buzzing sound replaced the silence. Intellectually, she'd known what he was going to do. Still, when he pressed the little bullet against her clit, she yelped.

"Now, I don't want you to come."

Her head snapped up, and she met his eyes. Was he serious? "You think I can control this?" Already her body was reacting to the vibrations being shot through her.

"Oh, you can. You're a strong-willed woman, Tarah, and you can control your body." His grin was quick and wicked. "I expect you to rein in your desire for release. Breathe through it, Mia."

"Why?" she wailed, not caring how it sounded.

Now he chuckled. "Because I told you I control your

orgasms. You thought they were just pretty words, but I was serious."

The pressure building in her overwhelmed, and she was powerless to stop it. As her body gathered, just about to tip over, he removed the vibrator.

She took a deep breath and tried to snap her thighs shut so he couldn't get near the impossibly sensitive tissue again. With the bands, however, she was stymied. For her trouble, he chuckled again.

"Maybe this time I might let you come."

That was all the warning she got before the wicked buzz resumed, and the vibe hit her clit. She barely had time to breathe before her body bore down. "Damn it, Sebastian, I'm coming."

He flicked a switch, and the machine notched up, making it unbearable.

She came.

He continued to hold it against her clit as she tried to flex her hips to get away from the vibrator. Now it hurt, but her body didn't care. Instead of fighting, she gave in to it. Heat suffused her, and a languor replaced the tension she'd been carrying when she was holding out. Now that she no longer fought, the pain was manageable.

He flipped off the wretched machine and hit her sensitized clit with the palm of his hand.

"You'll pay for disobedience."

"Whatever the price." Her heart was close to bursting. "I'm willing to pay it."

"Enjoyed yourself, did you?" Amusement tinged his voice. "Well, I think you're well lubricated."

That was her last lucid thought as he drove into her. She tried to pull away, but he was ruthless. His thrusts were quick—following in rapid succession. He used his hips to drive her thighs even farther apart, and impossibly, he seated himself even deeper into her. They were so close their pelvises fused as one.

Sweat dripped, dampening her hair. Her arms ached as she pulled against the restraints, desperate to touch him. Whether to push him away or pull him closer, she wasn't sure. She was achy but in an enjoyable way. Her body had missed this almost as much as her soul had.

She wouldn't have believed she had another orgasm in her, but he ruthlessly forced one from her. Her body clamped down on him hard, and he let out a growl and pressed in as far as he could. He bowed back and came right along with her.

She could think of nothing more glorious than simultaneous orgasms. Now that the exchange of pleasure was complete, she knew there was nothing more powerful in the world.

He collapsed on her, his weight a reassuring presence. His mouth pressed to her neck, and he nipped. "I'm not sure I can move." And he didn't try. "That was fucking amazing."

Hearing something like that from him made her heart sing. She didn't want to think about the women who'd come before her, but she wanted confirmation of something special with the man who had her heart, her love, and her devotion.

Without leaving her, he uncuffed her. He slid his hands up her thighs and released the rubber binding her legs.

She flexed her legs and her pelvis, then put her legs around his waist and held him in place. "Merry Christmas, Sir."

He pulled back to meet her gaze. "Merry Christmas, Mia. I have to admit this is the best Christmas present I've ever received."

She placed her hands on his cheeks and pulled him in for a kiss. What began as tender and gentle soon became more insistent. His tongue explored her, but instead of it being easy, it demanded.

What? He was still inside her and was getting hard. Again. *How the hell is this even possible?* "I thought…I mean, you know, don't you need time…"

He gazed into her eyes, and one of his hands stroked the damp hair away from her forehead. "Normally, yes. With you, though, I seem to need less recovery time. Shorter refractory period."

"Well, I need some time." In truth, her voice lacked conviction. Surely, she wouldn't be up for another round anytime soon, would she?

"There is something you can do for me."

"Anything." *You only have to ask.*

He pressed a kiss to her lips. "Those muscles around my cock? Could you move them?"

What? She stared at him in complete bafflement. When he moved a fraction of an inch, she understood his meaning. She closed her eyes and focused on her pelvis. Experimentally, she squeezed.

"That's it." The words were ground out. "Remind me later to explain about Kegels…" His voice trailed off when she clamped down around him.

She didn't care about Kegels or anything else. All she cared about was the hard cock in her.

He reached down to where their bodies met and pressed his finger to her clit. Desire she'd believed extinguished reignited. Muscles she'd believed exhausted rejoiced.

This time, the coupling was slow and gentle. The pace was languid, as if they had all the time in the world. And they did. Gradually, her body began to crest. She nipped at his earlobe, but he refused to increase the pace. Instead, he wrought from her an exquisite and breath-stealing orgasm that went on and on and on. This time she could wrap her arms around him and hold him to her. Keep him close. Like forever, if he'd let her.

When he came and emptied himself inside her, it healed her broken heart.

He placed his mouth to her ear, letting his warm breath tickle her. "I love you, Mia."

Chapter Fifteen

Sanity returned slowly but surely. Sebastian finally levered himself off her but dragged her along with him. She was half sprawled on him, their legs intertwined and her head pillowed on his chest. He gently toyed with her hair.

"I called a psychologist."

She tensed but didn't turn to face him. He needed her close but not too close.

"She's good. Both Rielle and Alessandra have seen her, so Smith had no qualms about giving me her name. She's out in Mission City, but I plan to see her Saturday mornings. Her name is Kennedy Dixon."

Swallowing the lump in her throat, she sought the right words. "I'm proud of you. It's hard to admit you can't do it alone."

The rumble in his chest was rueful or amused. "I've seen her twice already. I told her about you. About how I hurt you."

Now she rounded on him, turning her head to meet his gaze. "For God's sake, give up that bullshit notion. You didn't mean to hurt me. The bruise healed, and no one was the wiser. I withstood that, and I'd withstand more to stand beside you." She gave him a shy smile. "Well, maybe not beside you, but kneeling at your feet."

His expression was so sober, so serious, her heart went out to him.

"On this, Tarah, I need someone to stand next to me. In all other things I can be dominant but not with this. Kennedy said it's okay to lean on someone who is strong enough. I...um, got some pamphlets for partners of abuse survivors. My father abused me, Tarah, and I need to admit I didn't deserve it. I'd give my life to bring my family back, but I can't, and I have to find a way to live with that."

She scooted up and tucked her head against his neck. "There are no conditions on my support. I'll read the books. I'll do whatever it takes to prove I love you too."

He placed a kiss to her forehead. "I never thought...I mean, I always believed I was going to be alone." He fingered the collar around her neck. "Would you mind terribly if I asked you to wear my collar? Not this leather one, of course, I'll get something more subtle and elegant."

"But I can wear this one when I'm home, right?"

Chuckling, he ran his hand up and down her back. "I insist on it. I'd also prefer you wear fewer clothes."

Now her turn to laugh. "You'll have to jack up the heat."

"I can do that, Mia."

She levered herself up on one elbow. "What time is it?"

He checked his watch. "About three a.m. Why?"

"Because I'm starving. I was so nervous and angry earlier I barely ate anything at dinner." She placed a finger on Sebastian's jaw. "What did you eat?"

He gazed deeply into her eyes. "Not much since you've been gone. It's been sustenance, and not enjoyment, that's kept me going. I probably had a microwaved meal."

"You're hungry now?"

"Yes, I think I've worked up an appetite." He grinned. "Are you offering to cook?"

"Do you want food poisoning?"

"Um, let me think about that. Uh, no."

She pushed off him and rolled out of bed. "I was thinking about popcorn."

He looked at her disbelievingly. "We just went through horizontal gymnastics, and you want popcorn?"

"With lots of salt and butter."

"Whatever the lady wants, she can have." He squinted in skepticism. "Do I even have popcorn?"

"Since I bought some, the answer would be yes. You have a popcorn maker." She offered the information helpfully.

"Have at it." He put his hands behind his head and settled in. "I'm staying here."

Her heart soared. "We can eat popcorn in bed?"

"As long as you wash the sheets, we can do whatever you want." He quirked an eyebrow. "But if you spill the popcorn, not only will you have to clean it up, but there'll be a punishment."

She tipped her imaginary hat and went to the bathroom. A quick pass of the washcloth and she felt almost human. Limbs previously heavy now were light. Looking in the mirror, she wasn't surprised to find her face still flushed. How many orgasms had he pulled from her? Four? Five? It didn't seem possible. He might try to portray himself as selfish, but he was the most giving man in her acquaintance.

Pulling on his bathrobe that swamped her tiny frame, she padded to the kitchen. Sebastian wasn't the only one who hadn't been eating well. The hotel offered a vast variety of food, but she'd stuck to fruit and either shrimp or chicken salad, but even that'd been a struggle. She'd probably lost a bit of weight, but like everything else, it hadn't mattered.

This infatuation with Sebastian wasn't healthy, but if she was wearing his collar, her fears were alleviated, at least for the moment. He was encouraging her to continue to be independent so she wouldn't be reliant on him. What had he said? He couldn't be her everything. Well, she didn't expect him to be. She just enjoyed being with him rather than being without him.

Making popcorn and melting the butter in the microwave took little time. She made two bowls, one slathered with butter while the other had a sprinkling. After grabbing two napkins, she made her way back to the dungeon.

His eyes were closed, but he wasn't asleep. His magnetism carried across the room and hit her like a jolt of electricity.

As if sensing it, his eyes snapped open, and his lips curled lazily upward. "I'm smelling something delicious."

Waiting until he sat up, she handed him the bowl and a napkin. "Try not to make a mess." Her heart wasn't in the admonishment. She liked his corrections, his penalties, his punishments. She enjoyed knowing he cared enough to want to make her a better person. Sitting lotus style, she dug in to her popcorn, closing her eyes in bliss.

"If this is all it takes to get that look on your face, I'll make popcorn every day."

Her eyes opened, and she was met with his sparkling ones. "I might tire of popcorn every day, but how about every other day?"

The laughter rolled off him easily, and it warmed her.

"Did you sign the contract with Mercy and Shelley?"

"I did." His chest puffed a bit. "The rollout will be the first week of February."

"That quick?"

Sebastian nodded. "They put together the other seven packages in an amazingly quick time. Still, the quality was excellent." He tapped her temple. "I would've preferred to have your input, Mia, but I have the mock-ups in my office. Maybe we can look them over? They don't go to the press for another week, so changes are still possible."

She flushed under the assumption she might have something to contribute. "I'll look at them, but I'm not sure if I'll have anything constructive to add. Or that it would be appreciated."

"Oh, Mia, you should have seen the look on Mercy and Shelley's faces when I told them you were no longer working on the project."

"Really? I mean, I didn't think…"

"No, you didn't. You didn't give yourself enough credit. We're going to have to work on that." He pressed a finger to her nose.

When he pulled it back, she shot forward and nipped it. And upturned her bowl of popcorn. "Oh, shit!"

"Language, Mia."

Was he serious? "This from the man who called it *fucking semantics* and let rip at least a dozen f-bombs."

"More like half a dozen, but who was counting?" He wagged his finger. "And you were as bad, if not worse."

Her heart took a knock as she sobered. "I'm sorry. I mean, I'll take out a billboard telling everyone I'm not knocked up…"

His grin was wide and toothy. "Maybe it's good I'm the center of a rumor. It might upgrade my reputation when I'm seen courting you."

"They might notice when there's no baby eight months from now."

"By then the furor will have died down." His smile didn't diminish. "People have short memories. I hear the bad boy of rock 'n' roll will be staying in the building while he records his new album. I guarantee he'll be the center of all things gossipy within days of his arrival."

"Dare I ask who it is?"

Sebastian dropped the name.

She looked at him blankly. "I know little about these things."

"I'll download one of his albums for you, and you'll appreciate why I love the opera."

Her gaze softened. "I loved the opera."

"I have acquired season tickets for two."

"And if I hadn't come back? Would you have gone by yourself?"

The shake of his head was quick and sharp. "You think I'd want to sit there and think about how lonely I am? Hell, no. I would've donated the tickets to charity."

"Could you do that anyway? I mean, buy more tickets and donate them to charity?"

"For you, Mia, anything. Heck, I'll become a patron of the opera if it would make you happy."

Her eyes welled with tears. "It'd make me thrilled." She whispered the words reverently.

"Plus—" He waggled his eyebrows. "—it's a tax

write-off."

She lobbed a piece of popcorn and pinged it off his forehead.

It landed on his chest, and he popped it into his mouth. "The question is whether to punish you now or in the morning."

"What would be your pleasure?"

His grin was quick and wicked. "Both."

She squirmed as liquid pooled between her thighs. "Is it wrong for me to get turned on by that?"

Sebastian shook his head. "I told you submission can occur without sex, but it's awfully fun to add sex to the mix. Your body will come to associate the two."

"Like Pavlov's dog." Was she comparing herself to a dog?

"Exactly like Pavlov's dog." His expression was smug. "And I love that you know that little fun fact."

"I studied hard in first year psych class, and I got an *A*."

He reached for her empty bowl, put it with his nearly empty bowl, and placed them on the nightstand. Before she could reach for her napkin, he grabbed her wrist and tugged. She tumbled forward into his lap. The tips of her toes tingled as he licked each of her fingers.

"It just occurred to me that you're a southpaw."

"Left-handed in a world made for right-handed people. It can be a challenge." When he licked her fingers, her belly was full of butterflies.

"I found it interesting to watch you masturbate with your left hand."

"Well, now I'm proficient enough I can do it with both hands." At his quirked eyebrow, she shrugged. "I had to mix it up. To find ways to be creative."

"I like your idea of creativity." He raked a searing gaze over her body. "Now I think it's time for your punishment."

Again, she squirmed.

He rolled off the bed and loomed above her. "I want you on all fours with your ass hanging over the bed."

Didn't sound ominous, so she maneuvered herself exactly as directed. She wasn't prepared, however, when he smacked her ass.

He pressed his hand against the mark and squeezed. "Your ass is now a beautiful shade of pink."

"Are you going to mark it some more?"

"Not tonight, Mia." He paused. "Tonight I have other plans."

Holding herself steady, she waited patiently. Well, patiently might've been a stretch. She wanted whatever he was going to give her, but she knew he'd do it in his own time.

A snick as a bottle opened, a squishy sound, and soon a cold dollop of gel on her asshole.

Oh. This was his nefarious plan. First going down on her, and now taking her anal virginity. Could a girl get so lucky?

He started with one finger, but she was uncomfortable. He pressed his other hand to her back, rubbing it up and down her spine. "This can be a pleasurable experience, or this can be a very painful one."

"I like the sound of pleasure." She gritted her teeth, grinding out the words. "I choose that option."

"Then you need to follow my instructions carefully. You have to relax."

"With your finger up my ass?"

He chuckled. "Oh, we're just getting started."

As she flashed to the size of his dick, her sphincter clenched. "It's not going to fit."

Another chuckle. "I'm not going to do that to you tonight, Mia. We'll start small and work our way up."

She didn't ask how he knew what she referred to.

More lube was added, and he rimmed her with a finger. He used his other hand to continue to stroke up and down her spine. "Now, you need to relax, Mia. You need to let my finger slide into you without resistance."

Easier said than done, but still she concentrated on her breathing. She wasn't surprised when he added another finger. She was feeling used and abused and a bit aroused.

"Okay, Mia, I need you to take a deep breath."

She obeyed. His fingers pulled out, and something solid slid against her.

"Exhale slowly."

She obeyed. And sucked in a breath as he pressed something rock hard into her ass. Nothing gentle about it. He was ruthless, and pain rocketed through her body. After a *pop*, the plug wasn't being pushed any farther into her.

"Your instinct will be to bear down, but don't." The hand that had never left her back continued its strokes. "You need to keep your muscles relaxed and breathe through the discomfort. Soon your body will acclimate to the…intrusion."

She shot up on her haunches and rounded on him. "Intrusion? It's like an anal probe."

"Anal plug, actually, and it's serving a purpose."

She rolled her eyes. "Dare I ask?"

"It's preparatory. I could've taken you right then and

there, but I'm not a cruel man."

That assertion was highly debatable, but she bit back a retort. If she was hurting now, how much worse could it have been?

Sebastian walked over to the wall of pain and picked up a piece of plastic. "This is a larger version of what I put in you."

Now she gaped. "The one in my ass is smaller? Are you sure?"

His brow arched, and he grinned wickedly. "I have three sizes, and I gave you the smallest one."

Her insides clenched. "Promise me you'll never go bigger than this. I mean, this is enough, okay?"

He tisked. "I make no such promise, Mia. Trust me to know what's best for you."

She bit back another nasty comment. Then a realization dawned. "You expect me to sleep with this thing in my ass? That's crazy. I'll never sleep like this."

"Oh, Mia, you can and you will. Now, let's get you into bed."

She reclined and was settling in when he scooped her into his arms and made for the door. Immediately, she fought him. "You're not sending me away. If I go to the white room, you have to stay with me. You're not leaving me alone, goddamn it, and that's a hard limit."

He eased her from his arms, down along his body. When her feet touched the ground, he took her cheeks in his hands. "Tarah, the last time we slept together, the night ended as an unmitigated disaster."

"So what? The nightmare was after you had relived all of it. I'd think, after tonight's exertions, you'll sleep like a baby."

"But what if I don't? What if I hurt you again? God,

Tarah, I'd never be able to live with myself."

"Then let me sleep on the pallet. If you go the entire night without a nightmare, tomorrow I get to share your bed." In return, she placed her hands to his cheeks. "This is a hard limit for me, Sebastian." If he was using her given name, she'd do the same. "You said I could stay, and I intend to stay."

"But the pallet…"

"Is good for my back." She pressed a finger to his frown line. "Plus, you're not going to have a nightmare, and by tomorrow night I'll be sleeping in a nice big bed. Sharing an enormous bed." She pulled him down for a soul-searing kiss. "Now, I'm going to get the sheets and comforter."

"You'll need a pillow, and you're going to help me change my sheets. I sure as shit am not sleeping in grease and waking up smelling like popcorn."

"But I love popcorn." She licked her lips. "I might be obliged to lick it off."

"By all means, in the morning, you can cover my cock in butter. Tonight, however, you're going to help me change the sheets."

The entire process took about fifteen minutes, and then she settled down on the pallet. The bed wasn't as uncomfortable as she remembered, and every time she lay on her back, the plug seated itself deeper. She'd flex her hips to find a more comfortable position, but that was wasted effort. How she was going to get any sleep was beyond her, so she was startled when Sebastian hauled her into his bed.

"What time is it?" She was grumbling but didn't care.

"Noon." He gave her rump a slap. "Now, go have a

pee and come back."

An impish grin crossed her face. "May I remove Sir's toy?"

"No, you may not." He smacked her again. "And every minute you're away, the punishment will lengthen by that amount of time. Do I make myself clear?"

She didn't even respond as she ran from the room.

Ablutions completed in record time, she returned to the dungeon. Full-on daylight flooded the condo despite the gray day. He'd left the blinds open last night, not that she was going anywhere near the windows. She wasn't an exhibitionist.

He waited for her, buck naked and fully erect, a bottle of lube in his hand.

"Sir, I think you're going to be too big for me." She had to try, right? But then stopped when he gave her a warning look.

"Sir appreciates you worship his cock, but nothing you say will change the course of events this morning. I suggest you remember to practice your breathing and show your gratitude I gave you the night to prepare."

Her head bobbed. "Oh, Sir, I am grateful. Your consideration of my anal region is appreciated."

Lightning quick, he tossed the bottle on the bed and reached for her. He smacked her on the ass and thrust her toward the bed. "Same rules as before, Mia. Take the position."

Okay, she'd pushed a little too far. She got on her hands and knees on the mattress, sticking her ass in the air. Where she expected him to just pull the plug and plunge into her, she was surprised as those big hands gently explored her back. Fingertips sprinkled down as gentle as drops of rain, and she arched into the pressure.

His fingers rounded her ass and gently kneaded her cheeks. Where she expected pain, none emerged.

When his fingers delved between her thighs, she sucked in a breath. She was wet, willing, and ready to go. He let out one of his devilish chuckles as he worked her juices around her labia, touching her everywhere except where she needed it the most.

"Please," she begged, not caring if she sounded pathetic or not. "I need you."

His finger pressed against her and worked all kinds of magic. Her arms could no longer hold her up, and her elbows bent, landing her face-first into the mattress. It didn't hurt, but it meant she was no longer trying to balance on shaky limbs.

He pushed her higher and higher. Resistance was futile. "Please, Sir." The words were said through gritted teeth. "Let me come."

A few more flicks of his magic fingers. "You may come now."

She wasted no time in letting her body fall off the precipice. He was a musician, and she was his instrument. He knew her intimately and how to pull out every note with precision and grace. Then, as he milked her contractions, he withdrew the plug.

The relief was instantaneous, but a strange emptiness also settled. Overnight, she'd grown accustomed to the plug, and now she missed its presence. *Not for long*. It wouldn't be long before—

Sebastian's cold lubed fingers pressed inside of her. She had to make a conscious effort to relax, but his approval came through the fingertips massaging the small of her back.

He pulled both hands away, and the familiar sound

of lube being squeezed out of a plastic bottle again reached her ears. She chanced a glance over her shoulder and saw him applying the lube and fisting himself. He was huge. *It'll all be over soon.*

Or maybe not, given his stamina.

When his tip probed her, she tried to sigh into it.

"The first part is the worst, little one."

Little one? A reference to her or her ass?

He pressed against her, and she tried to ride the pain. Yes, painful. By the time the *pop* came, she was being torn in two. Tears filled her eyes. *You love him. You'll always share this.*

His movements were slow and deliberate, each withdrawal, then each thrust accompanied by soothing words and strokes. Soon her body was reacting to those magic fingers as much as she was reacting to the big cock. His hand delved between her thighs again.

He expected her to come? He must be out of his mind.

"You can do it, Mia." He was cooing, clearly having anticipated her refusal, her denial.

"I can't, Sir—it's not possible."

"You can and you will." His words were firm, timed with deliberateness to his thrusts.

Despite herself, her body reacted. She ground into his magic finger, focusing on the sensations being elicited as opposed to everything else going on in her body.

"Come, Mia." His words were encouraging. "Let go and feel it."

Seriously?

Insanity. The man was insane. No way could her body feel pleasure with the discomfort overwhelming her. Not possible.

Yet, like Pavlov's dog, her body reacted to the pain. Not so much that it became pleasure, but enough that the edge eased off. Not instantaneous, and it took a bit of work, but her body pulled up and let go. Pleasure washed over her as she arched into the contact. The contractions of her orgasm were so strong they shuddered through her.

Sebastian snagged her waist and thrust into her repeatedly. Tears stung her eyes, but they weren't tears of pain—they were tears of release. He pulled her hips to him and held himself in place.

The shudders transferred from him to her, and she reveled in them. Pride swelled in her that she'd withstood and, in the end, enjoyed losing her anal virginity. Just like before, it'd hurt and then been okay.

Tumbling to the bed, he left room for her to collapse onto her side, and he pulled her close. Their feet dangled over the side of the bed, they were sweaty and likely to chill quickly, but she didn't give a shit. His arm protectively held her tight, his breath warm against her neck. He lifted his head and bit her shoulder.

"Ouch, what was that for?"

"I'm marking you, Mia."

Even though he couldn't see, she rolled her eyes. "I think you've already done that, Sir."

"Master." He said the word quietly.

She turned in his arms, meeting his dark gaze.

"Once I collar you, I'd like you to call me *Master*. If it's okay with you, of course."

She cupped his cheek. "I'd be honored. Since I'm wearing your collar now, would it be okay if I started now?" She knew what a big step this was in their relationship.

He leaned over and placed a kiss to her lips. "Mia, nothing would bring me greater pleasure than for you to call me *Master*."

"Nothing?" She smiled wickedly. "Because I remember something about melted butter and a cock."

He groaned. "Not going to happen right now, Mia, but we'll keep it in mind for another day. After all"—he returned her wicked grin—"I know how much you love buttered popcorn." He kissed her, this time thrusting his tongue into her mouth.

The kiss was passionate and demanding, and she didn't hide her response.

He pulled back and looked at her with mock horror. "You're insatiable."

She guided his hand to her mound, an open invitation. "Just once more, Master. Then I'll be a good girl."

He quirked an eyebrow as his hand slid down her hips and between her thighs. She let her knees fall open and was pleased when he growled. *Seems he isn't the only one who knows how to play this game.* Awkwardly, he levered himself, his hand working magic with her clit while his mouth worked magic with her breasts. At times he could be reverential and gentle, but fortunately, this wasn't one of them. He nipped and bit hard, drawing a gasp from her.

Pleasure pulsed through her, threatening to take her away again. She ran her hands through his thick and silky hair, holding him to her breasts. They were sensitive, and his ministrations caused an ache. A good ache. Then she climbed again, this time to a place she was becoming well acquainted with.

"Oh God, Master, I'm coming."

When he bit her nipple extra hard, she took it as permission and let the climax rocket through her. His fingers pressed against her clit, as if holding her in place. Still, she bucked and tried to squirm away from his unrelenting presence. Her breathing was ragged as she fought to get oxygen into her lungs.

"Again." Another command.

The man had lost his ever-loving mind.

Her head thrashed back and forth, trying to deny and fight what her body was already climbing toward. She was sore, and this felt like work. On the other hand, she was good at work. Giving in one more time wouldn't be the end of the world, right? Alternately swearing and praising the deities, she orgasmed again.

This time, he let her go. Oh, he pulled her close to him and held her as if he couldn't bear to be parted from her, but he let her fall into the abyss of an apex so strong she didn't think she'd ever come back to earth.

As time passed and the tremors eased, he pressed a kiss to her forehead and laid the comforter across her. Her feet still dangled off the bed, but she didn't give a shit. She was warm in a way that only enveloped her in the afterglow of four mind-blowing orgasms. She'd never thought this would be possible. Multiple orgasms were the stuff of legends and male-created myths, right? Now she knew them to be true. In exchange, however, she found herself a little sore. But a good sore. Definitely a good sore.

Sebastian returned from his shower and went into the walk-in closet.

"I don't know why you're putting on clothes, Master, when I have all these wicked plans for you."

He chuckled. "Well, since you won't be wearing any clothes, you'll be happy to know I've raised the temperature." Something hit the bed next to her head. "I found this robe after you left."

She was *not* going to point out she hadn't left but had been summarily dismissed. She was too fucking happy to argue semantics. "It's a good thing you want me naked, because all my clothes are over at the hotel."

"Oh shit, I didn't think of that." He sat on the bed and pulled her head into his lap. "I hope you'll forgive me. And I hope Mme Veronique doesn't mind me calling her again."

"It's Boxing Day." She gave him a look of mock sternness. "How about we give the lady a day or two? I can wear my clothes from last night to go over and get a few necessities."

"Or you can stay here naked, and I can go get your necessities."

She gazed up at him. "As much as I appreciate the offer, I can manage. How about we go over together?"

Leaning over, he gave her a kiss. "After breakfast."

Wrinkling her nose, she did some mental calculations. "I think at one o'clock it's at least brunch if not lunch."

He tweaked her nose. "I'll give you that one. I'm making pancakes, so there's no rush. We'll eat, and you can have a shower."

"Or I can have a shower while you cook."

"Mia, are you seriously telling me you're ready to hop out of bed?"

She considered. "Breakfast in bed sounds good."

"Breakfast in bed you shall have. Just lie here, and I'll be back in a little while."

Snuggling farther under the comforter, she held on to the warmth of their love. "Yes, Master."

He left, and she closed her eyes.

****

The pounding on the door had her shooting out of bed. Sebastian hadn't closed the door to the dungeon, so she heard the sound echoing through the condo. God, had she been that loud last night? And to think he would've gone on ignoring her if she hadn't made the pregnancy threat.

She slipped on the robe, taking a moment to luxuriate in the satin against her skin. Only the best for Sebastian Merrick. She was pulling her hair into a ponytail when excited voices reached the dungeon. What was she supposed to do? Hide? Go greet the company? Find her clothes that were strewn everywhere?

"We're not taking *no* for an answer, Sebastian. You've been moping since your submissive left you, and it's time to stop."

The voice sounded familiar, but she was too miffed to give it much thought. She stepped into the hall and moved to the living room where she saw the backs of four individuals. Sebastian was on the other side, but he couldn't see her.

"His submissive didn't leave him—he sent her away."

All four guests spun around.

Uh, this might not have been the best course of action. Her gaze settled on Rielle. "What are you guys doing here?" She looked back and forth along the line Sebastian had now joined.

Rielle let out an ear-piercing scream, and Tarah spun around, searching for the reason for the outburst. Seeing nothing, she spun back, only to be pulled into a breath-stealing and fierce embrace by her friend.

"Oh my God, baby girl, you're Sebastian's submissive?"

Rielle's hands were all over her. Shoulders, arms, waist, then back up the arms, ending with her grasping Tarah's cheeks.

Tarah eyed her friend with some skepticism. "Do you think I'm not good enough for him?"

Now Alessandra stepped forward. "No, you're too young. You're too naïve."

She was about to respond when a god-almighty crash resonated. The painting had fallen to the floor because Gage had bodily thrown Sebastian against the wall and was now holding his arm against his windpipe.

"You fucking bastard. You chose Tarah? What the fuck were you thinking? She's an innocent. She knows nothing about the lifestyle. You had no right—"

She was about to step forward when Smith approached the other men, menace in his eyes. "We make you a bet, and you choose Tarah? That's fucking great."

Sebastian's gaze shot to her, and her stomach plummeted.

"A bet?" She closed her eyes for a moment, a growing despair gnawing her gut. "What's he talking about?"

"My stupid husband and his best friend bet Sebastian he could take a woman who was vanilla and turn her into a submissive." Now Rielle rounded on Sebastian. "A woman, you fuck, not a child. Gage is right—she's an innocent." She turned to Tarah. "It's not too late, right, baby girl? Let's get your things, and we'll take you home."

"This is my home." She said the words, but they lacked conviction. Her stare never left Sebastian's. "That's all I was to you? A bet?"

He wasn't fighting either Gage or Smith, telling her he'd done something wrong.

He tried to push Gage's arm from his neck, but the other man was strong. "It might've started out that way, Mia, but things changed. I changed."

Her temper flared red hot. "Never call me that." As quickly as it'd come, the flash of anger was gone. The lance across her breast staggered, and she was flayed open in front of her friends and the man she loved.

The man she'd thought she loved. Because no one she loved would hurt her this much. This hurt even more than when he'd sent her away.

She ducked her head. "My things are at the hotel—it's kind of a long story. Will you take me there?"

Rielle embraced her, almost smothering her in comfort. "Of course we will, baby girl. Where are your clothes?"

"In the dun—" She cleared her throat. "In the master bedroom."

"Okay." Rielle grasped her arm. "Allie and I will help you get organized." She propelled Tarah toward the dungeon.

When the women stepped into the room, her cheeks flamed. The butt plug and lube were clearly on display on the dresser, and the entire room reeked of sex. Oh, and chaos still reigned.

"What the fuck happened in here?" Allie's chocolate-brown eyes were wide in shock.

"I, um, it's really complicated, you know?" Tarah

snagged last night's discarded clothes. "Maybe I can explain on the way out of here?"

"Of course." Rielle offered the reassurance while helping Tarah gather her clothes. She and Allie turned their backs to give Tarah privacy, but they didn't leave her alone.

Once she'd secured her coat and grabbed her purse, she took a breath. "I'm ready."

The two older women spun.

The look of pity on Rielle's face was too much to bear, and Tarah tamped down the tears threatening to overflow. "Can we just get out of here?" Rielle's arm went around her shoulders, and she sagged into the proffered comfort.

When they entered the living room, Sebastian was no longer pinned to the wall, but Gage and Smith had put themselves firmly between him and the women.

"Just so we're clear," Gage said. "We're taking her away, and you are not to follow us."

Sebastian's eyes blazed in mutiny. "You can't prevent me from seeing her. She's an adult, and she can make her own choices."

"And she chooses to never see you again." She said the words quietly, even as her heart was breaking. The look on Sebastian's face almost—almost—had her rescinding her comment, but then she remembered what had put her in this situation in the first place.

A bet.

She laid the collar on the coffee table.

When Rielle and Alessandra bustled her out of the condo, she made no demur. When Gage and Smith followed, she walked, but found it a challenge. The fight had fled, leaving behind heartache and pain.

Gage was closing the condo door when another one opened.

Mrs. Wannamaker stepped out in the hallway, took in the group, and shook her fist. "You stay away from her."

Gage laughed and put his arm around Rielle. "It's too late."

Smith linked arms with Allie. "I put a ring on this one as well, so your warning went unheeded."

Undaunted, Mrs. Wannamaker shook her fist again. "You stay away from her." She went back into her apartment and closed the door.

The two couples laughed, leaving Tarah bewildered. Obviously, she wasn't in on this one.

Gage patted her back. "We'll explain it on the ride over to the hotel."

As soon as the doors of Gage's SUV were closed, however, Tarah, who sat in the back seat between Rielle and Allie, looked around. Really looked around.

Both women wore trench coats, and as far as Tarah could see, no sign of skirts or dresses. "Were you planning an orgy or something?"

The words were said in jest, but the heightened color on Gage's and Allie's cheeks told her she'd nailed it.

"Well, more like a foursome with Sebastian watching," Alessandra responded lamely. "Although we're never averse to him joining in the fun."

Tarah should've been shocked, but she'd long since learned that what happened in apartment 313 stayed in 313. And apparently, some freaky shit went on in that dungeon.

The rest of the ride was made in silence, and Gage pulled into the public parking section of the underground garage.

Rielle was slow to get out, and Tarah remembered. "You were going to play with them when you're…"

Rielle broke into a grin and rubbed her abdomen. "I'm four months along and still hardly showing. Plus, the doctor says I can play until month eight as long as I'm careful."

"Let me guess, Dr. Anthony?" Her voice was as dry as the Sahara.

Allie gasped, and Smith swore.

Rielle's brow creased in confusion. "No, my family doctor is Dr. Owen McCauley in Mission City. Who's Dr. Anthony?"

Allie's cheeks became a crimson color, and Smith's face was mottled in anger.

His hectic color showed he was absolutely livid. "That fucking prick." Smith ground out the words.

Rielle looked between everyone, baffled. "Dr. Anthony?"

Allie linked her arm in Tarah's as if sensing the younger woman might need support. "Dr. Anthony is a kink-friendly gynecologist." She offered the words as a way of explanation to Rielle. She glared over at Smith who had the decency to look chagrined. "I'm intimately familiar with the good doctor."

"He was nice to me." Tarah felt an odd necessity to defend the elderly gentleman.

"Oh, we know." Smith grimaced. "Sebastian's the prick. He should never have taken you there."

Tarah eyed the garage, suddenly feeling exposed. "Can we go upstairs?"

The group provided general murmurs of agreement, and they made their way to the elevators. She used her key fob to access the elevator that sped directly to the higher floors. Her mind was still boggled that she was staying on the twenty-sixth floor of a building. Until here, the highest she'd ever been was about the sixth floor. She still wasn't comfortable going anywhere near the windows.

She turned to Rielle questioningly. "Are you going to be okay? I mean I thought you were afraid of heights and—" She glanced around. "—elevators."

Rielle beamed. "I have a good psychologist."

"Actually, we both have the same psychologist." Alessandra said this as if it were no big deal.

"Kennedy Dixon, right?"

The elevator arrived at the destination just in time for all four occupants to gape at her. Instead of answering their unasked questions, she stepped forward and pulled out her key. Everyone followed her, so she opened the door and disarmed the alarm.

"Well, come on in." She walked through to the main room as if it were no big deal she was in this luxurious environment. She supposed for people like Smith and Rielle, who were rich, this was no big deal. Maybe Alessandra and Gage had also become accustomed to the wealth.

When Tarah faced the group, though, clearly they were impressed.

Rielle stepped toward the windows. "Oh my God, I've never been this high in my life."

Her words elicited titters and giggles from the rest of the group, and she whirled on them. "You know what I meant."

Gage stepped forward, then put an arm around her waist, placing a hand on her abdomen and pressing a kiss to her temple. "We know you're talking about height, my dear. Otherwise, my prowess as a Master and my ability to take you to sub-space might come into question."

They looked so intimate and so happy Tarah blinked several times. She'd had that. And she'd lost it for a second time. Christ, this wasn't fair. She cleared her throat. "Well, thanks for bringing me back here." She impotently waved toward the door.

"Oh, we're not leaving." Smith's blue-green eyes were bright. "Not until we get things settled."

Allie propelled her toward the master bedroom. "You have a shower, and we'll be waiting here when you get out."

Tarah glanced a little uncertainly around the group. Clearly, she had little choice. "Um, okay. Make yourselves at home."

As soon as she closed the bedroom door, she stripped. As much as she wanted to sink into the tub and into oblivion, she couldn't dawdle. Because...what? What were they expecting from her? What was she going to do? Staying here when Sebastian had been the one to send her away was easier, but now she was the one leaving? Somehow staying here was no longer right. Neither was taking his money.

Jesus Christ, what a clusterfuck she had gotten herself into.

After stepping into the hot spray, she immediately washed away any remnants of Sebastian. They'd been messy this morning because showers had been in order. She scrubbed and scrubbed and scrubbed. Would she never be clean? When her skin was raw and angrily red, she washed her hair. Even as the soap went down the drain, she was bombarded with images.

Sebastian between her thighs. Sebastian fisting himself before pressing into her ass. Sebastian as he came in her.

A bet.

Turning off the water with more force than necessary, she told herself she'd done the right thing. Sebastian had left her no other choice when he admitted all they had was based on a wager.

She wrapped the towel around her torso with another around her dark tresses. She shouldn't have been surprised to see Rielle sitting on the bed, but she was.

"How much?"

Rielle appeared momentarily confused, and her brow crinkled. "It's not really—"

"How much, Rielle?"

"A loonie."

The sharp shot to her chest was so painful she staggered. "They bet a dollar? I was worth a dollar?"

Steadying her, Rielle guided her to the bed. "I shouldn't have told you."

Tarah shook her head. "No, I needed to know. I need answers, Rielle. I need to know how badly I fucked up."

The other woman's arm went around her shoulders. "I'm so sorry, baby girl. I wish I could do something."

Tarah's brow furrowed as she faced Rielle. "Why do you call me *baby girl*?"

Shrugging, Rielle met her eyes. "Since we adopted Cara, I'm calling everyone *baby girl*. I mean it as a term of endearment."

"But I'm not a baby, Rielle. I'm twenty-five years old—old enough to make my own mistakes."

"But not schooled in the ways of the lifestyle, Tarah. The bet was to turn a woman from vanilla to submissive."

"Well, isn't that what he did? I mean, the guys are going to have to fork over a dollar."

"The assumption was the woman would be versed in the ways of the lifestyle and making informed consent."

Tarah's eyes widened. "He didn't force me. I mean, I agreed to do those things."

Now Rielle's eyes widened. "How much...I mean how bad..."

"Look, I knew about the dungeon. I knew what went on in there."

"Did you? I mean, did you really?" Rielle's gaze was incisive. "You had to go in there when you were helping me, but honestly, did you know what those things were for? Did you really understand the D/s lifestyle?"

She shrugged. "We had a contract. Two, in fact."

"Oh well, that makes everything okay." The words shot sarcastically from the older woman. "We just won't hold him accountable for deflowering a virgin."

She felt color drained from her face as she shot off the bed. "He told you?"

Rielle winced, clearly thunderstruck. "I was talking about the submission virginity. Are you saying he took your actual virginity?"

Tarah couldn't breathe. She was suffocating. "He didn't take it, Rielle—it wasn't rape. Consensual. What I did was consensual." She pressed a fist to her breast. "I didn't think it would hurt this much."

"Love hurts, baby girl. When I thought I'd lost Gage, I went out of my mind. He was the best thing that'd ever happened to me."

She didn't try to blink back the tears. Didn't try to hide the pain. "What if Sebastian was the best thing to happen to me, Rielle? Oh God, what am I doing?"

Rielle stood and marched over to the closet. She pulled out a pair of jeans and a blouse. She went over to the dresser and pulled out socks, a bra, and a pair of panties. "You get dressed while I pack a few things. You're coming home with us until we can figure out what to do."

"But…but…" Tarah sputtered. "I start classes in two weeks. I volunteer at a daycare. I can't leave. I need to find a new place to live because I sure as shit can't stay here." She paced. "Sebastian paid out my old lease, but maybe Ainsley hasn't rented out the room yet. I have to call her." She reached for her purse and the cell phone Sebastian had bought her, but Rielle snatched it away.

"All these problems will be here tomorrow. I promise. For tonight, come home with us and let us pamper you. You shouldn't be alone."

Oh, how tempting the offer was. To go where she could be coddled and cosseted. To go where she could share her burdens instead of facing them alone. Had it only been twenty-six days since Sebastian had insinuated himself into her life? Because before then, it would never have occurred to her to even consider the offer.

"You've got the baby…"

Rielle shook her head furiously. "It doesn't matter if I have Cara or not. Friends are friends. If you're not comfortable with us, go with Smith and Alessandra. Their house is easily three times as big as ours." She got a dreamy look on her face. "But I prefer cozy over space. Each to their own."

Was it that simple?

Gabbi Black

"Let me get dressed."

"Oh, go ahead." Rielle waved her hand breezily. She turned and opened the dresser drawer. "I'll start getting packed."

Of course she would. Because a woman who an hour ago was about to partake in an orgy wouldn't think of giving Tarah more than a modicum of privacy. And twenty-six days ago she would've made a beeline to the bathroom. Instead, she dropped the towel and pulled on her panties.

Once she was dressed, she picked up a brush.

Rielle stepped forward, palm out.

"I can brush my own hair—"

"Humor the pregnant woman."

Below the belt, but she acquiesced. What was the big deal? "I want to put it in a ponytail."

"But why?" Rielle drew the brush through the locks. "You have such beautiful hair." She looked more closely. "Are those auburn highlights?"

"Yeah." Her response was half-hearted, her chest still aching. "It went from dull brown to dull brown with red highlights."

Rielle tipped her head so their eyes met. "I've always been jealous of your hair."

Tarah gaped. The other woman had silver-blonde hair streaming halfway down her back. Along with her amber eyes and height, that made Rielle the most attractive woman Tarah knew. And Allie, with her dark smoky eyes and black hair, was a close second. "Why would you be jealous of my hair?"

"Because of the waves. My hair is as straight as straw. I've tried curling it, but it always goes back to straw. Oh, and Allie's hair, you should see it when it's long. Masses and masses of curls."

When Tarah had first met Allie, the woman's hair had looked like it'd been chopped off with a weed whacker. Now, with the hair several inches longer, Tarah could glimpse the curls Rielle referenced.

As requested, Rielle pulled Tarah's hair into a ponytail. She stood back to examine her handiwork. "I'm going to be such a girly girl with Cara. Gage is trying to argue not everything has to be pink, but I can't help myself."

Tarah grasped Rielle's hand. "I'm delighted for you." She fought against the tears. "You deserve to be happy."

The other woman's eyes misted. "I never thought I deserved happiness. You know where I came from and what I went through. Gage showed me I was worth more, and I'll always be grateful to him."

"I think, I mean, maybe in time I'll feel that way about Sebastian."

Pressing a hand to Tarah's cheek, Rielle offered a smile. "Regrets can eat you alive, but it doesn't forgive what he did to you." She straightened. "Now let's grab your bags and go."

Rielle had packed two suitcases full of clothes, and Tarah didn't have the heart to argue.

"I need to get my textbooks and my e-reader if I'll be more than a few days. I don't want to get behind."

"Of course, you can pack those while we throw out the perishables."

How long did Rielle think Tarah was going away?

Chapter Sixteen

Rielle opened the door to the main room, and Smith and Gage stood, then the latter grabbed the suitcases.

"I need to pack a few things for school." Tarah pointed to the second bedroom. "I set it up as a den. Give me a moment?"

Rielle waved off her request. "We've got all the time in the world. The babysitter isn't expecting us for another six or seven hours."

Just how long had they planned for this orgy to last?

She wasn't going to ask.

Instead, she went into the den and scooped up her books. A moment's hesitation over the laptop and e-reader, but her textbooks and notes were all stored on them. *Oh, fuck it.* Sebastian Merrick could afford them. She was taking many of the clothes he'd given her, but what was she supposed to do with them? Donate them to charity? Except now that she was without an income, she was the charity.

Oh God, she didn't even have a job to go back to.

"Tarah?" Gage stood in the doorway, watching her.

She dropped like a stone into the chair. Her head fell forward, and she put her hands to her face. "Oh, Gage, what am I going to do?"

In an instant, he was beside her, dropping to his haunches. "Smith and I got you into this mess, and we'll get you out. You needn't worry about anything, okay?

Money, clothes…don't think about it."

She wiped the tears from her cheeks. "I don't even have a job."

"Well, Smith owns, like, a hundred companies. I'm sure he can find you something. Otherwise, Rielle and I could use some help around the house."

"You looking for another submissive?"

The poor attempt at humor didn't have the effect she'd hoped. Instead of laughing, Gage's expression turned to stone. "I'm going to cut his balls off for what he did to you."

As much as she wanted nothing more in that moment, she shook her head. "I told Rielle, and I'll tell you, I'm an adult. I made my own choices, and I'll live with the consequences. I—"

Her next words were cut off by the most god-awful ruckus.

Someone was pounding on the door.

She shot out of her chair and strode to the living room, Gage hot on her heels. She indicated everyone should stay where they were. "He doesn't know I'm here," she whispered. "He'll leave." She said the words with more confidence than she had any right to feel, but the alternative was another confrontation with Sebastian, and no way could she emotionally deal with that.

Allie shrugged, Rielle cringed, and the men were clearly itching for a battle.

The pounding resumed. "Open the fucking door, Tarah."

At least *she* hadn't sworn. Still, it wouldn't be long before someone called security.

More pounding. "Open this fucking door, or I'll tell everyone I knocked you up and abandoned you."

Everything happened in slow motion. Allie gasped, Rielle dropped to the sofa, then Gage and Smith barreled into each other in the rush to get to the door.

Tarah didn't have a chance to say a single word before Gage opened the door, Smith yanked Sebastian in by the collar, and Gage decked him.

Sebastian staggered, but he didn't go down.

Smith's arm was back, about to take his turn, when Tarah leapt between Sebastian and the men. "I'm not pregnant, you goddamn Neanderthals!"

Both Gage and Smith looked at her as if she were speaking Greek.

"But he said—"

"Why would he—"

Tarah cut them off with a chopping motion. "Because last night I pounded on his door and told him if he didn't let me in, I'd tell the universe he got me knocked up and abandoned me."

Rielle stood. "But you just said you're not pregnant. I'm confused."

"A threat to get him to open the door and it worked." She glared at Gage and Smith. "Like it worked just now." She pointed at Gage. "Did you have to hit him?"

Sebastian, evidently recovered, pulled himself to his full height.

All three men were about the same size, and Tarah's short stature suddenly put her at a distinct disadvantage.

"I deserved it, Tarah." He regarded her as she gazed up at him. "I deserved it and a lot more." Carelessly, he wiped the blood coming from the side of his mouth with the back of his hand. "But no matter what you think, it was never about the bet. I wanted you long before we made the wager. I used it to justify my behavior, but I knew what I was doing was wrong."

"What if I said it wasn't wrong?"

"Tarah." A warning tone in Sebastian's voice.

"No, I need to be honest with everyone here. I was curious. Hell, I was more than curious."

Everyone appeared uncomfortable, but Smith spoke. "Sexual submission isn't something for the idly curious, Tarah."

"But you all started somewhere, didn't you?"

Five people all looked like they were going to speak, but none did, so Tarah pressed on. "I know, I'm ten years younger and probably far more naïve—"

"Not anymore." Gage snarled.

He stopped when Tarah shot him a warning look. "I still made the choice by consent. Safe, Sane, and Consensual." She dared anyone to argue. "I can't un-ring the bell. The horse has left the barn…" She struggled to come up with another trite saying but couldn't.

"You can't get back your virginity." Rielle's words were likely said for maximum effect, and they did the trick.

Tarah barely had time to think before Sebastian hauled her off to one side and stepped toward the other men.

He just stood there as if waiting for someone to deck him. This time, Smith's fist connected with Sebastian's face. Again, he staggered but didn't go down.

"What the fuck is wrong with you?" Tarah rounded on everyone, including Rielle. "I knew precisely what I was doing. Some people—" She turned to Sebastian. "— had scruples and wanted nothing to do with it." Now she pivoted to the other men. "If any of you lifts a single finger, I'm calling the cops because this is assault. You may think you have the moral high ground, but you don't."

Sebastian's face was already swelling.

"Allie, take Rielle into the kitchen and make three ice packs."

A chorus of *I'm fine* echoed in a cacophonous staccato.

Tarah's voice was louder. "I don't give a fuck what you all want." She pointed to Gage and Smith's knuckles. "Both of you have done damage that'll be mitigated by ice." She tentatively reached out to Sebastian. He flinched, even though she hadn't touched him. She held her hand steady until he relaxed, then she pressed it to his cheek. "You're going to have a hell of a shiner."

"Better me than them," Sebastian murmured. "Nothing happened here that wasn't warranted."

He looked despairing, and Tarah's heart broke all over again. When she was sure no one was going to hit someone else, she walked over to her purse and pulled out her wallet. She pivoted and walked back to the men.

She held out her fingers, the loonies visible.

"I don't—"

"It's not really—"

Exasperated, Tarah seized Gage's bruised hand and squeezed. Hard. He winced and opened his hand. She dropped the dollar in his palm. When she turned to Smith, she didn't even have to threaten. His palm waited for her.

"Now that the bet is no longer an issue, maybe we can start acting our ages?"

Rielle and Allie appeared with tea towels filled with ice cubes in hand. Allie glared at Sebastian. "There's a bag of peas in the freezer."

He inclined his head and made his escape.

With his departure, Allie and Rielle clucked over their men, encouraging them to sit on couches and chairs. Tarah rolled her eyes and strode into the kitchen. Instead of finding Sebastian with a pack of peas, she almost tripped over him. He sat on the floor, his knees bent and his legs drawn to his chest. After stepping over him, she retrieved the bag of peas. She sat next to him and then placed it to his jaw.

He hissed in pain.

"It's no less than you deserve." Her grasp on sanity was tenuous. "They only did what I wanted to do." Before he spoke, she continued. "Violence is never the answer. I've had to break up a few brawls in my time, Sebastian, and I would've done the same thing. You didn't have to protect me, and you didn't have to submit to being a punching bag on my account."

"What if they were justified?"

She shook her head. "I call bullshit. You gave me a million chances to say *no*, and I never did." She tucked her arm under his and laid her cheek against his shoulder. "When you sent me away, I didn't think I could bear any more pain. But this hurt more because I believed you."

"What did you believe?"

"You loved me."

Sebastian pressed a kiss to her hair. "Tarah, you believed me because it was true. Is true." His breath was warm against her scalp. "Present tense. Nothing will change my love for you, and I'll fight every man in Vancouver if that's what it takes to prove myself worthy of your love."

"See, you say stuff like that, and it makes it hard to

stay mad at you."

He cleared his throat. "Do you think, I mean, maybe could you…"

"Spit it out, Merrick."

"Do you think, in time, you might forgive me? I'm asking a lot—"

"Why did you really do it? Was I just a challenge to you?"

He shook his head, pulling his lower lip through his teeth. "The first time I saw you, you were in uniform and wearing that ridiculous cap. But those eyes…" He swallowed. "They are spectacular in color, but that wasn't what I saw. I saw something that mirrored me. Loneliness, longing, desire."

"I'd love to contradict you, but you're exactly right. I think I would've gone with you if you'd offered me a quickie in the janitor's closet."

"Please tell me that is not how you lost your virginity."

She glanced up to find Gage gazing over the kitchen counter at them.

Despite herself, she smiled. "No, we did it like civilized human beings—doggie style on the couch."

"Fuck, Tarah, are you trying to get me hit again?"

She kissed his cheek. "Gage knows I'm pulling his leg."

Gage, after a long moment, offered a slight smile. "I think Rielle has had too much excitement today, and I want to get her home." He surveyed Tarah and Sebastian whose arms were still entwined. "Do I take your suitcases down to the truck?"

Slowly, she shook her head. "I can't run away, Gage, as tempting as the offer is." She paused. "Will you give my regards to the others? I can't face them right now."

He nodded. "They'll understand." His gaze narrowed on Sebastian. "Fuck this up, and there won't be a place in this country where you'll be safe."

Sebastian inclined his head. "I'd rather cut off my right arm than hurt her again."

Gage placed two loonies on the counter. "None of us wanted to hurt her."

"I'm right here, you know."

Sebastian interlaced their hands and drew her knuckles to his lips where he placed a kiss. "Five people who care that much for someone might occasionally differ on what's best for her, but it doesn't mean they can't also find common ground." He met Gage's stare. "I'm not going to get up so we can hug it out, but she's my everything."

Seemingly satisfied, Gage inclined his head to Tarah. "I'll give them your regards."

"Maybe one day we can have that orgy."

Sebastian's hand tightened against hers, and Gage's mouth gaped.

"Jesus, Tarah, how much did he corrupt you?"

She lifted one shoulder haphazardly. "The thought of the six of us makes me wet."

Gage's hands clapped to his ears, and two bright spots of color appeared on his cheeks. "I'm not sure I'll ever be able to un-hear that. I'm leaving." With a final tilt of the head, he was gone.

She sighed. "He is so easy to read."

"Why do you think we could only bet on submissives? We can't play poker because there is no one with less of a poker face than Gage." He paused.

"Okay, well, maybe Allie."

"Or me." She helpfully offered the words with a wicked grin.

"Maybe." His acknowledgment was grudging. "But when you told me you were leaving me, I believed you didn't love me."

Now she brought their entwined hands to her lips, then pressed a kiss to his knuckles. "No matter how angry I was, it'd never diminish my love for you."

Sebastian shifted the ice pack from his jaw where Gage had hit him to the cheek where Smith had nailed him. "Did you have to tell them about your virginity?"

"That was your fault."

"How do you figure?"

"Rielle said you'd deflowered me. I assumed you'd been boasting to Gage and Smith."

Sebastian let out a howl of laughter. "They came to Vancouver about a week ago, and we went down to the pub. We all got shit-faced, and needless to say, the guys had to crash at my place."

"I'm sure Allie and Rielle were impressed." Tarah rolled her eyes.

"Oh, better than them drinking and driving."

Well, he was right on that count. "You guys got shit-faced…"

"And in the morning, when we were all desperately hungover, I told them about losing my submissive. God, Tarah, you should've heard me. The guys didn't even mention the bet because I was goddamn miserable."

She rolled her eyes. "If you suffered that much, why the fuck did you not come back and get me?"

He stiffened. "I'm still not sure I'm good enough for you, Tarah."

"Mia," she corrected him softly. "It's Mia."

He pressed another kiss to her hair. "Can we go home before this black eye develops? I can imagine what Carlos is going to think."

Likely as he'd intended, she laughed. "I'll tell him you were defending my virtue."

"Stealing it would be more like it, but I like the way you put it." His eyes were a turbulent storm.

Please open your heart to me.

"Will you come home with me?"

"Oh Christ, yes." Her relief mingled with joy. "A thousand times yes."

Conveniently, two suitcases and a knapsack were already packed and ready to go. The descent to the garage took mere moments, and they held hands all the way home.

Going straight from the garage to the third floor, they bypassed the security desk. Probably just as well, as his face was turning some nasty colors. As soon as they were through the door, she pushed him to the couch and pressed an ice pack from the freezer to his eye. "I'm afraid it might swell shut."

"Tarah, it's not like I haven't been hit before."

She sank down to the couch next to him. "That's why you didn't fight back? Being in a brawl was like that with your father." She fought the bile rising in her throat. He'd taken the beating for her. Because of her.

"Mia, you're not responsible. I should've told you about the bet from the first, and I should've told them about you before they found us *in flagrante delicto*."

She couldn't help it—she laughed. "Well, at least you didn't have me tied up. That might've been a little tough to explain."

He joined her merriment and chuckled. "It would've been hard for you to come to my defense if you were tied up." He turned to her. "Brave of you, to step between Gage, Smith, and myself."

"And yet you're the dickhead who pushed me out of the way to take the second blow. You know very well neither man would've thrown a punch with me in the middle."

"And the tension would never have been broken if I hadn't let Smith take his turn."

She rolled her eyes. "It's a guy thing, right?"

"Probably, although I've seen a few catfights in my day."

Now she laughed. "You'll never see me in a catfight. I love you and will be protective of you, but you can defend yourself against other women."

"I don't have to worry, Mia. The women will all see I'm in love, and they'll leave me alone. When I go out with Gage and Smith, no one hits on them."

Snickering, she rolled her eyes. "Might be because they're wearing wedding rings."

"What if I wore one as well?"

She turned so quickly her neck snapped. Since he was looking off into space, she had to tug his chin, forcing him to face her. "Don't joke, Sebastian. I agreed to wear your collar…"

"Would you also be willing to wear my ring?"

He was dead serious. "It's been, like, a month."

"How long before you're comfortable with it? Because I'll die if we're ever apart. Collar, ring, the whole deal, Mia."

"Are you proposing?"

The ice pack fell unheeded to the floor, and he

dropped to one knee. He took her hand in his and gazed up at her. "Will you marry me?"

Her breath whooshed out of her as she read the seriousness in his eyes. Well, one of his eyes. The other one was pretty much swollen shut.

She wanted to touch his face but was afraid she wouldn't be able to find a place she could touch that wouldn't hurt.

"Yes, Sebastian, I'll marry you." She pressed a broken kiss to his lips. "And yes, Master, I'll wear your collar."

Her words elicited a smile, pursued by a grimace.

"Oh, for God's sake, get up off your knees and put the ice pack back on your face."

He rose but didn't rejoin her on the couch. "Stay right here."

As he left, she snickered. Where the hell might she go?

He returned quickly and handed her a jeweler's case. "Open it."

Her hesitation must have been clear, because he clarified. "I'll put the ice pack back on my face if you open the box."

She quirked an eyebrow. "I hardly think you're in a position to blackmail me, but what the hell…" She opened the box, and her breath caught. Wow, what an exquisite and intricately designed necklace. The braided strands were roots with little animals etched into the trees.

"This is like Allie's watch." The words came unheeded.

"I know and I thought…shit." He swore. "You liked the watch, so I thought I'd get you something similar, but of course you'd want something unique." He tried to pull the box away, but she held tight.

"I love Allie's watch. I don't want to give this back, because I love it." She gave him a sly grin. "A collar that looks like a necklace." She turned so her back was to him. "Will you put it on?"

He hesitated.

She twisted around, arching an eyebrow, tamping down frustration. "What can I say to make you okay with this?"

His hands rose over her head, and he tucked the necklace snugly against her neck, finally securing the clasp around the back. His hands lingered, fondled, and pressed. Then his lips replaced his hands.

"Sebastian." The protest was feeble. *His lips must be in so much pain...*

"Shh, Mia, don't fret." He nipped at her earlobe. "It's eighteen karat white gold. It's tough, so you can wear it all the time."

"Even in the shower?"

"Even in the shower." His eyebrows wiggled. "When we play, however, we'll use the other collar."

Pleasure traveled up and down her spine as she shivered. How could so few words have such an effect on her?

"Your face." A whisper—part plea, part prayer.

"There are lots of things I can do to you that don't require using my lips, teeth, or tongue."

Turning to meet his gaze, she clasped the necklace. "But you have such talented lips, teeth, and tongue."

"Well, my hands escaped unscarred."

She grasped them. "Tell me you wouldn't have fought them."

He considered her. "Them insulting me was no big deal. But if either of them had impugned you, fists would've flown."

"Gage and Smith would never—"

"I know, Mia, which is why my hands stayed at my sides. Now, do you think we can continue this in the bedroom?"

She shook her head. "Nope."

"I told you, Mia, my hands work perfectly well…"

"And neither of us have eaten anything since popcorn last night. As desperate as I am to discover what your talented hands are capable of, I need food." She pressed her hand to his forehead, the only place not swollen. "I'm going to make you a protein shake."

"Fuck that." He heaved an indignant sigh. "I've at least earned the right to masticate a cow."

She gazed deeply into his eyes. "All right, big boy, I'll run down the street and grab burgers from White Spot. Good enough?"

"I would prefer steak, but I'm not fussy." He obviously tried to lift his eyebrow but failed spectacularly. "Plus, I need to clean up the dungeon."

Her laugh coaxed a smile from him.

"Try some air freshener." Her nose wrinkled. "I don't want to know what you were doing in there."

"Missing you." He offered the quick and sure response. "Now go get food before I attempt to ply you with tales of torrid lovemaking techniques."

She quirked an eyebrow. "I'll just grab my purse."

Night had fallen when she stepped from the elevator into the lobby. Carlos was speaking to another tenant, so she ducked her head and escaped outside.

The first few flakes of snow hit her in the face.

Grateful for her winter coat, she walked up toward Georgia Street. By the time she made it to the restaurant, she was cold and wet. Once she had her order, she flagged a cab to take her home.

Uncannily, Carlos was at the door when she arrived. He held it open for her so she didn't have to maneuver with the drink tray.

"Thank you, Carlos."

"No problem, Miss Peters." He walked with her to the elevator but didn't push the button. "I hate to ask, but an incident on the third floor was reported last night during Gus' shift. You wouldn't know anything about that, would you?"

Since she was incapable of lying, she pasted on her best smile. "I might, but I can promise you it'll never happen again."

The older man appeared relieved. "Oh, I'm sure glad to hear that. Because you know how much I hate getting into other people's business…"

"And your discretion is appreciated."

He pushed the button and held the elevator door open for her. "Thank Mr. Merrick for our bonuses."

"I will." She was never as grateful as when the door to the car closed. Of course Mrs. Wannamaker would make a complaint. Would anyone complain about today's escapade at the other condo? She still hadn't forgiven Sebastian for the pregnancy comment. Rielle had looked like she was going to pass out, and Allie's eyes had been wider than saucers.

What would've happened if she had gotten pregnant? The pill was pretty darn effective but wasn't foolproof. If Sebastian was dead set against having kids, then maybe they should look toward something more permanent.

Except if Sebastian was sure he never wanted kids…

She balanced the tray and open the door. Oh good, Sebastian was there to take the bag of food from her hands.

"Why did you never have a vasectomy?"

He dropped the food. "What?"

"Why did you never have a vasectomy? Simple question, Sebastian."

He moved her hip so she was no longer holding the door open. "First pregnancies and now vasectomies? Mrs. Wannamaker is going to have a heart attack." He flipped the lock, then swept down to grab the bag of food. He searched in it. "Probably still edible…"

"Answer my question, Sebastian. You're thirty-eight years old and told me you didn't want to have kids. Why—"

"I lied." He spat out the words.

"When did you lie?"

His eyes closed, and he took a deep breath. "Can we do this somewhere other than the front hall?"

"Sure." She could be reasonable, right? "Where would be best?"

Without another word, he headed for the kitchen.

She followed him, then tapped her foot as he took down two plates from the cupboard and sorted the food.

"Do you think it's warm enough? I mean I can nuke it, but the lettuce will get soggy."

"I hate lettuce and plan to take it out—now, when did you lie to me?"

He took a breath, not meeting her gaze. "I loved being a father to those kids, Tarah. I was there for all the firsts—steps, words, bike rides—you name it, and I was

321

there. How I didn't die from the anguish of losing them, I'll never know."

The image of him standing next to seven caskets overwhelmed her. Not as he had been, but as he now was. Proud, tall, strong…and heartbroken. "I know you loved them, Sebastian, and nothing will ever take away that pain."

Suddenly, he seized her upper arms. "But don't you see, Tarah, when I'm with you, I don't feel that void. I don't feel empty of hope. I'm full of optimism."

Her eyes blurred with tears. "It'll be enough, just the two of us. I shouldn't—"

He pressed his index finger to her lips. "I want kids. I want to honor what I shared with them. I just never thought I'd meet someone who'd make me want them. I guess my subconscious was looking for you, because about a dozen times I almost called Dr. Anthony to make the appointment." His gaze softened. "And I shouldn't have freaked out when you said you might be pregnant, because it would've been okay. It will be okay." He repeated the words with more conviction. "But it's too soon. You need to go through school first. By then I'll be forty. You might think I'll be too old to father your—"

She cut him off by pressing her lips to his. She was gentle with the kiss when what she wanted was to seal their deal. Pulling back, she settled for ruffling his hair. "Gage is over forty—he's got an infant and another one on the way."

"And Smith and Allie are trying as well."

"See, it's not an issue." She gazed deeply into his eyes. "Do you want kids, or are you saying this because you know I want them? Because I don't want you to resent—"

He pressed his index finger to her lips again. "Fuck, Tarah, I'm hungry. I told you I'd never lie to you, and about something so important, I wouldn't. The day you finish teacher's college, the pills go in the trash."

His words warmed her in a way a fire on a chilled night never could. She threw her arms around him, and he grunted as her shoulder connected with his cheek. She pulled back, and the top of her head connected with his jaw.

A few muttered curses later, he set her away from him. "You are proving hazardous to my health today, Mia."

She managed a smile. "There's another ice pack in the freezer for when we're finished with dinner. And we never finished watching those movies."

He rolled his eyes. "You agree not only to marry me, but to wear my collar, and you think I want to celebrate by watching a science fiction movie?"

"Well, I'm thinking of you." With acute regrets sexual escapades were out for a bit. "You must be in a lot of pain."

"I took an ibuprofen."

"You need to eat, because they're hard on your stomach."

He looked heavenward. "Finally, I'm going to get my food."

They nuked the burgers and fries, then settled at the dining room table. Most of the meal was consumed in silence as they were both famished.

"Do you have enough of your things to last a few days?"

"I think Rielle was packing so I could move in permanently with them."

"You realize how big a step that would've been?" He said the words casually.

She understood the gravity of what he was saying and nodded again. Good, he was on the same page. "I thought the same thing. You never could've convinced me I had friends, but today showed me I was wrong."

"Loyalty and fidelity."

"You make me sound like a dog."

"I like dogs." He offered a lopsided smile.

"I love dogs." She ducked her head shyly. "Since having a baby is out of the question right now…"

"We'll go to the animal shelter tomorrow." He swooped in for a hard and fast kiss. "It's a good thing this building allows pets."

"And big pets. I always wanted a lab or a shepherd or a husky or—"

"Enough, Mia." He took her hand. "I'm sure we'll be able to adopt a big dog, but if not, I'll buy you a big dog."

"Do you think the dog will be confused to see his mistress wearing a collar?"

He laughed. "Speaking of collars, I think it's time to put yours on." He rose and left.

She took the plates and put them in the dishwasher, then met him in the living room.

Taking her hand, he paused to press a kiss to her knuckles, then guided her to the dungeon.

He'd done an amazing job. Everything was back in its place, as if the whole kerfuffle hadn't happened. Things were right again in the world, and she could breathe again.

When he presented her with the leather collar, she knelt at his feet. She held her ponytail to one side so he could attach it. When he stepped back, she tugged at it experimentally.

"It's well attached, Mia, trust me."

He held out his hand, and she took it and rose.

He went over to the chair and sat. "Now, strip for me."

She waited for clarification. Was this a get-out-of-your-clothes-as-soon-as-possible strip or a striptease?

"Your Master wants to watch you unveil your beauty."

Oh, *that* kind of show. She began a slow revelation, starting with the buttons on her blouse. She shed the garment and shimmied out of her jeans.

"Hold it."

She had been reaching around to unhook her bra, so she stopped mid-movement.

"You picked that lingerie set?"

What? "Well, it arrived with all those other clothes—"

"No, I mean today."

"Oh no, Rielle chose them. I was too upset, so she picked all my clothes. Why?"

He chuckled. "Nothing, except you look virginal in white satin."

"Probably because Rielle was trying to shove me back in that *innocent* box." She released the clasp and let the bra slip from her arms and to the ground. "I think she was trying to put the cart before the horse."

As intended, he smiled.

She tugged on the elastic, and her hair tumbled out of her ponytail. A veil cascaded down. "Rielle told me she envied me my wavy hair."

"You have beautiful hair, Mia." His shining eyes

offered confirmation. "I especially like it when it's fanned out against my pillow."

His words caused a frisson of desire to sweep through her, and her nipples tightened painfully. Without conscious thought, she hooked her thumbs in her panties and slid them down until they landed on the ground. Feeling uncertain, she fidgeted.

"What's wrong?"

"Should I pick up my clothes or kneel or present myself—"

He rose from the chair with lightning speed. "Let's leave clothes folding for later, shall we?"

She noted his crotch, and her lips twitched. "I take it my dropping to my knees would be appreciated."

He scowled. "Just ignore that—it's something that comes up when I watch my woman undress."

My woman. The butterflies in her belly went ballistic.

"But I can wait." The words were uttered through gritted teeth. "I said I wanted to pleasure you."

Her eyebrow quirked. "This is one of those times when I point out that servicing you makes me as wet as anything else you might do to me."

She could've sworn his jeans got tighter.

"Jesus, Mia, you're killing me."

At the sound of her name, she dropped to her knees. She understood the unspoken plea in his words. With deft fingers, she unsnapped his jeans and undid the zipper.

Commando again.

She needed to do laundry. Except this meant taking less time for her to place her mouth around him.

He let out one long groan as she deep throated him.

Then, as quickly as it had started, he hauled her off him.

"What the—"

He had her facing the wall in one fluid motion. His hand connected with her ass. Oh, she would've finished him off too quickly, and now he wanted her to catch up.

His hand connected against her other cheek, and she rocked up on the balls of her feet. How had he known this was what she needed?

He rained down another series of blows and then stopped as suddenly as he'd begun.

She waited, her cheek pressed to the wall and her eyes shut tight.

Those clever hands snaked around her waist, and one went lower. Much lower. She let her head fall back, mindful of not hitting his face. His left hand splayed across her abdomen and held her securely in place while his right hand slid lower still, delving between her thighs. A couple of passes against her clit had the orgasm rocketing through her. Then those clever hands were on her ass, pressing against the warm heat. He eased her back against the wall, scrutinizing his handiwork. Was he pleased with what he saw? God knew her ass was sore.

"God, Mia, I need to be in you."

"Does my Master want to be in my pussy or my ass?"

He swatted her. Hard. "That's for impudence, little one. Now, go to the bed and get on all fours."

She hadn't thought she could get any wetter, but she was wrong. Even she could smell her own arousal as she dropped to her hands and knees on the bed. This time she didn't bother to try to get her arms to hold her up, instead placing her forearms on the bed, creating a pillow for her head.

He came up behind her moments before he thrust into her.

Her pussy it was. And said pussy contracted and clamped onto his cock.

"Jesus, Mia, keep that up, and this will be over before it starts."

"Well, I seem to remember a certain someone is capable of a short recovery time."

"That was last night." His words were choppy, matching his thrusts. "I'm not feeling so…oh my God."

Kegels. This was something she could do.

As he pistoned in and out, she fought to match his rhythm. He grasped her hips as he continued his barrage on her senses. Each time his hips hit her sore ass, pain blossomed and spread. Each time he thrust into her, brief explosions happened behind her closed eyelids. He'd lost control, and soon she did. Hard to tell who climaxed first as her shouts mingled with his.

He dropped to sit on the bed next to her and gathered her into his arms, pulling her across his lap. Pressing a kiss to her forehead, he grunted. "I'm sorry, Mia."

She pulled back, mindful of not hitting either of his bruises. "Whatever for?"

"I…I lost control again. I hate losing control."

She laughed. "There is nothing I love more than when you lose control, because then I know I've done a good job. I did a good job, didn't I?"

As she had hoped, he pressed a kiss to her forehead. "Yes, Mia, you did an exceptional job. I hope not too much work…ouch!"

She had elbowed him in the ribs. "That's for making stupid comments. Now, it's time for you to get into bed.

I'm getting the ice pack."

"Are you trying to order me around?"

"I will if I have to. Your health will always come before my servitude."

He chuckled. "I feel the same way, Mia. I'll get into bed and let you take care of me."

She eased off his lap and guided him into bed. A silly thing to do, for sure, but she enjoyed knowing he could be vulnerable with her. She went to the kitchen and retrieved the ice pack from the freezer. She scooped up her phone on the way back.

"I think I should call Gage and let him know I'm okay."

She placed the compress to his face with great tenderness, but he hissed.

"And I should probably tell him you're okay."

"Well, what if I'm not okay?"

"Don't bullshit the bullshitter, Sebastian." She feathered her hand through his hair. "Just keep quiet while I make the call."

He relented, replacing her hand with his as he pressed the ice pack to his face. "I won't say a word." His eyes closed.

She dialed Gage, and it rang four times before he picked up. "Tarah? Is everything okay?"

He was breathing heavily, and odd sounds filtered through from the background.

"That's not baby Cara I hear, is it?"

"Uh, no. We might have taken advantage of the babysitter and come back to Smith and Allie's to…um…"

"Play?"

"Uh, yeah." She heard him placing his hand over the

handset. "Rielle wants to talk to you."

"Sure, if it's not a bad time—"

"It's never a bad time for you, baby girl." Rielle's breathing was as ragged as Gage's.

"Look why don't you call me tomorrow?"

She heard something sounding like a whip strike.

Rielle giggled. Actually giggled. "Yeah, that might be best. Around noon?"

"Sounds perfect, Rielle, and tell Allie and Smith I hope they're enjoying themselves."

"Always, baby girl. Later."

The line disconnected, and she giggled like a schoolgirl.

Sebastian eyed her with amusement. "What was that all about?"

"Oh, I just interrupted a foursome."

He groaned. "Don't tell me that…"

She pressed her hand to his twitching cock. "The thought of a…wait, what is the name for five people?"

"An orgy." He offered the word through gritted teeth.

As she continued to stroke him, she used her imagination. "I bet you like girl-on-girl action the most, eh? I mean guys need time to recharge, but women can just keep going and going…"

"Fuck, Tarah, keep it up, and I'm going to embarrass myself."

As if she hadn't heard him, she continued. "Or maybe you prefer to be the voyeur. How much would you love to see Gage in my ass and Smith in my pussy?"

He was rock hard in her hand.

"Oh, then you could take my mouth…what's that called?"

"TP."

"TP?"

"Triple penetration, look it up on Google—just, for God's sake, let go of me."

His face was contorted, but she wasn't really hurting him. Her movements increased in pace as she mimicked the action that'd take place if he were inside her.

His balls drew up, and the end came quickly.

She giggled as cum sprayed everywhere. She tried to keep it confined, but what was the point? Hopefully, he had more clean sheets. After rising, she walked to the bathroom to get a warm wet washcloth. His eyes were closed when she returned, and they remained that way as she washed his abdomen.

"I think that takes at least two more things off the list." She whispered the words huskily. "But you know what I want?"

"Whatever you want, you can have, Mia. A Porsche? It's yours. A million dollars? Not a problem."

She rolled her eyes. "Just a hand job, Sebastian. God, what a pushover you are."

"What is it you want?" He had cracked his good eye open.

"I want you to whip me."

A sharp intake of breath. "Oh, Mia, you have no idea how long I've waited for you to say that. I wanted to ask, but whipping was on your hard-limit list." He laughed ruefully. "Except I can't whip you right now."

"Well, you're in post-orgasmic bliss, so I wasn't meaning this exact moment."

"You're going to have to wait longer than a recovery period, Mia. I can't whip you until I can see clearly out of both eyes."

"Fuck Gage Clayton and Smith MacLean." She spat out the words.

"A minute ago you had one of them in your—"

"Oh, shut the fuck up."

He chuckled. "What made you change your mind?"

"I've wanted you to whip me since the night we went to Club Kink." She feathered his hair again. God, he was sexy. "I think I had to learn to trust you."

"And do you, Mia? Do you trust me?"

"If I'm willing to let you whip me, then I'm saying I'm trusting you." She considered her next words, wanting them to have maximum effect. "But I want to put something on my hard-limit list."

"Okay."

"This bed." She glared mutinously. "Me sleeping in this bed is nonnegotiable. I'm not sleeping in the white room, and I sure as shit am not sleeping on that fucking pallet again."

His laughter barked out. "I thought you said sleeping on the floor was good for your back."

"Fuck me, Sebastian, you know very well I was lying through my teeth. Now, do we have a meeting of the minds, or do you need a signed contract?"

He pulled her down and into his arms. "My bed is your bed, Mia, for better or for worse."

She snuggled up close.

Exactly the way it was meant to be.

A word about the author…

Even though Gabbi Black is a firm believer in happy endings, she makes her characters work for it in every romance she writes, no matter what the genre. From contemporary to BDSM, they are penned early in the morning in her home in beautiful British Columbia while her trusty ChinPoo dog and her cantankerous Himalayan cat keep her company. She also writes gay romances as Gabbi Grey.

~*~

Visit Gabbi online at:
www.gabbiblack.com

www.ingramcontent.com/pod-product-compliance
Lightning Source LLC
Chambersburg PA
CBHW050035030726
47506CB00001B/285